Luther
A Luther LaMotta Tale
Book I
42

Luther

Luther LaMotta, Volume 1

David Larson

Published by David Larson, 2024.

LUTHER

First edition. July 31, 2024.

Copyright © 2024 David Larson.

ISBN: 979-8227672438

Written by David Larson.

Also by David Larson

Luther LaMotta
Luther

Tyler Stone
Powder Keg

Standalone
One Crowded Hour

1.

Luther LaMotta was an extremely complex man. On the surface he was a borderline simpleton who had difficulty completing the most rudimentary tasks. He also saw the world through a most literal lens. If a person were to tell Luther to beat it, he would punch the closest thing to him. If he was told to get lost, he would spend the entire day trying to find someplace he didn't know and would have a hard time finding his way back from. At one time Luther had trusted people openly and honestly without question. Unfortunately, the world Luther lived in was filled with nothing but people living by lies, deceit, and lawlessness. The Luther of old may have referred to these people as scoundrels, but the new Luther simply called them friends.

On the outside Luther was a third-level button man of sorts, for the mob, and parttime cleaner's assistant. His childhood friend Tony "the tongue" Ferrari had risen through the ranks of the Manchini crime family, achieving the rank of second-level button man. Tony felt responsible for Luther and had received permission from his boss, first-level button man Big Benny Amato, to take on Luther as a sort of an assistant to. Tony didn't want Luther to feel as though he was extra baggage, so he bestowed the made-up title of third-level button man on him. Luther loved the perceived honor of an actual title, and he also loved Tony. Third-level button man Luther was the Luther the realm of the real world knew. Luther referred to *outside Luther* as *Bad Luther.*

Bad Luther could feel the coolness of the tile on his knees as he knelt on the floor, but his mind was a thousand miles from where his physical self currently was. His head was tilted back, and a look of complete resigned placidity softened his face. A slight smile served as a juxtaposition to the lines of anxiety on his forehead and the soft rivulets of emotional tears flowing down his cheeks.

Through Luther's ever-present Aftershokz headphones, a crystal-clear haunting guitar was picking across a kind of easy Spanish riff. Each note complemented the last and left him craving the next.

Then came the thing that broke him down completely every time he heard it. The deep throaty voice of Susan Said began like a spectral gift asking Luther personally, "If there's a strong wind blowing will you hear me call your name?" "*Oh my God Susan,*" Good Luther said inside his mind, "*I am shaken to the very core of my emotions when you sing so beautifully. I lay prostrate at your feet pleading for more.*"

A few more notes rang through his mind, then Susan was back, "And when the skies turn black and grey, will you be able to find me?" "*Yes. Oh, my sweet Jesus, yes, I will Susan,*" Good Luther moaned in the deep recesses of his inner self. "*I'll not only find you my beautiful angel, but I am also you. We are one in the universe, and we will float on the angelic sound of your voice for ever and ever.*" Susan answered Good Luther, "You cannot leave behind the problems that you made, Luther." Luther was confused and descending out of his cloud-like bliss like a man falling from a plane. "And I am sitting waiting for this time to fade away, Luther." Susan continued.

"*What in the world?*" Good Luther thought. Good Luther abhorred foul language. He was being sucked backward out of his cocoon of romance, beauty, and unbridled emotion. "In my mind I see you trying to climb mountains you fuck wit." *Hey, hey, hey, miss Said. What's with the language?*" Good Luther chastised.

"Hey," a loud and crude voice demanded, jerking Luther all the way down out of heaven and back into the skin of Bad Luther. "Hey, fuck wit!" The ugly earthbound voice demanded again. "Get to work goddamn it. We don't have all fucking day." As Luther opened his eyes the voice said "Jesus Christ! Are you crying?"

Luther realized he was holding someone's hand. Someone that was extremely cold, but very light. As he looked down, the reality of where he was slammed into him and jarred him back to what he was supposed to be doing. The hand he was holding was dead fish white, flaccid and, judging by the bloody termination mid forearm, seemed not to be attached to anything else. In his other hand he held a Hublot Big Bang watch. The 1,282 diamonds and three 3-carat emerald cut diamonds set in the face set the price tag for this particular watch in the vicinity of $50,000.

"No," Bad Luther answered glumly. "That acid is tearing up my sinuses." Next to him was a giant bathtub filled with smoking sick colored liquid. A femur was busy disintegrating just below the surface.

The man currently shitting on his Chi was Mick Murphy, dressed in a large rubber apron, steampunk goggles, a painter's respirator, and rubber gloves. His receding hair was thin, white, and stringy, giving off a strong Lemony Snicket vibe. The breather on his face made his voice sound like Darth Vader after a castration.

"Then get your breather on," Murphy chided. Then he murmured, "Shithead," for effect.

It wasn't that Murphy didn't like Luther specifically; Murphy hated everyone on the planet equally. Murphy grew up on the south side of Chicago and as a teenager found a job killing cattle with a penetrating captive bolt at the stockyards. He had no further prospects than that in his life and had been certain he was going to die an old man with that fucking gun in his hand.

The older cattle killers on the floor were merciless in their harassment of Murphy. They pushed him around, called him names, beat him up and made his life miserable. Eventually the harassment became unbearable, and Murphy was at his breaking point. One of the more aggressive abusers stood behind him dishing out massive doses of ridicule as he jabbed Murphy in the back with a meaty index finger. Murphy spun around and shot his antagonist right in the forehead with the bolt gun.

He was pretty sure his career as a stock killer was officially over, and next stop would be prison for life. He ran as fast and as far as he could, ending up in New York City, a place he hoped would be the perfect mass of humanity amongst which to get lost and start over. It also turned out to be a perfect place for him to get beaten, raped, robbed, and nearly killed. Through a series of unfortunate events, he found himself at the mercy of Paul "Cutter" Manchini, godfather of the Manchini crime syndicate. The Manchinis saw the value in a person who was at the bottom of the barrel, had a background in death, blood, and guts, and also owed the family a ton of money. Murphy became the family's number one cleaner.

"You don't plan on taking that with you. Right?" Murphy said indicating the Hublot. "Not even you can be that stupid. Cutter would rip your dick out by the roots and force feed it to you."

"Shut the fuck up Murphy," Luther said flatly. "That acid horseshit of yours won't burn this. You know that. I'll put it on his dresser before we leave."

Murphy's eye's burned through Luther. It was rule number one when you were cleaning for the Manchini family: do not, under any circumstances, take *any* personal items from the scene. The reason for this rule was sound enough. If someone were to take expensive personal effects from a hit and pawn then there might be something about that individual piece that was identifying and would lead police back to the Manchinis. The thing that would top the list of shit not to take would be a $50,000 Hublot watch. There weren't a lot of those floating around, and even if there were, they certainly would not be pawned.

"You better, asshole," Murphy said as he turned back to the pile of hookers and Wall Street traders lying on a plastic sheet in the dining room. "Because if I *ever* find out you took something you'll be the next lump of shit in that tub." Murphy picked up a saw from the table and bent over a legless torso. Luther dropped the watch in his pocket, and it made a muffled ping sound as it hit the two diamond rings that were already in there.

Luther couldn't stand the thought of all of this wealth going in an evidence box or to some family member of the deceased. He wasn't stupid, he knew if he tried to pawn it, he would be caught almost instantly. With most of the jewelry he pilfered, he removed the jewels from them and melted down the gold. Most of it anyway. On a very few occasions he gave some of the smaller, less noticeable stuff to his girlfriend, Candy Barr, a stripper at the Golddiggers strip club. If he couldn't trust her, then who could he trust?

2.

Luther, back when there was only one Luther, and Tony Ferrari, before he was Tony the Tongue, became fast friends from the very first day they met at Sacred Heart elementary. Tony and Luther had almost nothing in common. Tony came from a broken home, but not a broken home in the classic sense. In Tony's home his parents were still together, and his father was home every single day. Tony's type of broken home meant everything in his home was broken from constant fist fights.

His father was home every day because he didn't work, and at night all of the gin in the Bronx wasn't going to drink itself. His father was on a mission. His parents were very close, but close in the manner that they had world class MMA cage matches every day. You can't get closer to a person than that. They also lived by very strict rules. There could be no ceramic dishes or glass glasses in the house. They seemed to shatter too easily when they hit the wall, floor, or people. Knives were kept in a cabinet with a combination lock on it. It took too long to get the lock off and stab your partner in a fit of rage. It also gave the other combatant a head start.

At night Tony's mother would go off to work in a run-down building that made boxes, and his father would go to his job of ridding the world of gin and chasing women that didn't run too fast but charged a lot. It was the only peace Tony had in his life and he cherished every moment his family spent apart.

Tony was in trouble all the time at Sacred Heart for doing things he thought were actually quite clever. For example, spray painting over the word "Heart" on the sign in front of the school then writing "Fart" in large red letters above it. He released a full jar of odorous ants under Sister Mary Catherine's desk. When the sister accidently smashed a few, the smell was horrific. When she panicked, the rest of the class also panicked, and the stampede to the exit crushed thousands more of the rancid insects. There was little or no question who the culprit was when the only one in the hallway laughing so hard that he cried was Tony.

Consequently, the sister's wooden ruler and Tony's knuckles spent a lot of quality time together.

Luther became Tony's best friend the day Tony got caught passing a note to the girl sitting next to him, Terry Ajello. Sister Mary Catherine was standing directly behind Tony and jerked the folded notebook paper out of his hand. Assuming the note was some type of juvenile crush, Mary Catherine ceremoniously unfolded the note and began to read out loud in the hopes she would embarrass Tony. "Terry the turd fu…" the sister stopped in horrified stasis. The note read *"Terry the turd fucked a bird then blew a wizard."* The note fluttered to the floor as Sister Mary Catherine raised her ruler above her head ready to deliver the righteous vengeance of our Loar and prince of peace on Tony's hand.

"Excuse me sister," Luther said stopping her in mid-swing. "Tony didn't write that note."

"Oh really," the sister was indignant, and suffering from severe violence interruptus, but she loved Luther. Everybody did. "Then pray tell me Mister LaMotta. Who wrote it? You?"

"Oh no sister," Luther said laughing and blushing a little. "I would never write anything like that. Terry is my friend". Terry smiled at him.

"Who then?" The sister was losing patience.

"I have no idea sister," Luther said sweetly. "It was stuck under the foot of my chair. Well, I hate to admit it, but I thought it was funny, so, I passed it to Tony."

The sister's face began to soften from black and white clad berserker to something more benign. "Are you telling me, Mister LaMotta, that someone, in another class, wrote something horrible about Miss Ajello who is in *this* class then left it on the floor under *your* desk."

"Oh no ma'am," Luther said spreading on the innocent act as deep as he could get it, "I'm not saying that at all. That would be conjecture, Sister Mary Catherine, and you've always taught us conjecture and supposition are the devil's hand maidens. I'm just saying the note was there when I got here, I found it, and instead of giving it to you immediately I passed it to Tony. If anyone should be punished it should be me for laughing at something so crude, then dragging Tony into my sin." Luther closed his eyes and laid his hands on top of his desk waiting for the pain he knew would never be administered.

"Don't let it happen again Mister LaMotta," Sister Mary Catherine chastised. She slid her ruler back up her sleeve and floated down the aisle like a ghost in a Stephen King book.

"*Thank you,*" Tony mouthed.

The friendship forged from that single incident would last for as long as the two of them were alive. Tony understood the value of a friend that would take a hit for him when there was nothing to be gained. Tony watched Luther's back and Luther in turn kept Tony out of trouble for the most part. Tony also showed Luther the wilder side of life, albeit not the criminal part. Luther helped Tony with his schoolwork and got him to see the value within himself. Tony got Luther his first beer when they were fourteen. Luther took Tony's final exams for him. Tony got Luther laid when he was fifteen. Luther helped Tony get a job at the local grocery store.

When the boys were juniors in high school, Tony came to Luther asking for a favor that would change Luther's life forever. They were sitting on the steps in front of Luther's house.

"Brother," Tony said, leaving his voice uncharacteristically low, "I'm in a tight place and I really need your help. I wouldn't ask you if it wasn't a matter of life or death."

"That seems a bit overly dramatic," Luther smiled. "We're just juniors in high school. How can *anything* be a manner of life or death to us?"

"This is, Luther," Tony whispered as his eyes darted up and down the street like he was waiting for something horrible to happen. "For all I know there's someone watching me right now. Man, I wouldn't ask if I wasn't in such a tight place."

"What did you do?" Luther asked in an accusatory fashion.

"Man," Tony began. It looked like he was going to burst into tears. "Oh man. I think I've really done it this time. You have to help me."

"Jesus Christ," Luther said as he grabbed Tony by the shoulders. "I'll help you already. What is it?"

"Me and some other dudes knocked over a dealer," Tony was shaking now. "Goddamn it! How the hell were we supposed to know who he was?"

Luther looked horrified and moved back a step.

"Focus Tony," Luther demanded. "What exactly are you talking about?"

"We were just hanging out by the liquor store smoking a little weed," Tony began.

"I TOLD you to stop smoking weed and get rid of those jerks you were hanging around with," Luther scolded. Then he realized this was not the time or place for correction. "Go on."

"There was this guy on the corner selling," Tony continued. "Man, he didn't have a look out, or a money man, or nothing. How could we pass up a chance like that? We rolled this guy and took his pack."

Luther sat down hard on the steps.

"When we got it back to the apartment this guy had a literal shit ton of coke in there. Dude, I've never seen that much coke in one place in my life!"

"What'd you do with it?" Luther sounded like he was in a daze.

"We sold it to a guy we know," Tony was looking at Luther with pleading eyes. "He paid shit for it, but we just wanted to get drunk and buy weed. We didn't fucking know man! I swear to God we didn't know."

"Didn't know what Tony?" Luther was afraid to hear the answer he was sure was coming.

"Who it belonged to."

"Jesus," Luther ran his hands through his hair. "Whose was it?"

"Barbie Blue's." Tony was wide eyed in terror when the name came out of his mouth. "We already pissed the money away man, and they know we were the ones that took the coke."

"Where are the other two guys?" Luther asked. "Why do you need me for this?"

Tony looked at Luther for a moment not wanting to say what had to be said. "They're both dead." Tony was apoplectic now. "I have to get the money back man. I can't get the drugs, so it has to be the money."

Luther paced back and forth for a few steps then stopped. "What do you need me to do, hide you?"

"No man," Tony was weeping now. "They'd find me eventually and I'm a dead man."

"So, what's the plan then?" Luther was growing impatient.

"I need you to help me boost some cars," Tony pleaded. "Just two, three at the max. I have a guy that will chop them for me. I can get the money back and a little more, take it to Barbie Blue and beg for forgiveness."

"That plan is worthless," Luther reasoned.

"Then give me a better one asshole," Tony hissed. "Because it's all I have. They will probably beat the shit out of me and maybe cut something off anyway, but I'll be alive."

Luther bent over at the waist with his hands on his hips. He had to get Tony out of this, but it could all blow up and destroy his life. "All right," Luther finally said. "But no more than three and you owe me huge."

Tony was surprisingly good at boosting cars, especially for someone as young as he was. He knew Barbie Blue would have people out looking for him everywhere, and if he got caught, he was a dead man. He may not have taken a lot of coke by mob standards, but volume wasn't the issue. The fact that *anyone* had ripped off a dealer working on Barbie Blue's crew had to be dealt with swiftly. The longer Tony was allowed to breathe, the weaker it made Barbie Blue look to the other crime families.

Making Leonardo "Barbie Blue" Barbieri look bad wasn't that difficult. He did an outstanding job of that himself just by getting dressed in the morning. The first part of his nickname, which he loathed, was a lifelong anchor, as Barbieri was naturally going to be shortened to Barbie. However, the second part didn't come into being until Barbieri became a king pin. As a mob boss Barbieri could let his freak flag fly as much as he wanted to. If anyone ever gave him just a little bit of shit about what he looked like, he would have them beaten to death.

Barbieri had always been a fan of Elvi Presly and always wore blue suede shoes with giant gold TCB buckles on them, hence Barbie Blue. But after he got the top seat with his mob operation Elvis was most definitely in the building. Barbieri wore blazing white suits with pants that flared out to an impossible bell bottom, a patent leather rhinestone-encrusted belt, a gold TCB necklace, and a blue silk scarf that ran underneath the lapels of his suit jacket. If he had stopped with that, he would have just looked like a very short clown with a shitty attitude. Almost as a dare to make people say something nasty to him, he constantly wore giant gold sunglasses, had his hair dyed jet black and swept up in a pompadour that should have had its own zip code, and carried a black cane with a giant gold tiger head on top.

Tony and Luther had taken two very expensive cars to the chop shop on the first night of the theft-for-freedom operation. Luther's job was simple: just be the lookout, giving Tony plenty of time to get the car running. Luther never warmed up to the real-life grand theft auto game they were playing and couldn't wait for the third car to be stolen so he could put this nightmare behind him.

The last car was nearly too good to be true. Parked about two car lengths off the street next to a flashy nightclub sat six-million dollars' worth of black Bugatti Divo. The lights off the street and night club didn't reflect off the slick roadster; instead they flowed in technicolor stasis around and through the car. Only forty Divos had ever been built, and this one was going to make Tony extremely flush.

"Holy shit dude," Tony whispered to Luther as they stood in the shadows of the alley across the street.

"You have got to be kidding me," Luther whispered back. "How the heck would you even get started on something like that?"

"Oh," Tony said, still ogling the Bugatti. "I had an old-timer teach me everything there was to know about boosting cars. He told me that every car on the planet can be stolen. Some just take a little more time is all."

"So, you know what you're doing then?" Luther asked hesitantly.

"I sure do partner," Tony sounded overly confident. Then turning to Luther, "Same as before dude. You watch the street, I boost the car, we drive away rich men."

The two walked across the street, heads down, hoodies up, telegraphing to anyone paying attention that these two needed watching. As soon as they got to the car Luther walked a few feet behind it, taking a position that would afford him the widest view of the main street. Tony immediately dropped to the pavement and stuck his head under the car. He lay there for several minutes while Luther stood uneasily with his hands jammed into the pockets of his jacket.

"Come on Tony," Luther hissed, "this is taking way too long."

"Calm down Nancy," Tony said as he stood back up by the driver's door. He did something on or near where the door handle should have been, then opened the door. He looked back at Luther smiling. "Presto," he said as he got in the driver's seat. After a few more minutes in the car, Tony got back out and reached under the car again.

"Come on," Luther muttered to himself.

Tony got back in the driver's seat and started the engine. "Let's go!" He shouted to Luther.

Luther took one step forward and then the street erupted into the brightest blinding white light he had ever seen. Things seemed to slow down to a near standstill. Luther felt like he was still standing upright, but he could see the pavement rising up to crush his face. In a foggy effort to protect himself from the inevitable broken nose, he forced a slight twist with the body muscles that were still functioning and slammed hard into the street on his shoulder. He blinked once and saw a very large man in a black suit holding a bloody baseball bat. Then he heard the Divo rocket away from the building. The last thing he saw was the leather bottom of a dress shoe smashing into his face, and then things went black.

Luther woke to a world that held nothing familiar for him to latch onto. He was handcuffed to a bed, and a constant whistle was screaming through his head like a shard of ice. He could remember quite a lot of things from his past, for example, his name and his address. That was a good place to start. Get to the easy things first. He could remember his friend Tony and the trouble he got himself into with the mob, as well as what his role was in helping Tony get out of the hole he had dug. He remembered that beautiful liquid color speed demon on wheels. He remembered Tony rolling underneath it. All Luther remembered after that was the world going blinding white like a nuclear weapon exploded in his face. He also understood he was chained to a bed in a hospital.

When the detectives questioned him, he gave them careful lies, careful answers, and honest confusion. He said he didn't remember being in that alley, a lie. He told them he didn't remember who the guy was that drove the car away, a lie. He told them he didn't remember anything after getting hit, the truth. He told them he had no idea where the car was going, the truth. And he told them he found it almost impossible to understand what people were saying to him, absolute truth.

Luther had no problem understanding the words people were saying, but he couldn't get a grip on nuance. Shortly after he regained consciousness, he asked a nurse if he was in some sort of trouble. "Not at all honey," she had answered sweetly. "We handcuff all of our patients to their beds." He was very relieved when she said that. When the detectives came to question him, he asked why they were there and if he was under arrest or something. "Why do you think you're handcuffed to the bed?" the detective asked in a practiced cop monotone. "Well," Luther slurred groggily, "My nurse told me they handcuff all their patients to their beds." The detectives shared an incredulous look and said they would come back the next day when he felt a little better.

As Luther's trial progressed, the fog persisted. Luther had a hard enough time understanding side conversations behind him and the lawyers' and judge's general conversation. The technical discussions might as well have been in Mongolian. After Luther was sentenced and was being led out of the courtroom, he asked the officer if he was going to jail. "Not at all my friend," the officer replied cheerily. "We're just going to put you in this taxi so we can be sure you get to your new home safely." Luther thanked him.

Luther learned quite a lot during his time in prison. He learned the meaning of sarcasm and that truth was subjective. He learned to trust no one. He learned that there is no end to the sexual depravity or violence humans were capable of exacting on fellow inmates. Luther learned how to fight and how to survive. Then he realized the good side of him had been responsible for being repeatedly raped, being beaten, being robbed, and being humiliated. Good Luther would never be allowed out in public again. Only Bad Luther existed when there were people present, and Bad Luther was confused, angry, and suspicious.

The only person that either of the Luthers could count on was Tony. Good Luther tried to object to that, pointing out that not only was Tony not sharing Luther's pain in prison, but for the entire time Luther was in prison, Tony had never once visited.

Luther's parents had disowned him the second they found out he had been arrested—not convicted, just arrested. That left Luther with nothing and nobody. No matter how much Good Luther argued, Bad Luther would never turn his back on Tony.

On the day Luther was released, it was Tony who was waiting for him at the gate, and it was Tony that gave him a place to stay. Tony had made a name for himself with the Manchini crime family and currently held the position he liked to call "second-level button man." In fact, he answered to Big Benny Amato, the family's actual button man. Tony was the muscle Big Benny used when he didn't want to get his hands dirty. Tony also served as a helper for the family's torture expert Dante "pretty boy" Pesci. Pretty Boy was not a boy, and he definitely was not pretty.

Pretty Boy had been captured by a rival gang as a teenager and tortured for information about the Manchinis' coke supplier. Over the course of several days, the gang tied Pretty Boy to a chair, cut off his balls, knocked out his teeth, cut off both pinkies, sliced an eye in half then scooped it out with a spoon, cut him across the face with a box cutter several times, and then left him to die in an abandoned warehouse that had at one time been a pet food storage facility. Now it was a breeding ground for the biggest rats in the state. Not once, as he endured all of that agony, alone, did he give up a morsel of information.

During the time he languished in that chair after his abusers had left, rats chewed through the ropes on his hands, freeing him. Unfortunately, before the rats went after the rope, they ate three toes and took out a large section of his nose, along with chunks of his cheeks. He crawled into the parking lot and collapsed, resigned to the fact that this was where his last moments on earth would be realized. Cutter's crew had been frantically searching for the boy, and it was Enzo Armani who found him as close to death as a person could be without actually walking into the light and took him to a mob doc.

Unfortunately, that doctor hadn't been an actual doctor because shortly after he finished his residency, he gave up a bright future for a bottle and a gambling addiction. He basically taped, stapled, and sutured Pretty Boy back together. On the other side of Pretty Boy's long recovery, he had become a speed freak, dropping both speed and molly together. In what must have been a dare to see how much more horrible he could look, Pretty Boy always wore an eyepatch with a picture of a bloodshot eyeball painted on it. He resembled the result of the Crypt Keeper and Riff Raff's copulation.

Tony got Luther on the Manchinis' payroll as a "do boy." Tony told Luther he would be a third-level button man and would answer to him just like Tony answered to Big Benny. Also, like Tony with Big Benny, Luther was there when Tony didn't feel like getting his hands dirty. Luther was also a helper for Mick Murphy, the Manchinis' cleaner.

Luther knew how to keep his mouth shut and stand in the corner. Due to those traits he was eventually allowed to stand in the background at meetings and look menacing when the Manchinis' needed to show strength.

Life was good for both Luthers.

3.

Since his prison time there was only one person on the face of the earth, other than Tony, Luther had allowed himself to get close to, and that was Martini Conti. That person was a pale, diminutive man who had shriveled to a nearly unrecognizable version of his former self. For many years he had been forcibly sequestered in the basement of the Manchinis' office building, leaving him with skin so white he was nearly translucent. Conti had been an enforcer for the Manchinis, and he was very good at it. All Conti had to do was be present at a meeting and everyone knew how to stay in line. His brutal tactics were known and feared throughout the New York crime world.

As is usually the case with successful gangsters, Conti began to think he was untouchable within the family, and he began to get close to Paul "Cutter" Manchini's daughter Evangeline. They both knew the gravity of this situation, not only because Evangeline was Cutter's pride and joy but also because she was eighteen and Conti was thirty-five. Evangeline was petite at five foot four and painfully beautiful, with very long, lustrous raven black hair, dark brooding eyes, and a "come hither" look that melted most men. She was also a connoisseur of the finer things in life, such as fine cocaine, alcohol, and ecstasy.

Conti and Evangeline were celebrating the fact that Wednesday had dawned right on time in Evangeline's room. They had begun with several lines of the powder that destroys critical thinking abilities, and, as everyone knows, the only thing that can round off a great coke high is two fifths of Elijah Craig Barrel Proof bourbon. Through alcohol-soaked cocaine eyes, Evangeline began to temp Conti in ways she knew he would never be able to resist. They both knew if they ever got caught, one of them would be torn apart and the other would be shipped off to a convent. But the coke knew better. Several tabs of ecstasy told both of them that chastity in the Manchini house was a stupid rule. The bourbon assured them they would never be caught.

Cutter was walking past his daughter's door when he heard an odd slapping noise coming from inside. That was followed by the life-changing words uttered by his teenage daughter in a low, nearly animal tone. *"Please, stick it in my ass baby."* Then *"Oh Jesus Christ yes! Slam it, slam it as hard as you can!"*

The door of Evangeline's room splintered, and Cutter was rewarded with a head on view of his sweet and innocent daughter being sodomized by his old and vicious muscle man. First Cutter dragged Conti off his daughter by the hair and drug him into the hallway. Evangeline's protest and pleading granted her a vicious backhand, knocking her unconscious. Cutter beat Conti until his hands hurt too much to continue. A crowd had gathered in the hallway, so Cutter told Enzo "Toothpick" Armani, Cutter's right-hand man, to continue. Cutter's son Richy "Junior" Manchini pushed through the crowd, instantly understood what had happened, pulled Toothpick off Conti, and continued the beating.

Conti was cared for and carefully brought back to full health. During that time, he had no misguided thoughts that he was given medical care because Cutter felt bad. He knew full well that he was being brought back from the brink so he could spend the rest of his life in some horrible hell he could never get out of.

That life was realized in the dank, musty, fowl-smelling basement of the Manchini office building. The basement itself was about the size of a medium parking garage with only one feature breaking the severe right angles and the soul-breaking dull grey of the concrete walls, floor, and ceiling. That feature was a pit the size of a three-car garage. Half of it was a swimming pool and the other half a habitat for Bianca. Bianca shared the basement with Conti and was the only living thing he had contact with other than Luther. Bianca was the reason it was kept so warm and humid down there. Bianca was also Cutter's best cleaner.

Cutter's wife Bianca Manchini had looked like a twin to her daughter, just twenty years older. Cutter was the exception to the misogynistic, philandering, profile of his peers. He was deeply in love with Bianca and would have done anything for her. He took her with him on all of the business trips he could, and for the ones she couldn't make, he called her every single night just before they both went to bed.

Any perceived flaw or frailty in the mob business left a person open to scrutiny. Cutter was no exception. He had been dealing with a cartel in the small town of Mapire, Colombia, on the Orinoco River that ran between Venezuela and Colombia. Cutter felt as though his contract with the cartel was not being honored and that their prices had risen too high. The Cartel in turn didn't really care what Cutter thought and demanded they get back to business. Only this time, business would be at a reduced percentage to Cutter due to the inconvenience the Cartel had had to endure at Cutters hands.

Cutter was having none of it and told the Cartel in no uncertain terms their business was done. Shortly after that, Bianca went missing. Cutter assumed correctly the Cartel had her, and he was making the necessary arrangements to have the entire town of Mapire burnt to the ground. Unfortunately, before Cutter was able to launch the rescue mission, he received a small package by courier. The package contained a single thumb drive with a label suggesting Cutter watch the video.

Cutter, Enzo, and Junior watched in enraged horror as the video opened to Bianca tied to a chair in a filthy, dimly lit room. She had been beaten, and she was apparently drugged. Her clothes had been ripped and torn in strategic locations, telling the story of repeated fierce rapes before the video started. A well-dressed Colombian man Cutter recognized as Manuel Ortega, the leader of the cartel he had cut ties with, walked in front of Bianca and addressed the camera.

"Buenos Dias Mister Cutter." The man sounded very pleasant, with a smooth Colombian accent. "I am very sorry things had to come to this. Lo siento mucho my friend. I will say this, though; I understand why you love beautiful Bianca so much," Ortega said easily. Then he nodded his head toward someone off camera. A large man, shirtless and sweating, stepped between the camera and Bianca, dropped his pants to his knees and grabbed Bianca by both sides of her head. She began making gagging noises. Ortega leaned back into the shot. "She is a *very* willing partner mi amigo."

"The good news, Mister Cutter, is that this is *not* a ransom note. No, Dios nos libre. I mean why would she even want to come back to you after being treated to tanta pasión," Bianca continued to gag behind him. "Mister Cutter, this," he waved behind him and his tone grew gradually coarse and angry, "is simply a reminder of what happens when a gringo pedazo de mierda like you fucks with Manuel Ortega!" The gagging stopped and the look on Ortega's face grew into one of mock despair. "Oh, Dios mio Mister Cutter. It would seem Bianca, no matter how much training we have given her, cannot suck cock and breath at the same time."

Ortega backed out of the frame as the man in front of Bianca pulled his pants up and stepped away, leaving a limp and lifeless Bianca in the picture. "Oh well," Ortega said off camera, "at least the crocodile will be happy." The man who had sodomized Bianca to death reappeared, cut Bianca's dead body free and flung her into a pit behind her. The camera moved to the pit and pointed down, showing a huge Orinoco crocodile dragging Bianca by the head into a slimy green pool of fetid water.

Of course, Cutter hired as many Venezuelan and Colombian mercenaries as he could, then personally supervised the murder of every man, woman, and child in the Ortega compound. Manuel Ortega was captured and taken to the crocodile pit, where Cutter sat the entire time Pretty Boy Pesci cut small pieces off Ortega and fed them to the croc. The thing that was most time-consuming was keeping Ortega alive and aware as toes, fingers, sections of limbs, lips, eyeballs, etc. were removed and tossed into the pit. Blood transfusions weren't something you just hurried through.

Cutter spent quite a lot of money packing that crocodile up and shipping it to New York. The line of bureaucrats that needed to be paid off seemed to be endless. Cutter loved the croc, imagining that the essence of his beautiful Bianca lived within the beast. He built a perfect habitat in the basement floor of the family office building for an Orinoco crocodile and named her Bianca in memory of his lost love. Her only job was to disappear the body parts of people Cutter needed to get rid of.

4.

Before Cutter exiled Conti to the realm of the croc habitat, he decreed Conti would forever be referred to by his new name "Croc Turd," and anyone referring to him in any other way would have an eye cut out and fed to them while they watched with the good one. Croc Turd had grown extremely close to Luther and Bianca. Not just because they were all he had, but also because they were both the most honest beings he had been in contact with since his childhood. Luther had no idea how to be deceitful, or treacherous, and Bianca lived only to eat and shit. In fact, Bianca shit was the very most important thing generated from that hell hole.

"Hey," Luther said cordially as he walked toward the pit. Croc Turd was sitting in a hobo-quality lawn chair, wearing boxer shorts, a Hawaiian shirt, sandals, and a Corona sun visor. "I brought Bianca marshmallows."

"They better be Stay Puff Luther," Croc Turd said sullenly, "you know she won't eat that Campfire or Jet Puff bullshit. They give her the shits."

Luther smiled, "Only the best."

"Big ones?" Croc Turd asked suspiciously. "That tiny shit just pisses her off."

Luther held up the family size bag of large Stay Puff marshmallows and jiggled it back and forth a few times as he raised his eyebrows.

"How's life down here buddy?" Luther asked as he sat next to the pit with Croc Turd. Luther would never call Croc Turd by his new name, and he knew better than ever to say his actual name. Cutter had the uncanny ability of finding out *everything*, no matter how small the information might be. He showed the marshmallow bag to Bianca, and she hissed her approval.

"Is there anything I can bring you?" Luther asked as he tossed a treat into Bianca's open mouth. Her huge jaws slammed shut, she blinked once in ecstasy, shook her head, and opened her mouth again. Luther tossed in another treat.

"Well, the powers that be"—Croc Turd tilted his head and shifted his eyes toward the ceiling, raised one finger off the corroded arm rest of the lawn chair, pointed up and mouthed "*them*,"— "Don't seem to have an issue with me reading. How about anything by King or Peter Stroud? None of that dark tower shit though," Croc Turd quickly pointed that same index finger at Luther and frowned. "Man, I don't know what the hell King was thinking when he wrote that bullshit."

"I'll see what I can find," Luther answered nonchalantly as he tossed another treat into Bianca's gaping maw.

Croc Turd gazed into the pit for a minute, then asked Luther, "what's on your mind big guy?"

"Man," Luther answered, laying the Stay Puff bag at his feet. Bianca hissed in disapproval. "I don't know. I just can't seem to get the hang of this Mafia thing."

"Shhhhhhh," Croc Turd held a finger to his lips and shifted his eyes back and forth. "There is no such thing as the Mafia."

"See," Luther said looking at Croc Turd with pleading eyes. "That's the kind of bullshit I'm talking about right there. I know what it is, you know what it is, the people that brought me on board know what it is, but everybody says what it is doesn't exist."

"It's better to not put too much thought into it Luther," Croc Turd advised. "Too much thought around these people can get you hurt," Croc Turd lowered his voice and added, "or killed." Then after some inner reflection he said, "Well except in my case. In my case not enough thinking got me into *my* current position."

"Right?" Luther agreed. "How can you know how much thinking is enough? And these people never say shit. I mean do you want me to punch this guy in the face or do you want me to give him a cookie? How the hell am I supposed to know? And I'm going to tell you something brother, in this world there's a Queen's shit ton of difference between a punch in the face and a cookie."

"I'm pretty sure that's the same way it is in the straight world," Croc Turd explained.

"I know that" Luther replied sullenly. "But in the straight world if you punch a guy in the face who's expecting a cookie, they just look at you all stunned and shit while they sit there bleeding. If you give a guy a cookie that expects a punch in the face, they're all like, 'Oh, hell yeah. That worked out better than I expected.' But in this nut house the boss might be talking to someone, and he gives you the head nod. What the fuck does a head nod mean? Everybody else in this life seems to get it. The boss nods to Tony and he sticks his gun in someone's ear. If he tilts his head, Tony takes the gun back out; if the boss raises an eyebrow, Tony pulls the trigger. How in the hell does he know the difference?"

"Well," Croc Turd replied thoughtfully, "I think you might find the answer to your question in the nuance of the conversation."

"Nuance?!" Luther asked incredulously. "Do I have to take a fucking dictionary to all the jobs I'm on? When Cutter raises his right shoulder and I say, 'Hang on boss I'll be right with you,' I think he would shove my dictionary in my ass."

"OK Luther," Croc Turd said, "why don't you give me a real-life idea of exactly what you're talking about."

"Alright," Luther said, looking at Croc Turd intensely. "The other day Big Benny Amato was negotiating with this small-time dealer. Big Benny tilted his head, so I handed the guy a cup of coffee, then Tony hauls off and slams this guy in the face. He spilled coffee everyplace."

"That seems pretty radical even for Big Benny," Croc Turd said as he scratched his chin. "Why don't you tell me what was being said."

"Well," Luther began reflectively, "Big Benny was telling this dealer that he was going to be working for the Manchinis now. This guy says, 'Just what would make me do something like that?' Big Benny tilts his head toward the guy. What the hell was I supposed to think? I thought

'What would make me feel more comfortable when I was beginning a new partnership?' So I handed him a cup of coffee. You know, kind of like a peace offering, like I was saying to the guy, 'See, we're not all that bad.'"

"And?" Croc Turd asked.

"And?!" Luther said. "What the hell do you mean *and? And*, Tony smashes him in the face. The coffee goes flying, blood is squirting everywhere, Tony picks the guy off the floor and slams his ass in a chair and gets ready to punch the guy again. Then Big Benny tilts his chin up and Tony stops mid swing, then steps behind the guy. I mean, what the hell?"

"Do you see the difference between those two things?" Croc Turd asked slowly, like he was talking to a child.

"Uh, yeah, "Tony said sarcastically, "one ends in a shitload of blood and the other ends in a pleasant cup of coffee and a conversation."

Croc Turd mulled this for a second, smacked his lips and looked up at Luther, "Okay, let's break this down buddy. Was Big Benny asking this gentleman if he was interested in a partnership, or was he telling him there was *going* to be a partnership whether he liked it or not?"

"I guess he was telling him," Luther sounded confused.

"Yeah," Croc Turd agreed. "I think that makes the most sense also. So, second thing, was this guy receptive to the idea, or was he hesitant?"

"I gotta say he was pretty hesitant," Luther was catching on. "In fact, now that I think of it, he was kind of acting a little hostile."

"Hostile," Croc Turd's eyes went wide. "Now we're getting some place! And with this hostility, would you say this guy seemed even tempered, or would you say he was being a little bit of an asshole?"

"Well," Luther began slowly as the lights came on, "I think he was actually being a little bit of a dick."

"And," Croc Turd prodded.

"And," Luther's eye's started to brighten, "and I think he was kind of asking for it."

"Asking for what Luther?" Croc Turd asked.

"He was asking for a punch in the face," Luther said triumphantly. "In fact, this little asshole was begging for it. Holy shit! I never thought of that before. He was begging to get punched in the face, and I gave him a cup of coffee. What a dickhead," Luther slapped himself in the forehead hard enough to leave a red mark.

"Exactly," Croc Turd said as he leaned back in the lawn chair spreading his hands wide. "See, this shit's not that hard at all."

"Yeah," Luther confided, "but I don't have the time for someone to give me a play-by-play so I can react right when the time comes."

"Just read the room buddy," Croc Turd sounded defeated. "It really isn't that hard." Croc Turd regretted those last words as soon as they came out of his mouth. He realized that he had just told Luther the world was a simple place, for everybody except him.

"What the hell does that even mean? *Read the room,*" Luther sounded hurt and exasperated.

"Why don't you just wait next time and do what Tony does?" Croc Turd suggested.

"Tony says I have to be more pro-something," Luther said searching for the word. "I don't know, *protective*?"

"Maybe proactive?" Croc Turd was trying to be gentle.

"Yeah, uh, pro—what you said," Luther said snapping his fingers.

"If that makes Tony happy, then you should do that," Croc Turd suggested.

"Yeah, yeah," Luther said smiling, "I'll do that." Then to himself. *"Productive, how hard is that?"*

Luther reflected on that for a second, trying to commit everything Croc Turd had said to memory, then said, "Thanks man. I always know you'll straighten me out." Croc Turd smiled thinly. "Hey," Luther continued, "I hate to cut this short, but Tony wants me to go with him to back up Big Benny for something so I gotta get going. Do you have the bucket?"

"Yeah," Croc Turd said as he pulled a stainless-steel bucket adorned with a gleaming gold bail from behind the lawn chair. "She's been a little backed up, but everything broke loose this morning. Go get the box, and I'll get the net."

"Cool," Luther said as he stood up and walked toward a closet near the pit.

Croc Turd walked to the wall, retrieved a long-handled pool skimmer net, and began to walk around the pit like he was searching for something. After a few steps he stopped, dipped the net into the pit, and came up with a net full of crocodile shit. He swung the net out of the pit and dumped the reptilian scat into the silver bucket.

Luther went into the closet and stood in front of a row of shelves full of hundreds of identical stainless-steel boxes that were each twenty-four inches wide, twelve inches deep, and twelve inches high. Each box had ornate gold hinges, gold handles on the sides, a gold hasp and pad lock, and a golden butterfly attached to the peaked lid. A gold and pewter plaque on the front of each box bore the word *beloved*. Luther solemnly chose one of the boxes, lifted it off the shelf, and walked back out to the pit.

"Is there enough, or too much?" Luther asked Croc Turd.

"Looks like just enough," Croc Turd answered as he dipped out more scat. Luther set the box next to the bucket, and Croc Turd slowly poured the contents of the bucket into the box, making sure he didn't spill the least bit. Luther closed the lid, locked the hasp, and dropped the golden key in his pocket.

After the incident in Colombia, Cutter had seemed more than just a little off. He tended to be more violent, while at the same time being overly benevolent. A staunch Catholic, Cutter believed deeply in the resurrection of the soul and the meaning of religious signs, like a blue bird on your windowsill, which might hold the essence of your mother, who is watching out for you. That was Cutter's frame of mind when he brought the crocodile back to New York and named it Bianca. He was convinced that the essence of his precious wife was contained in the persona of the croc, but more than that, he believed that Bianca was physically still in the croc's excrement. Consequently, every particle of croc shit was carefully removed from the pit, laid to rest in silver boxes, and shipped to Miami, where it was stored in the family crypt.

"I wonder if he understands that whatever parts of his wife were actually in this thing at one time were probably shit into the shipping crate on the way here?" Croc Turd mused.

"I wonder about that too," Luther agreed. "I know if I eat corn, I shit it out one, no more than two days later. I don't just keep shitting corn for the rest of my life like some kind of circus freak."

"So," Croc Turd continued with the conjecture, "I wonder who *this* is that's about to live in the lap of luxury in Miami then."

Luther looked up at the ceiling and ran that around in his head for a second. "Actually, I think it might be the guy I just told you about that I gave coffee to, and Tony belted."

Croc Turd raised his eyebrows.

"Yeah," Luther explained, "turned out that guy was a real asshole. Big Benny folded his arms and Tony shot the guy in the head. I damn near lost a finger because I thought Big Benny wanted the guy slapped."

"You know," Croc Turd said folding his arms, "Pigs would be much better for this kind of work. I hear they'll go through bone like butter."

"Well," Luther said as he hefted the weight of the shit-filled box, "I guess unless someone face fucks Evangeline to death and then feeds her to pigs, we'll never know."

"You do have a point my friend," Croc Turd said slapping Luther on the back. "Take care of yourself Luther."

"You too buddy," Luther said cordially.

"Hey," Croc Turd said to Luther's back as he reached the exit, "remember, none of that Dark Tower bullshit."

"I got ya dude," Luther answered, then disappeared through the door, taking with him a silver and gold box full of small-time drug dealer who had recently been filtered through an endangered species of South American crocodile.

5.

The exterior of the ragged and disintegrating warehouse stood indifferently in the center of twenty other exact replicas of itself. From a distance, they all shared a precise military straightness and uniform rate of dilapidation, making them look like an army of vagabonds standing at attention, awaiting inspection by the chief derelict. Large holes dotted the roof, into which tattered sheets of rolled asphalt bent inward as though they were trying to escape the elements. Where the roof had exposed the superstructure, the rusted steel skeleton was sadly losing the battle of keeping the roof off the floor.

Most of the windows had been smashed out by rock-throwing hooligans who had taken a break from stealing bikes and robbing old ladies to devote time to their other job of destroying property. Shards of broken glass covered the floor and glinted magically as the sun reflected off the edges. Large pools of fetid water lay stagnant beneath the gaping ceiling. A carpet of slick, stinking green slime lay on the surface of the concrete floor, causing revulsion in anyone who got near it, like a naked fat man sitting in his lounger eating chili with his fingers. A beautiful black and green palette of moss and mildew added a swath of color to the portions of walls that were never exposed to the light. The smell would chase the stench of death screaming into the night.

In a small damp back room that made the rest of the warehouse look like a ballroom, four men were having a spirited conversation. Well, actually, three men were conversating; the fourth had a sock stuffed in his mouth held in place by a strip of grey duct tape. The man tasting his own feet was held in an armless office chair by copious amounts of silver duct tape wrapped around his chest. He was slight of build but muscular. Religious tattoos like the Madonna and Christ on the cross, intermixed with tattoos of naked women, slid from under his white tank top undershirt and flowed down his arms. With his arms taped behind him such as they were, the Madonna did a little dance every time the man struggled. Black dress trousers flowed beautifully down to the tops of ankles that were taped to the chair legs. Very expensive Italian leather shoes angled out every time the man was hit in the head. Blood ran freely down his ruined face and over the tape, dripped off his chin, and then pooled in his lap.

Big Benny was facing the man in the chair. His camelhair overcoat had a speck of blood just under one of the buttons. Benny's hands were stuffed deeply into the coat's pockets, and he rocked back and forth on his shoes slightly after he asked each question. Tony stood behind the man on one side and Luther on the other.

"Do you have any idea what the amount is now?" Big Benny asked. The man's pleading answer was incoherent against the sock and the tape. Big Benny nodded to Tony, and Tony punched the man so hard in the face it knocked him over backwards. Tony and Luther bent down to pick the man up.

"*I don't think he can answer with that sock in his mouth,*" Luther whispered to Tony as they righted the chair.

"*Shut the fuck up!*" Tony hissed at Luther. Big Benny nodded toward Luther, and Luther shot Tony a questioning look, slightly shrugging his shoulders.

Tony leaned his head toward Luther and stage whispered, "*Take the tape off.*"

"*Really?*" Luther mouthed as he squinted. Tony tilted his head toward the man in the chair and raised his eyebrows in a gesture that telegraphed, *yeah really, and now.*

"Are you two shit heels about done?" Big Benny asked as he spit on the ground for emphasis.

Luther reached over, ripped the tape off, and the man spit the sock on the floor.

"Honest to God Benny. . ." the man started to plead.

Benny nodded to Luther. Luther looked at Tony with his forehead knitted in indecision. Tony made a fist, cocked his elbow back slightly, and nodded toward the man in the chair. Luther instantly broke the man's jaw. The resultant howling scream reverberated through the halls of depression that marked the boundaries of the warehouse. Big Benny tilted his head toward Tony, and Tony replaced the tape. Luther looked at Tony confused.

"Can you keep your shit together?" Big Benny asked the man in the chair. The man nodded ferociously. Big Benny shot Luther a look. Luther smashed the man in the chair in the temple.

"What the hell is wrong with you, asshole?!" Big Benny yelled at Luther. "Take the fucking tape off?!"

Luther immediately ripped the tape off. "*He could have just said that*" Luther muttered to Tony.

"What the fuck did you just say?" Big Benny bellowed at Luther.

"Nothing Benny," Tony quickly answered, "He just said that this guy is a real asshat. That's all." Big Benny glared at Luther. Luther shrugged, held his palms out, and let a look of subservience spread across his face. "Yeah Benny," Luther verified, "what Tony said."

Big Benny turned his attention back to the man in the chair.

"*What the fuck?*" Luther mouthed at Tony as more of a question than an exclamation.

"How long did you think you were going to be able to walk around town laughing at us?" Big Benny demanded of the man.

"Honestly," the man pleaded, "I would never think of laughing at you guys."

Big Benny blinked at Tony, and Tony slapped the man in the back of the head.

"You're laughing at us every time you breathe, ass wipe," Big Benny shot back. "Do you have *any* idea how much you're into us for?"

"Benny. . ."

Big Benny turned his head toward Luther. Luther started to put the tape back on the man's mouth. Tony quickly knocked the tape out of Luther's hand and smashed the man's toes with the heel of his shoe.

"One more fucking time," Big Benny warned Luther. "Get with the program." Then turning his attention to the man in the chair "You're down one point five mil in *our* books, ass licker," Big Benny said darkly.

"*What?*" the man was astonished. "I only borrowed seven fifty."

"I don't give a syphilitic rat's ass what you think," Big Benny cut him off. "Have you ever heard of vig?"

"*Who's Vig?*" Luther whispered to Tony. Tony shook his head in a short choppy motion. Big Benny appeared not to have heard the question.

"Yeah Benny," the man tried to explain, "But I never thought. . ."

"Shut up!" Big Benny roared. "You're right about one thing: you didn't think. I'm sure one thing you *did* think about was that we wouldn't snuff your ass because you owed us money. I bet you thought that just wouldn't be good business sense. By the way, what's the name of that whore shit bag you're banging now? It's Loretta, isn't it?" Benny's cell phone rang, and he turned his back as he answered it.

"Yeah," Benny said into the phone. Then he laughed and shook his head, "Of course he did." Benny hesitated a second, "No, don't worry about it, we'll send Luther and Murphy over when they get done here." Big Benny pocketed his phone and turned around chuckling. "Dude," Big Benny said to the man, "You are absolutely amazing. We went to your shit hole apartment," Big Benny paused and laughed as he rubbed his mouth with his hand. "Uh, yeah, we went to that dump because we heard a rumor you were flush and planned on skipping the country with what's-her-twat." Big Benny looked at Luther and Tony and asked, "Do you know where this fucking rocket scientist hid two million dollars?" Luther shrugged. "He hid it," Big Benny was laughing again, "He hid it under his bed. Yeah, no shit, under his bed."

"By the way, shitbag," Big Benny directed his anger at the man again, "you aren't going anyplace with Lucinda or whatever. She doesn't travel well with a bullet hole in her eye socket."

The man began to cry and plead. Big Benny looked at Luther and tilted his head toward the man in the chair. Luther began to cut him loose. Tony quickly pulled his gun and shot the man behind the ear.

"You fucking moron," Big Benny spit at Luther, "what the hell is wrong with you?"

"I'll talk to him Benny," Tony said stepping in front of Luther. "He just gets a little confused is all."

"You do that," Big Benny growled, "Or the next time there's going to be two extra bodies for Murphy to take care of."

Big Benny looked toward the ragged hole in the wall where the door to the office used to be and tilted his head toward the body in the chair. Murphy walked into the room wearing steam punk goggles on his forehead, carrying a large duffel bag in one hand and a toolbox in the other.

"Clean this shit up," Big Benny muttered to Murphy as he walked out of the room.

Murphy laid the duffle and toolbox down and started to put his rubber apron on. "I swear to Christ, dip shit," Murphy said to Luther, "if you don't get your shit together, you're going to get a one-way ticket to Miami riding in a silver shit box."

6.

Good Luther placed his Aftershokz over his ears, adjusted them for comfort, and pushed the power on button. "Battery high, connected," a soft female voice whispered in his ear. "*Thank you so very much Beth,*" Good Luther said to his headset. Good Luther closed his eyes and bowed his head in reverence. Music was just a single part of the holy trinity that gave Good Luther life and meaning. The others were poetry and good wine, in equal parts. He drew in a deep Zen breath, allowing the warmth of black bamboo–scented wax from his warmer to roll completely through his sinuses, float around his soul, and nuzzle against his extremely emotional heart like a white longhaired kitten.

Good Luther steadied himself to allow the opening notes of the morning's first taste of beautiful music to marinate in the space between his ears, then cover him in syrupy comfort. He reached up to his left ear, gently pushed the play button, and braced himself.

♪♫♫♫ George Harrison spirited the opening notes down through his fingers and onto the strings of his 1961 Sonic Blue Stratocaster, each note living a life of its own, which complemented the next, and the next, and the next. Crisp clear beauty rang in his head like a golden mist of painful ecstasy. Then came the mind-crushing elegance as John easily started the cotton soft lyrics, and George and Paul laid the foundation with the harmony. "There are places I remember, all my life, though some have changed. . ."

Good Luther tilted his head up, eyes still closed, and swam in a silken sea of harmony. "*Oh, my merciful heavens, yes,*" Good Luther swooned. "*Yes John, yes, I can feel it.*"

"Some are dead, and some are living. In my life I've loved them all."

"*Ummmmmmm,*" Good Luther moaned in sensual rapture. Good Luther spun in a small circle, allowing his socks to glide on the cheap linoleum floor, then waltz stepped to the kitchen counter, left foot, sway left, right foot, sway right, in perfect time with the beat Ringo was laying down. Thick scarred and bruised hands floated through the air in time, drifting left, then drifting right, filled with expression, joy, and solemnity like the graceful flight of a butterfly.

Good Luther stopped at the kitchen counter, bowed, and lifted his watering can to his chest, his right arm elevated and curved in a large loop in front of him. The harpsicord interlude began, and Good Luther pointed his right toe at an outward angle, knee slightly bent, then moved into a beautiful natural spin. Around the apartment he spun while George Harrison's fingers danced on the keyboard.

With each practiced step, Good Luther dipped and rose again like a beautiful sea bird riding a wave on the open ocean. Oh yes, Good Luther could dance, and dance beautifully. Good Luther talked and read poetry out loud; he sang and wept openly and freely without shame or hesitation. That was why Good Luther was never ever allowed outside the apartment. Out there lived loutish brutes, vagabonds, and horrible drug-addled specters of the humans they once had been. They were constantly watching and waiting to exploit any weakness in people such as Good Luther.

Out there people could hurt you, beat you, and rob you. Out there Good Luther would be laughed at and ridiculed, at best, or beaten, at worst. Sometimes Good Luther would seep out of the recesses of Bad Luther's mind, where he would stand quaking in numbing terror as he watched Bad Luther move through the terrifying world. In public Good Luther existed only in Bad Luther's head and occasionally was so deeply horrified by the violence he saw Bad Luther commit he would chastise and beg Bad Luther to stop. Good Luther and Bad Luther were constantly struggling for control of physical Luther in the outside world. Bad Luther was locked in a soundproof box while he was in Good Luther's apartment.

Good Luther spun through the apartment, stopping at each plant to deliver water and a greeting. *"Hello, my lush Philodendron,"* Luther said as he poured water around the pot. *"And good day to you Mister Pothos,"* Good Luther crooned as he stroked a leaf. *"Why would anyone ever call you Devil's Ivy? I mean, just look at you."* Good Luther spun and danced through his dining room, living room, and bedroom, encouraging plants. Cacti, succulents, vines, variegated leaves, deep green leaves, pale green leaves, and jade plants covered every flat space in every room.

The last note of "In My Life" floated into the past, and soft sterling notes of violins drifted in. Good Luther set the watering can back on the kitchen shelf and held on to the edge of the counter with both hands, bolstering himself for the sensory assault of emotion he was about to be treated to. The violins dipped and weaved into his mind for the short interlude. He bowed his head again and squeezed his eyes tight as the violins stepped back like a curtain revealing the Venus De Milo and an acoustic guitar whispered on.

"Love will abide, take things in stride. Sounds like good advice, but there's no one at my side." Linda Ronstadt's voice rolled sweet and melodic in Good Luther's head and coated his personal realm in a sheet of doleful beauty. Good Luther didn't move, afraid he would lose the magic of her voice. His head swayed lightly back and forth. ". . .and I think I'm gonna love you for a long, long time." Tears welled up in Luther's eyes, then slid to the edge of his burning cheeks and splashed bitterly on the white Formica. Good Luther sniffed back the passion that was being sucked out of him.

He stood up and blinked, forcing white hot tears to run down his face and neck, but he didn't rub them away. They were an integral part of what he felt when he was moved like this. Wiping away that part of him would be akin to ripping out his heart. He reached into the refrigerator and removed a plate of small cheese squares and sections of various sausages. He set that on the counter and retrieved a box of crackers from the cupboard.

"And I think I'm going to love you for a long, long time." Violins escorted Linda past the veil, leaving Good Luther broken and euphoric. He reached up and pushed the pause button on the headset. He didn't want whatever was coming next to be released until he got his things together. With the tray in one hand, the crackers under his arm, and a wine glass and bottle of 2019 Stolen Owl Malbec in the other, he made his way to his fire escape.

Good Luther lived on the fourth floor of a shabby apartment building in the middle of a shabby New York neighborhood, but his fire escape platform was worlds away and resting in another dimension. He placed the plate, bottle, glass, and box on a small cast iron café table. The tabletop was a mosaic of flowers that had been created using broken ceramic tiles. The railing was covered in plants that writhed and folded around the rusted railing, hiding the grotesque reminders of where he actually was. Good Luther pressed the play button on his headset, and the light lilting notes of an orchestra began, then melted into a clarinet solo. Good Luther smiled against the sun.

Edith Piaf spoke the opening lines, then slid into the music and began the haunting melody. "Quand il me prend dans ses bras, Qu'il me parle tout bas, Je vois la vie en rose." Good Luther held his wine glass high, swaying it back and forth, and sang along, because Good Luther spoke both French *and* Italian. Luther smiled and sang as he languished in the warmth of the sun and the beauty of La Vie En Rose. He sipped wine and held it in his mouth, savoring every note and flavor, then he swallowed, taking in each aftertaste as they resurrected themselves in his throat and on his palate. He took a small bite of cheese and added a bit of summer sausage, chewed them, appreciated them, tasted them deep and fully, then washed them down with a bit of wine.

On the grimy streets of New York, the city clawed and scratched at one another, trying to gain purchase within the elusive American dream. Four floors above those streets, an emotionally damaged third-level button man for the mob danced with a beautiful French café singer and dared the world to interfere.

7.

The Manchini family conference room was cavernous and appointed with enough highly polished walnut woodwork to redeck an aircraft carrier. Walnut walls, cabinets, window frames, chairs, and flooring gave one a feeling that one had wandered into a very shiny hobbit hole that had been dug into the side of a giant walnut trunk. The only thing that wasn't walnut in that office was the runway-length, smooth, semi-oval desk in the center of the floor that screamed overcompensation. That desk had been had crafted using only the finest of the most endangered and illegal hard wood on the planet, Madagascar rosewood. Black floor-to-twenty-foot ceiling chiffon curtains hung on gold rods and were tied back with gold braid tasseled ropes.

Locked glass doors covering a shelf on one wall protected a 2.7-million-dollar bottle of Macallan Adami 1926 Scotch, a bottle of $55,000 Old Rip Van Winkle twenty-five year old bourbon, a bottle of $5,000 Morus LXIV gin, a $25,000 shipwrecked bottle of Juglar vintage, circa 1820, and a handmade 24kt gold and sterling platinum bottle encrusted with 6,500 diamonds containing 100-year-old Henri Dudognon Heritage Cognac Grande, cheap at twice the price of two million dollars.

Paul "Cutter" Manchini sat at the head of the table, leaning on his elbows with his fingertips touching in front of his mouth. Cutter had earned his nick name when he was just sixteen years old and his Don asked him to *take out* a rival, making sure he *felt it*. Cutter went after the target with a box cutter while he was tied to a chair. When Cutter was done the victim had received 1,826 small one-inch razor cuts all over his body. Cutter sat in a chair for two hours, wiping away clotted blood, watching the man slowly bleed to death.

Now Cutter was the head of the biggest crime syndicate anywhere in the world. On his right sat his number two, Enzo "Toothpick" Armani. Enzo had received his nickname in an obvious way: he constantly had a toothpick sticking out of his mouth. Once Enzo had risen to the rank of number two, he replaced the standard wooden toothpick with a sterling silver one. However, with an overly romanticized name like Enzo, the slovenly nickname never really stuck.

If you were to imagine a strikingly handsome pure Sicilian with long, sensuous jet-black hair that had been haphazardly greased back, swarthy skin, and green eyes in a rakish face that would fit perfectly on a Grand Prix driver, you had Enzo. He had come to New York from Sicily to look after a certain organization's interests there. Five years after Enzo started working for Cutter, the Manchini family made a successful move against the main family in Sicily, and now Enzo was the guy that kept the Sicilians honest.

To Cutter's left was Richy "Junior" Manchini. Junior wasn't actually a junior, and nobody ever called him that to his face. It had begun as a derogatory handle when the coke sniffing, alcoholic, womanizing fuck-up had begun to work for his father. Richy, as most fuck-ups do, thought he was smarter than his father and everyone else around him, so he started an underground coke business that, if run correctly, *should have* undermined Cutter's own businesses. Richy was unable to get good coke from the suppliers his father used, for obvious reasons, so he got *his* product from Vietnam. Unbeknownst to Richy, the Vietnamese got *their* product from Cutter's suppliers. By the time it got to Richy, the coke had been stepped on more times than the doormat in a two-dollar whorehouse.

Richy's coke was shit, his distributors were shit, and his product was shit. The only people that were buying Richy's coke were people who didn't know any better and high school kids. Hobos wouldn't even touch it. Richy worked his ass off ineptly trying to hide his backdoor operations from Cutter, but Cutter had known all along what Richy had been doing. Cutter's approach to the problem was kind of like setting a toddler in a sandbox. The kid could work all day long doing meaningless shit and stay out of the way of the adults.

When he was high and drunk, which was the majority of the time, Richy bragged to his nightclub friends that he was cleaning up in the drug trade; however, Richy was actually losing his ass. He *thought* he was making huge money because large amounts of cash kept coming into his office. He had never considered that the cash going out was almost twice as much as the inflow. Cutter financed and tolerated Richy's shortcomings while the rest of Cutter's crew laughed at Richy behind his back.

Standing ominously behind Cutter in the shadows was Alessandro "the Monster" Bianchi. No one knew where the Monster came from, what his background was, or how he and Cutter had met. One day the Monster wasn't there, and the next day he was, with no explanation of who he was or how he got there, or even an acknowledgement that he was in the room. Everyone in the family knew better than to attempt communication with the Monster. First, the Monster had had his vocal cords damaged when his throat had been sliced open in a murder attempt, and he was left mute. Second, and most importantly, if anyone other than Cutter, Enzo, or Richy tried to talk to him, they might get one word in and maybe half of another before the Monster punched them right in the face. Cutter said that was because the Monster took his bodyguard duties very seriously and, in the Monster's mind, the only reason someone would speak to him was so they could distract him from his duties and attack Cutter. Everyone else was pretty sure it was just because the Monster really liked to punch people. Kind of like a hobby.

The Monster had been shot five times, stabbed eight, and even hung once while in service to Cutter. Every one of the assailants, including the hangman, had been brutally murdered by the Monster—most of them while they were in the process of shooting, stabbing, or even hanging him. The Monster was more like a weapon; Cutter pointed his finger and people died.

Around the table sat the four crime bosses that made up Cutter's New York operation. They all posed in various forms of seated pantomime as they tried to convey a certain aura without having to actually say anything. Perpetually pissed off, dangerously stoic, morbidly irritated, and murderously aloof demeanors were plastered on brooding faces that strove to look anywhere in the room except in the general direction of Cutter. Behind each one of the bosses stood a slightly less terrifying version of the Monster acting as personal protection. Luther and Tony guarded the door. The men at the table were all legends in the crime world.

Leonardo "Barbie Blue" Barbieri in his gleaming white attire, pompadour, and blue suede shoes represented the area of Staten Island. He sat easily, leaning his weight against the left armrest of his chair as he strummed the fingers of his right hand impatiently on the golden lion's head of his cane.

Frank Russo, representing Manhattan, basked in relaxed excessive opulence. If it wouldn't have made him look far too much like comedy legend Minnie Pearl, he would have left the price tag on everything he was wearing. A white hand-woven straw Brent Black Panama hat positioned at a deliberate rakish angle sat above chiseled Italian features. The fusion of the finest Mongolian cashmere and handpicked Chinese Mulberry silk (made only by the Bombyx Mori moth) used in the creation of his ostentatious Stuart Huges R. Jewels Diamond edition suit draped immaculately over his strong, lean physique. The rows of .5 carat diamonds in the jacket seams danced and glittered discreetly each time he moved. A platinum and diamond time edition iPhone 15 pro sat on the table positioned next to his ring laden right hand sporting an Omega Speedmaster Moon Watch Professional. Beneath the table, Testoni diamond buckle alligator shoes rested flat on the walnut floor, the left one tapping in mostly hidden impatience.

Frederico "Red Fred" Esposito, representing Brooklyn, wore his signature red silk scarf around the neck of his Greek embroidered guayabera. He loved Panatela slacks from the '70s and had a local tailor make them for him. There were fifteen pairs of identical black Panatela slacks hanging next to fifteen black Greek embroidered shirts in his closet and fifteen red silk scarves in his dresser drawer. When he spoke, he did so around an eternal soggy, fat, unlit cigar that had possibly been clenched in his teeth since birth. Esposito had murdered, cheated, and lied his way to the top of an Italian mob in an area that had only a 6% Italian demographic.

Last, and pretty much least, Aldo "Hookens" Ray, representing Queens was the epitome of non-descript. As the first page in L. Frank Baum's *Wizard of Oz* described everything in Kansas as gray, the word that would describe Ray was *meh*. Even his nickname had a depressingly boring back story. Hookens was the last name of the character Aldo Ray played in the movie *Battle Cry*. His manner of dress was irrelevant, his mannerisms made him look as if he had just finished his last chemo treatment, and his eyes would have made a Bloodhound look damn near giddy.

He was murderous, although no one could remember the last person he was responsible for killing. He was treacherous, but people trusted him instantly and implicitly. Most could never imagine that anyone so outwardly depressing was dangerous in any way. He was ruthless, but no one gave crossing him a second thought. Even the bodyguard behind him was slouching and pasty white; his suit hung on him like he would have been better served guarding a cornfield with a pole shoved up his ass. Now Ray simply existed in the world of organized crime and had to finish most of the orders he gave to his men with the words "yes, really."

"Any great nation," Cutter addressed the room, "has a beginning, a flourishing, a time of turbulence and then an ignominious end. Our *family* has had a beginning and, currently, a time of flourishing that has left us all basking in the well-appointed lap of luxury. Life is, as they say, sweet." Cutter placed his palms on the edge of the table and reclined back in his chair.

"They also say familiarity breeds contempt, and good fences make good neighbors." The bosses shifted uncomfortably. "Now, we find us here on the precipice of turbulent times, with pissing contests and *"Ooooops I killed one of your guys, my bad,"* incidents, boarder disputes, real or imagined, and disrespect that I have to deal with, and the disappointingly small tributes coming back to me are all out of control. All of this has led me to the conclusion that you motherfucking children have it too good and refuse to play well without adult supervision."

"What the hell is this?" Barbie Blue demanded. "Are you accusing any of us of shorting you on the kick up?" The Monster began to take a step forward, but Cutter raised a hand to stop him.

"I find it amazing Barbie," Cutter knew Barbie Blue hated his nickname, "that out of *all* the issues I just mentioned, the only one you focus on is a short kick up."

"That's because all of the other bullshit was just that," Barbie Blue fumed.

"Although Mister Barbieri disagrees with my level of irritation," Cutter said dismissing Barbie Blue, "I can assure you that things are about to dramatically change for future operations. This pissing and moaning, and the shoving matches are going to stop right fucking now. I am going to institute guidelines for each of the boroughs."

"This is horseshit," Esposito said under his breath. Cutter chose to ignore it.

"Each one of you," Cutter went on evenly, "will have specific areas of entrepreneurial action you'll be allowed to participate in." The men around the table began to murmur dissent.

"Allowed?!" Barbie Blue asked incredulously.

Cutter slammed his palm down on the table. "Enough of this bullshit!" Cutter chastised. "What about our operations or our charter makes *any* of you bitching shit birds think this is a Goddamned democracy?!" The room became quiet, and Cutter let that sink in for a minute. Then he stood up and leaned on the table. "This is *my* organization. This is only a small part of *my* worldwide operation. If any of you assholes can no longer accept that, there's the door."

"That's great by me," Hookens said. Cutter glared at him.

"Now," Cutter went on, "I don't personally care what you guys do with your protection business, numbers, theft, gambling, or any of that kind of shit as long as you stay in your own shitty areas."

"You aren't actually going to tell us what we can and what we can't do in our own territory, are you?" Russo asked as he adjusted his watch so it would be more visible to the others.

"I just said I didn't care," Cutter said like he was talking to a child.

"Yeah," Esposito had a New York accent so deep it made it nearly impossible to understand him, "But, with all that other bullshit it sounded like there was a 'but.' So, let's hear it."

Cutter leaned back and played with his wedding ring for a second as he surveyed the room. Finally, he looked toward Enzo. Enzo moved the toothpick from one side of his mouth to the other and tilted his head slightly.

"As I said before, you people can't seem to stay out of each other's backyards when it comes to the important operations," Cutter sounded almost threatening. "Every time I turn around, one of you is coming to me, wanting me to give you permission to hit one of the other ones."

"Which one of these motherfuckers wanted me hit?!" Esposito demanded.

"Look," Cutter smoldered, "Every single person in this room has asked me to kill one of the other ones."

"Motherfucker!" Barbie Blue exclaimed.

"SHUT THE FUCK UP!" Cutter commanded. "All of you, just shut your moronic mouths for a single second, get your ignorant ass heads out of your fat asses and pay attention!" Cutter stood up and walked behind his chair as if he were either contemplating his next words or trying extremely hard to not shoot every single person at the table. Finally, he moved back to the table and pushed his forefinger down on the endangered tabletop for emphasis. "This," he jabbed his finger into the desk with each of the next three words, "this, right, here, is exactly the kind of shit I'm talking about. You assholes should have been opera singers. It's always ME, ME, ME, ME with you dicks and I am FED, THE, FUCK, UP!

"Since *you* people can't play nice, I guess I have to tighten up the rules a little. Keep in mind that you *all* still work for me, and in that light, if any of you have an issue with what I'm about to say, I assure you there will be a different ass in your chair for the next meeting we have."

Four pairs of eyes blazed at Cutter.

"First," Cutter went on, ignoring the dissent, "I'll lay out who gets what action. First, Frank, you get trafficking. . ."

"What the hell?" Ray was incredulous. "We have the biggest trafficking business anywhere on the east coast."

"There was one thing I forgot to say," Cutter added. "This list wasn't simply pulled out of my ass. I actually put quite a bit of thought into it. In that light, if you would be so kind as to shut the hell up until I'm done, I would greatly appreciate it. Now, for you Ray, Queens also gets trafficking."

"Great," Barbie Blue whined. "I guess all you have to do is bitch and you get what you want."

"Goddamn it!" Cutter slammed his palm on the table again, "I'm not going to say it again, Barbie, let me fucking finish!"

"That's twice," Barbie Blue fumed at the use of his nickname.

Cutter held Barbie Blue in an icy glare for a long second, "Now, that leaves prostitution for you in Brooklyn, Fred. You already have the biggest stable of whores in the western hemisphere. A few of them are even fuckable."

"Everything is fuckable," Esposito said.

"And finally," Cutter hesitated for effect, "that leaves the other prostitution slot for Staten Island. Is that good with you. . . Barbie?"

Barbie Blue slammed his hands down on the table as he stood up. "That's the last time motherfucker. I don't have to sit in this bullshit tree trunk of yours and listen to you constantly insult me." He ripped his gold sunglasses off the table and slammed them onto his face. "This is all going to blow up in your face, you sanctimonious shit." Barbie Blue turned towards the door. "I'll tell you what," he said turning back to Cutter again, "how about you get your own house in order before you start dicking around with us. This whole goddamned town knows somebody is shorting you. Well, everybody except *your* stupid ass, that is."

Barbie Blue started for the door again with his body man right behind him. Cutter tilted his head toward Luther. Luther reached into his jacket and began to pull out his pistol. Every hand in the room reached for their weapons.

"Goddammit Luther," Tony said as he quickly grabbed Luther's arm and escorted Barbie Blue through the door. Once in the hallway Tony pushed Luther against the wall. "One of these days your dumb ass is going to get someone killed."

"How the hell am I supposed to know what a head tilt means?" Luther was irritated and tired of this Marcel Marceau bullshit. "Jesus Christ, just say it. Why is that concept so hard for you people? Here watch this, 'Tony, shoot that piece of shit in the forehead.' How hard was that?! I just told *you* to do something *specific* with my words. Here, watch this, 'Tony, let that guy out of the room.' Piece of cake. Hey, now watch this," Luther glared at Tony then tilted his head to the right and winked. "Now, you go take care of *that*."

"Take care of what?" Tony asked blankly. "You never said anything."

"Suck a fat baby's ass!" Luther yelled, "That's *exactly* what I'm saying. How could you possibly know what I want? Do you get me a doughnut, or do you ass rape my dog?"

"Get your shit together Luther," Tony said as he began to turn around to leave. "That's not the same thing and you know it."

"NO, I FUCKING DON'T!" Luther screamed at Tony's back.

8.

Hanna Petersheim was a good girl who had been raised in the bosom of Amish simplicity and discipline. She graciously lived by the communities *Ordnung,* the book of rules governing Amish families, and was baptized at the age of sixteen. Her jet-black hair, which had never been cut, falling between her shoulder blades in a silken braid, stood in stark contrast to the ever-present starched white kapp on the back of her head. Her navy blue, long-sleeved dress hid her womanly form, as it was meant to, and stopped just above the toes of her plain black shoes.

Hanna dutifully attended church services that were held in the neighbor's barn every other Sunday and freely accepted the lack of electricity, telephones, and cars. She believed, as did the other Amish, that these *trivialities* were worldly and distracted from one's ability to worship and be closer to God. For transportation the Petersheims had an Amish buggy that looked like a black cracker box on wagon wheels, for general transport, and a black buckboard used to haul supplies and feed. Hanna loved riding these buggies into town and felt somewhat special. The family had two identical black Friesian geldings that traded off the duties of pulling the family transportation and accomplishing farm work. That black buggy pulled by a dazzling black Friesian with black tack, high stepping down the road with long black mane and tail floating on the wind, was a beautiful sight, and Hanna was proud to be a part of it.

However, as any good Christian of any denomination knows, the more devout a person is, the more Satan works to turn them. Satan hates the devout more than any other people on earth and loves to fill hell with the souls of those he can pry from the flock. Hanna's secret sin was vanity. She tried every day to pray the evil thoughts away that had seeped into her mind like oily black mucus and contaminated her soul with prideful thoughts.

Hanna knew she could sing, because everyone told her she had been blessed with the voice of a songbird, and why would they lie? In the privacy of her room, Hanna would dance, whirling around as her dress flowed around her like she was the center point of a giant parasol. She imagined being in the arms of a very handsome young Amish boy who might make her feel safe and secure, and they would spend the rest of their lives together. But *together* doing what? Raising children, working on the farm, tending to livestock? Satan was constantly present in her mind making her ask those difficult questions.

Those questions became the vehicle that put her on a bus to New York City with the dream of becoming a famous singer. As soon as she stepped off the bus at her final destination, she was met by a smooth-talking flashy dresser who told Hanna his name was Mack, "with a K". Mack with a K took her to lunch and explained all of the dos and don'ts that came with living in a giant metropolis like New York. He told her he knew some music producers that were looking for talent just like hers and that if she stuck with him, he would make sure she made it to the big time.

He set her up with a place to stay and made sure she had money. He taught her about fashion, custom, how to talk and how to walk, and of course how to make love. Hanna was deeply in love with Mack, and she would do anything he asked to make him happy. Thanks to Mack she also learned about drinking, taking drugs, smoking, abuse, and domestic violence. Once Mack had her completely beaten down, she learned men would pay for sex, but only men that Mack had personally picked out for her. She learned that there were as many different sexual proclivities as there were men. She learned that sixty per cent of all the money she made went to Mack, and she learned that Mack would hold *her* money for her because it was a wicked world out there and you couldn't trust anyone.

Hanna was eighteen when Mack died. No one other than Hanna knew how or where he died, and no one cared. One day there was just one less shit bag in the world, and life continued to move forward nonchalantly. Hanna retrieved her money from Mack before he passed, as well as quite a bit of money that he had apparently been holding for other people. She found a ratty apartment in a ratty part of town and was able to secure a ratty job as a stripper at a ratty strip club called Gold Diggers. Always one to look at the bright side of life, Hanna, now to be forever known as Candy Barr, could dance as much as she wanted. The money was good, she kept all of her back-room money for herself, and she didn't have to fuck anyone unless she wanted to. Life was great.

Azriel 'Azi' Applebaum was a man of many hats. He was an accountant by education and a degenerate gambler by trade. These two attributes found him deeply in debt to the Manchini crime family, which the Manchini family used to sequester Azi from the rest of the world as a kind of indentured bookkeeper. In that vocation Azi had become a devoted abuser of cocaine and cocaine products and a constant fixture at the stage seats of the Gold Digger. That was how Candy came into his life. Candy brought sensuality to their relationship, and Azi brought Luther LaMotta.

Through family connections Azi and Luther had become friends. Luther was simple and listened to Azi's bullshit, and Azi was non-threatening and a little pathetic to Luther. The magnet that had drawn the hapless trio together had been the strip club. Azi brought Luther there once because for all practical purposes, Luther was Azi's only friend in the world. Luther kept coming back to the Gold Digger because he had fallen deeply in love with Candy at first sight. Candy constantly had sex with Luther because he was a sweet, kind of "special" guy, and Azi LOVED to talk to her about what she and Luther had done sexually. Actually, Azi adored it when Candy would talk about *any* of the men, or women, Candy had sex with. It was a win, win, win, and life was even greater.

If the champagne rooms at the Gold Digger strip club were given a human quality, it would be schizophrenic. Thick red shag carpet that had been professionally installed decades ago started life as a "classy" accent in a room devoted to romance. Now it lolled indifferently across padding that had long ago been trampled into paper-thin submission. The grubby shag filaments lay in prostrate submission to the years like quills on a sedated porcupine. Flat dark charcoal paint on the walls had been carefully chosen by the original designer as a complement to the carpet. Now scuffs, smudges, handprints, and stark white gouges exposing the inner core of gypsum in the drywall offered the same allure you might find in an unattended toilet in a turnpike shithouse.

The dim lighting served several purposes. First it helped hide the crushing depression of the room and the less-than-exotic look of the down-and-out "dancers" employed by the Gold Digger. If that light had ever been replaced with a black light, the decor of dried DNA from floor to ceiling would have looked like a Jackson Pollok masterpiece. A bench that had begun life as booth seating at a thankfully defunct Sambo's restaurant was bolted to the back wall. A folding chair and chilling bucket for the more discerning degenerates guarded a far corner of the room.

Luther sat in the folding chair, forearms resting on his thighs, passively listening to the ice melt in the chilling bucket. Across from him on the ex-Sambo's bench, a man leaned back with his arms spread wide. His head was tilted back, and a look of sensual ecstasy mixed with debilitating inebriation was plastered on his alcohol- and coke-infused face. Luther was mesmerized by the size of the coke boogers in the man's nose. A rumpled white dress shirt, unbuttoned at the neck with a partially loosened black tie, covered the upper half of the man, and black slacks, unzipped and pulled down to mid glute, draped lazily over black dress shoes.

Candy sat casually next to the customer, topless, clad only in a faux brocade red and gold g string, disinterested as she slowly stroked the customer's package. The long black braid had been cast aside for a short pixie cut, with dark eye makeup and fake lashes finishing off her Liza Minelli theme.

"Is Azi with you?" Candy asked Luther. The customer let out a long, low moan.

"What?" Luther asked, irritated. The customer was beginning to piss him off.

Candy stopped the pumping motion and asked again, "Is Azi with you?" The customer's eyes flittered open and he lifted his head. Candy started pumping again and his head fell back onto the back of the bench.

"No," Luther answered indifferently. He frequently had conversations with Candy while she *worked* in the champagne Room. "Azi had paperwork or some shit to do. Does he ever sit in on one of *these*?" he asked, indicating the moaning man Candy was connected to.

"Azi?" Candy said smiling. "He never comes in here. He doesn't like to watch. Actually," she hesitated, "I'm not sure that's true. I never asked him. But, trust me, he's just fine with it."

"What's he get out of it?" Luther asked. The customer moaned and thrust his hips forward. Candy slowed down. She wanted more time to talk to Luther.

"He gets what he wants, Luther," Candy said as she looked deeply into Luther's eyes. It was almost like her hand was working independently of the rest of her body as she manipulated farm machinery.

"And what could he *want* that has to do with this?" Luther asked cynically.

"Azi has absolute shit for self-respect I think." Candy said thoughtfully as the customer's head flopped over toward her, and his eyes rolled back in his head. Candy stopped again. "I don't know if he likes to abuse himself, or if he likes to abuse me. It could be either I guess. It's complicated if you think about it."

"And I guess you don't think about it." A coke booger drifted out of the customer's nose on a slight stream of snot and rolled down his cheek.

"Why should I? That's his thing. He wants me to tell him what men do to me while we have sex. The more depraved it is, the quicker he gets off. He's happy, I'm happy. Win, win."

"What about me?" Luther wasn't deluded enough to think he and Candy had an exclusive relationship. The dick she currently had her hand wrapped around pretty much spoke to that. Luther was okay with her *job*, and he was okay with whatever the thing was between her and Azi. His relationship with Candy had all of the things Luther craved. It wasn't complex, everyone was honest, and he was getting laid by a beautiful woman that kind of reminded him of someone in the movies, but he couldn't put his finger on who.

"What about *you*, honey?" Candy asked. The customer let out a long, guttural, "*Ooooooooh yeah, just like that.*"

"Do you two talk about me when we—you know," Luther didn't want to say it. It wasn't that he was jealous, he just felt like that would be intruding on Candy and Azi.

"When we fuck?" Candy asked playfully as she tilted her head down and looked up at Luther, biting her bottom lip slightly, alluring white teeth set stark against deeply sensual red lips.

"Yeah," Luther answered. Candy twisted her busy hand side to side at the wrist gently as Luther said that. Clearly, she liked some of the same things Azi did.

"Of course we do. Well Azi does most of the talking, I just answer what he asks me. Does that bother you?"

"No," Luther said honestly. "Do you tell him everything?"

"Well, yeah. If that's what he wants. He pretty much controls that aspect of it." Candy started to pump a little faster as she gazed at Luther. "Does this turn *you* on baby? I think I'm going to make him cum now. I know he wants it *soooooo* bad." Candy squirmed seductively on the bench. Luther swallowed hard.

Inexplicably Luther found himself staring at Candy's hand as it worked on her customer, and then he looked back into Candy's eyes.

"Do you want me to give it to him?" she asked in a low throaty whisper. "I won't let him have it until you say you want me to."

Luther nodded slightly and shifted in his chair. The customer moaned again, "*Ooooh holy shit. Please don't stop.*"

"I'm going to have to hear you say it lover." Candy raised her eyebrows at Luther and stopped her hand in mid stroke. "Come on baby," Candy said alluringly, "Nothing's going to happen unless you *tell* me what you want to see."

"I want to see it," Luther whispered.

"See what baby? Exactly."

"Jerk him off till he comes," Luther whispered again.

"Okay baby. But only because that's what *you* want." Candy began to apply the finishing strokes to her masterpiece.

"God Damn!" the customer exclaimed. "Put it in your mouth. Please for the love of all that's holy. Suck my cock!"

"That costs more honey," Candy advised as she brought him closer to the end.

The customer reached behind Candy's head and tried to force her face into his lap.

"Come on bitch," the costumer snarled. "Suck me off you fucking slut." Candy had both hands on the customer's leg and was trying hard to push herself back up.

Luther let out an exasperated sigh, stood up and punched the customer/rapist directly in the center of his face. The customer's head bounced off the back of the bench, releasing Candy's head, and she stood up. "You motherfucker!" Candy growled, "I'll kill your stupid ass." She lunged at the customer as he was trying to stand, and Luther stopped her with a hand to her chest.

"I'll take care of it," he promised. Luther grabbed the customer by the back of his still unzipped pants and shirt collar and high-stepped him toward the front door. His now apathetic penis bobbed back and forth as if it were checking out the other clientele as its human was escorted toward the door. As they passed the bar, the customer yelled at the manager, "Do you have any idea who I am?" The manager shot a look at Candy, then back to Luther.

"He tried to get free head," Candy pouted. The manager looked back at Luther. He feared Luther because he thought Luther was a big wheel in the Manchini family. He thought that because Candy told everyone who would listen that's what Luther was. Luther nodded back, affirming Candy's accusation.

"You're the guy that's about to get tossed in the street," the manager told the customer. With that, Luther used the customer's head to open the door and tossed him into the street.

"You want to go get a car from the valet?" Candy asked Luther. "You know, to *talk* about what just happened," she added playfully.

Luther simply nodded and walked back to the champagne room so he could wait while Candy got dressed.

9.

Azi Applebaum had already been working for the Manchini family for a little over a year when Candy Barr showed up at the Manchini-owned Gold Digger. In an effort to ensure Azi understood what an insignificant pustule he was, Cutter had given him a room, in a manner of speaking, above the strip club. In a different manner of speaking, shortly after the Monster had smashed Azi in the face, breaking his nose, Cutter informed Azi that he would, from now until the second coming, be living in a shitty efficiency apartment above the strip club. Cutter also let him know that if Azi even thought about moving out of that place, or running away, Pretty Boy would be paying Azi a visit. Not to kill him or anything—that wouldn't be good business sense. Pretty Boy would just make sure that when Azi *did* go out in public, he would have to wear a hockey mask.

Of all the positive attributes Azi had, which were few and far between, resolve and self-esteem were absolutely not on the list. He was terrified of every member of Cutter's crew; well, except Luther, that is. He saw Luther as a buddy and confidant. Due to his unremitting frightened state of mind, Azi lived his life self-confined to a three-block radius of the club. That included a few convenience stores, a liquor store, two restaurants, and a coke dealer. Azi had all the things he needed in life and never had to worry about straying so far from home that it might warrant a visit from Pretty Boy.

Azi had "dated" a few of the strippers in the Gold Digger, if you could call paying some of them to come up to the depressing dump he lived in dating. His *free* time mostly consisted of sitting at the bar in the club during slow times and pounding away furiously on his laptop as he carefully constructed caustic comments on Facebook posts. He didn't care what the post was; he just took the other side of the argument and got as derogatory as he could. It was the only outlet he had to blow off some aggression without the danger of getting punched in the throat.

When he wasn't doing that, he was sitting in front of an ancient Videocon CRT TV set watching porn and pounding his dick into submission like it had threatened a hostile takeover. His pud pulling palace looked like a degenerate's throne room. A Naugahyde La-Z-Boy, resplendent in silver duct tape covering wear holes where the elbows met the armrest sat back from the Videocon just enough to allow the footrest to be raised. Old fashioned, very off-white TV trays sporting elegant decals of a rose bouquet rested on flimsy gold chrome folding frames that flanked each side of the La-Z-Boy. These tables made sure everything Azi may need whilst having *self-induced sex for one* were available and within reach.

The table on the right was filled with toys. Overly mistreated silicone, nylon, and the finest rubber molded into various parts of human anatomy lay haphazardly on it. Two dildos, one lime green, the other neon pink to ensure the anal one was never accidently confused with the oral, a few flesh-toned pocket pussies, vibrators of all sizes and colors that stood in a row like a display of different caliber rifle ammunition, two rabbits, and one each of the "spring fling" and the "adventurer" had all been wiped down, emptied where appropriate, and disinfected. Azi wasn't some kind of barbarian, after all.

The other table contained a cornucopia of lubes. Silicone, water, oil, and natural base types were all represented, as well as enough flavored lube to make Willy Wonka giddy. Pussy Licker Strawberry, all four flavors of "Fuck Sauce," and cum-scented lube were lined up like terracotta solders next to two rolls of paper towels and a box of tissue paper. In front of that table was a tall kitchen trash can.

In this same La-Z-Boy, Azi had contemplated ending this humiliating degradation of a life far more times than he could count. He thought pills would be a good and peaceful way to cross death's threshold, but he had no idea where to get them. His coke dealer refused to help, saying he didn't want to be responsible for someone's death, but in fact he didn't want to lose his best customer. A bullet in the brain pan was weighed, but when he asked Luther to get a gun for him, Luther balked. Azi was a good guy, as far as Luther was concerned, and he didn't want Azi dead, cut to pieces for killing a member of the mob, or arrested for robbing a bank or something. Hanging was out, due to no rope. Slicing his wrists was a no go because he was pretty sure that would hurt. The only things he had left were coke or alcohol. He drank until he puked and passed out, so another failed attempt, and he snorted enough coke to paralyze an elephant, then he forgot what the original plan was and went to bed—two days later.

The day Azi saw Candy working the pole at the Gold Digger, he was hopelessly and dangerously in love. The combination of a pristine figure, big tits, the Liza Minnelli theme, playful innocence covering dark eroticism, and the fact that she hadn't charged him when he took her upstairs turned Azi into weaker jelly than he already was. Azi and Candy complemented each other as a couple. She needed a place to stay, and Azi had a place. She needed to feel secure, and Azi worked for the mob. She needed someone she could manipulate, and Azi was malleable to a fault. She needed someone she could dominate sexually, and Azi would have eaten the corn out of her turds if she had asked him to. It was the proverbial match made in scuz heaven.

Candy had redecorated their little efficiency hacienda when she moved in. The La-Z-Boy had been dropped off at the curb, and it sat there forever like a Naugahyde monument to masturbation. Even the hobos wouldn't get near it. The happy couple's bed was the focal point of the room's pathetic *feng shui*. It was a queen size four poster affair they had found in a Goodwill, and Candy had attached sheer red mosquito netting to the ceiling that surrounded the bed and gracefully flowed to the floor. Bits of that same red cloth covered all three of Azi's lamps. The ambiance was great, and it seemed to make Candy happy, but Azi couldn't see shit in the dim light and constantly walked into door frames, stubbed his toes, and stepped on sharp things. But it was all a small price to pay to keep the love of his life content.

In the beginning of their relationship, Candy wanted to set some ground rules so there would be no surprises or unspoken issues further down the road. That translated into, Candy didn't want to hear any shit about what she did for a living. They agreed that downstairs would be kept downstairs, and upstairs would be kept upstairs.

That agreement lasted until the day Azi was sitting at the bar fucking with tree huggers on a Facebook post while shouting down Neo-Nazis and January 6th supporters on another. Candy was working the pole for the few customers that were the types to be in a strip club at two o'clock in the afternoon. She spun around the pole upside down once, then squatted down to say something to a man who was "making it rain." Still squatting, Candy looked directly at Azi, winked, and deftly pulled her G-string to one side as the man moved his head to within 6 inches of her knees. She stood up, the man helped her off the stage, and they walked hand in hand into the champagne room. Just before Candy closed the door, she looked over her shoulder towards Azi, bit her lip, and blew him a kiss.

Azi was drowning in a sea of emotion, and he was going down for the third time. That night he asked Candy what had happened between her and that guy when they were in private. At first, she spoke in generalities and vague hints, leaving Azi to slog through a seedy bog of conjecture. Then she noticed the lids on Azi's eyes begin to droop a little, as animal lust began to take over and kick reason right in the nuts. She ventured closer to specific actions, like hands above cloths, probing both mammary and genitalia. Azi never flinched. As the one-sided conversation went on, Candy became more and more specific until she was telling him every feeling she had and every sexual act they had committed, inventing some that hadn't actually happened, as well as all of the filthy things they had said to each other in the act of coitus. Azi picked Candy up in midsentence, tossed her on the bed, and subjected her to violent dispassionate mating. In the after-glow, Azi was left confused and hating himself. He also loved Candy even more and couldn't wait for her to bang someone else so they could do it all over again.

After another round of humiliating intercourse, Candy was lying on her back stretched across the bed, naked and resting her head on Azi's thigh. Azi, also naked, sat with his back against the headboard smoking a cigarette.

"What about Luther?" Azi asked absently.

"What about him?" Candy answered as she turned her face up toward Azi.

"Have you ever—you know."

"*You know?*" Candy sounded surprised and a little irritated. "What are you, six? Is there a question or comment in there someplace?"

"Have you two ever done *it*?" Azi said, his voice nearly a whisper. He didn't want to piss Candy off, but he felt odd talking about sex when it had to do with Luther. It was almost like kiddy porn.

"Done what baby?" Candy tilted her head down slightly, smiled, pursed her lips, and blew a small puff of warm air at Azi's testicles. Azi closed his eyes and remained quiet. Candy rolled on her stomach and ran her tongue along the inside of Azi's thigh, near but not touching his awakening penis.

"Come on baby," she said dreamily. "Say it. You know you want to."

At this point in their relationship, Azi wasn't ever actually certain what he wanted until Candy told him. Then he *absolutely* had to have it. "Does he fuck you?"

"Oh," Candy said as she dipped her tongue into his naval, "yes, he certainly does. Repeatedly."

"When?" His blood was making him feel warm and dizzy as it raced, nearly at the speed of sound out of his torso and into his loins.

"Well," Candy said as she looked at the top of the mosquito netting like she was calculating, "pretty much whenever he wants to." She moved her hand up to his crotch and fondled his testicles playfully. Azi moaned gutturally.

"Where?"

"You mean where on me, or *where*, as in a location?"

"Location," Azi whispered as he tilted his chin up a little.

"Oh, Luther knows a valet at this super nice restaurant. He pays off the valet and we fuck in very expensive cars."

Azi looked down at her, "Really?" He sounded a little incredulous.

"Oh yeah," Candy said as she raised up on her palms and dragged the end of a nipple across his chest. "It gets me off every, single, time." She allowed her lips to brush against his. "He fucked the holy hell out of me in a Bentley after a client tried to force me to suck his dick." She stroked his erection slowly.

"Why didn't you?" Azi was riding a wave of exotic euphoria.

"Suck his cock?" Candy asked playfully as she ran the side of her index finger slowly around the tip of his penis. "Did you want me to?"

"Oh yeah," Azi moaned.

"I was saving that for Luther. I love it when he fucks my mouth hard."

"Did he—oh shiiiit—did he cum down your throat?" Azi was losing control quickly.

"Oh, yeah. Hard and hot. I nearly couldn't take it all," Candy stopped and pushed herself up on her hands again and gazed into Azi's eyes. "But I did," she leaned up to whisper directly into his ear. "Every, single, drop." She ran her tongue around the inside of his ear.

Azi grunted and rolled out from under her. He grabbed a small bottle of coke off the nightstand, pulled Candy's ass up by her hips so her butt was on her heels, carelessly laid a line of coke into her butt crack, then snorted it back out from bottom to top.

Candy moaned and pushed her ass harder into Azi's face. The love making that followed was animal-like and did not last long.

10.

Cutter stood near the head of the conference table staring through the window as he absently rolled ice cubes around in a highball glass full of bourbon. Enzo and Richy were sitting on either side of the desk waiting to hear why Cutter had called them into the room, and the Monster stood to one side like a statue of raging indifference with his hands folded in front of him. Enzo leaned back in his chair and raised his eyebrows toward Richy. Richy shrugged his shoulders.

"What's up Pops?" Richy asked, trying to get the ball rolling. He had important things to do, like gamble and snort coke.

"Gentlemen," Cutter said as he turned toward them and took a sip from the glass. "We have some—issues that need to be dealt with."

"Anything we don't already know boss?" Enzo asked carefully. If Cutter was talking about something Enzo should have already fixed, he wanted to prepare for the ass chewing he was about to get. Richy kept his mouth shut.

"Yes and no I guess," Cutter said as he sat down and unbuttoned his suit coat. "Lately things just don't seem to be adding up."

"In what way?" Enzo asked.

Cutter took another sip, leaned back, and pursed his lips. "In the worst way, Enzo," Cutter said as he contemplated the ceiling. Richy swallowed hard. "I can't put my finger on it," Cutter went on, but things seem—I don't know what," Cutter said.

"Je ne sais pas quoi," Richy said smiling nervously. Enzo glared at him and raised an eyebrow.

Cutter looked at Richy then back toward the other end of the room. He tapped his glass on the table a few times lost in thought. "To begin with, the protection income seems light."

"Do you want me to muscle our collectors a little?" Enzo asked. He checked the Monster in his periphery, trying to read the atmosphere of the room. Money issues unquestionably meant someone was about to die an agonizingly slow death.

"Not yet," Cutter dismissed Enzo with a wave of the hand. "See, that's too easy of an answer. When things are fucked up in some way in our family business, I always can feel it before anyone else even considers whether there's a problem." Cutter swiveled his chair back toward the window, propped his elbows on the overly padded arms of his office chair, touched his fingertips together, and laid his index fingers on his lips. He stayed that way in thought for a long second then turned back to the table. "Someone is ass raping us in a way that's not conventional."

"As if ass raping were ever conventional," Richy said lightly. Enzo looked at the ceiling wishing Richy would shut his mouth.

"Who do you think it is boss?" Enzo finally asked.

"I want you two to take care of the protection thing," Cutter said as though he were just brought back to reality from a trance. "I want to know if the marks are shorting the collectors or if the collectors are skimming off the top."

"We're on it boss," Enzo instantly assured Cutter.

"Yeah," Richy said as he started to get up from the table," Yeah, we'll get right on that. Right Enzo?"

"Sit down," Cutter commanded his son.

"Sure Pops," Richy said nervously.

"If you should find nefarious activity being exacted against this family by *anyone*," Cutter said, "bring them directly back to me. Pound on them if they give you any shit at all, but I want them in one piece when they get here."

"Sure boss," Enzo said. "Do you want us to follow the collectors, or just make their pickups for them?"

"Start with taking over the pickups. That should be quicker. If anyone has the balls to short our collectors, they'll short you too. If you find someone fucking up, don't stop there. I want each and every one of our marks tested. That way we'll know how deep this goes."

"You got it Pops," Richy said as he put his palms on the table and pushed back a little. Cutter glared at him, and Richy scooted back to the table.

"Is there more boss?" Enzo asked.

"Yeah," Cutter was considering his next words. "Nobody in this business ever says anything just for shits and giggles. Especially when that thing could get them killed. That asshole Barbie Blue got my attention before he stomped out of here."

"That guy is nuts," Richy offered. "Just look at the way he dresses. Who does that?"

"You need to stop jumping to conclusions just because of the way someone looks," Cutter advised Richy.

"He was pretty pissed off when he left here, Boss," Enzo said nervously. "Don't you think he was just trying to get to you?"

"Oh, there's no question he was trying to get to me. But the way he said it told me he was shoving actual facts up my ass."

"How can you be sure about that?" Richy asked.

"Like Freud said," Cutter said, still deep in thought, "sometimes a turd is just a turd."

"I think he said. . ." Richy started, but Enzo cut him off with a slight headshake and stern look.

"Barbie Blue said, '*someone* is shorting you,'" Cutter said as he finished his bourbon and set the glass on the table.

"Yeah but. . ." Richy started to say.

Cutter cut him off. "He said, *someone*, specifically, not *people* are shorting me, or you're getting shorted. That prick knows something and has no problem rubbing my nose in it. That means it's big. If it was just marks holding out on protection money, he would have just said that. He knew that whatever came out of his mouth next could have gotten him killed."

"I see what you're saying boss," Enzo agreed. "Where do we start looking?"

"That Elvis-looking prick knows something," Cutter said again. "It's going to take some time to work this out. I've had a few people come to me asking to fix issues in Barbie's crew, so it shouldn't be really difficult. Most people have had enough of him making us look like a bunch of cosplaying shit birds." Cutter thought for a moment, "When I give the word, bring his ass in here. We'll find out what he knows and who's sticking it to us."

Richy put his hands on the table, then hesitated for a moment. He didn't want to jump the gun again. Cutter tipped his chin up slightly in a gesture saying, "*The meeting is over.*" Both men got up and left the room, closing the giant doors behind them.

Outside the conference room door, Richy stopped Enzo. "Is he actually talking about hitting a boss?" Richy asked. "That's crazy."

"He's talking about getting Barbie Blue's crew on board, then finding a replacement."

"Then what?" Richy asked in a whisper. "Do we hit Barbie Blue?"

"Then," Enzo eyed Richy suspiciously, "we drag Barbie's fat ass in here and pound the shit out of him till he tells us what we want to know."

11.

The stench of blood, mold, and crocodile shit permeated the air of the dank concrete-shrouded room, but no one seemed to notice. Their attention was directed to a chair in the center of the room resting directly above an iron floor drain. A jet-black wig lay on the floor next to the chair, resembling some type of roadkill, as its owner slummed forward against his duct tape restraints and moaned softly. His bald head swayed slowly, rhythmically back and forth. A crumpled white blood-smeared suit jacket rested a few feet in front of a pair of equally bloodied blue suede shoes.

Bloody spit and mucus drooled from Barbie Blue's lips and landed on a growing blood puddle in the middle of his bright white slacks. One eye was deep purple and completely swollen shut. The ear that should have been next to that eye was lying next to the wig on the floor.

"Fuck you," Barbie moaned through bloody swollen lips that made the words sound like *fug ya.*

Pretty Boy stood between Barbie's chair and a stainless-steel surgical tray. A light green sterile towel draped across the table held various surgical instruments as well as a few things he had picked up from Home Depot on the way to work. Next to the tools of the trade was a black and red bottle of Ward, Bottled Insanity smelling salts, several packages of Celox Hemostatic clotting crystals, several North American Resue NAR CAT tourniquets, and an innocuous looking saltshaker. Allowing a *client* to pass out or bleed out before the boss was done torturing/questioning was a rookie mistake, and Pretty Boy was no rookie.

Pretty Boy also loved to set some type of a fun theme as he performed his work. If you couldn't have a little fun in your workplace then you were just beating, dismembering, or maiming with no flare or panache. The theme for *this* session was *steampunk surgeon.* To that end he was dressed in a long, knee-length, light green surgeon's jacket and like-color scrub pants. He wore elbow-length red rubber ShuamgAn linemen's gloves and black battered combat boots. A green surgeon's mask was plastered across his face below a pair of thick black plastic "birth control" glass with one lens missing. The eyeball-adorned black eye patch lay at an angle behind the lens-free side of his glasses and peered steadily at nothing. A green surgeon's cap perched just above Pretty Boy's wild eyebrows.

Luther was serving as Pretty Boy's surgical assistant. Tony stood to one side of the broken Barbie Blue, ready to beat on him when directed, and Richy sat on a stool in front of him. Murphy waited next to Bianca's pit with his cleaning supplies ready to go. When the word came to start cleaning up the mess that would be left where Barbie Blue used to be, he wanted to be Johnny on the spot. Murphy was a professional too, and as Lions' running back Barry Sanders had said about celebrating in the end zone, Murphy wanted to "act like he had been there before."

Richy contemplated Barbie Blue for a moment as if he was trying to decide what to do next. He looked at Pretty Boy and tilted his head back toward Barbie.

"Scalpel," Pretty Boy demanded as he held his hand out to Luther. Luther retrieved the scalpel from the table and slapped it in Pretty Boy's waiting hand, handle first. Pretty Boy placed his free hand on the side of Barbie Blue's head and leaned back as though he were an artist trying to decide how a certain spot of shading should be applied to his masterpiece.

"Hold this," Pretty Boy said to Tony. Tony held Barbie Blue's head by the front and back and kept it tilted. Pretty Boy held the top of Barbie's ear tightly with his thumb and forefinger, then quickly cut a line all the way around it.

"*Ahhhh,*" Barbie sobbed. "You bastards."

Pretty Boy was a craftsman. He knew it took seven pounds of force to rip an ear off the side of someone's head. However, if you were to make an incision around that ear, you could tear it off with as little as four or five pounds of force. Pretty Boy handed the scalpel back to Luther, placed his now free hand on the side of Barbie's head, and yanked as hard as he could.

"Huh," Pretty Boy thought as he examined the hear in his hand, *"That might have been only three pounds of force."* He smiled and tossed the ear next to the one already on the floor.

"Ahhhhhhhhhh!" Barbie screamed in pain. *"You miserable cock sucking lumps of cowardly shit!"* Red spittle flew from Barbie's lips as he howled. He had lost several appendages before anyone had even asked him a question. Now Barbie parts were scattered around his chair like someone had blown up Mr. Potato head.

"Salt," Pretty Boy demanded of Luther. Luther slapped the shaker into Pretty Boy's outstretched hand. Pretty Boy pushed Barbie's head to the side again, shook ten servings into the bloody oval wound, passed the shaker back to Luther and ground the salt in with the palm of his red rubber gloved hand.

"Holy Jesus!" Barbie begged. Giant bloody tears ran down the front of his ruined face and dripped off his quivering chin. "Please, I can't take anymore! Just fucking shoot me! I'm begging you!"

"Come on Barbie," Richy said flatly, "that's some pretty un-American shit right there. If I were to put a bullet in your head, that would put Pretty Boy out of business. Ain't that right Pretty Boy?"

Pretty Boy answered by slapping Barbie on the fresh ear wound. "Clotter!" he called out.

Luther slapped a package of clotting agent into Pretty Boy's hand. Pretty Boy glared at Luther and continued to hold the package in front of him and raised his eyebrows.

"Damn it Pretty Boy," Luther said. "Not you too. What the hell is that supposed to mean?"

"I think he can't open the package with his gloves on," Tony offered.

Pretty Boy jabbed the clotter toward Luther again. Luther took the package, tore the top off and placed it back in Pretty Boy's hand. "You assholes need communication classes," Luther pouted.

Pretty Boy crammed the clotter into the wound just like he had the salt. Barbie Blue produced a pathetic moan from deep in his throat.

"Just tell us what that shitty comment meant when you ran away during the meeting," Richy said calmly. Barbie Blue was blissfully unconscious. Tony slapped him on the back of the head. Barbie didn't even flinch.

"Did you kill this shithead?" Richy demanded of Pretty Boy.

"I, beg, your, pardon." Pretty Boy was aghast. "I *know* what I'm doing here." Then to Luther, "Salts." He stomped his foot slightly as he thrust his hand toward Luther like a Nazi asking Poles for their papers. Pretty Boy snapped a capsule in half and shoved both halves into Barbie's nostrils. "You're making me look bad," Pretty Boy hissed into Barbie's ear hole. "Don't you dare pull that shit again or I'm going to hurt you."

Pretty Boy smacked his hand over Barbie's mouth and punched him hard in the stomach. Barbie blew both bloody capsules out of his nose then looked up at Richy. Richy raised his eyebrows and raised his hands, shrugging. "What are we going to do with you?"

"You already know the answers, you prick," Barbie wheezed. Richy looked at Tony, and Tony punched Barbie in the back of his head. Richy stood up and took a few steps toward Barbie.

"What did you just say?" Richy's mood went instantly dark.

"You heard me, retard." Barbie spit blood clots at Richy's feet. Richy gave Pretty Boy the look.

"C-clamp," Pretty Boy demanded. Luther pushed a large automotive C-clamp into Pretty Boy's hand. Pretty Boy carried the clamp to the side of Barbie's taped-down arm, positioned the clamp above Barbie's hand and below the arm rest, then tightened it down as far as he could. Barbie screamed, then clenched his teeth and jutted his chin toward Richy. His eyes were bright and wild as he strained against the tape. He bared his clenched teeth like a rabid dog protecting a pork chop in an alley. As the clamp was slowly turned one revolution at a time, blood oozed up through the gash it left.

"*Grrrrrrrrrrr.*" A low, animalistic noise crawled up through the deepest recesses of Barbie's resolve.

"Electrical tape," Pretty Boy announced. Then he taped the only finger Barbie had left to the arm rest.

"Come on dude," Richy prodded.

"Cleaver," Pretty Boy demanded. He carried the cleaver around to face Barbie, glancing over his shoulder at Richy. Richy nodded and Pretty Boy slammed the clever length wise through Barbie's finger, splaying it like a Polish sausage at the fair.

Barbie growled through bared teeth and shook his head violently. Blood flew onto Pretty Boy's surgical jacket.

"YOU KNOW!" Barbie screamed at Richy as he continued to strain against his bindings. "YOU KNOW, YOU KNOW, YOU KNOW. YOU BLITHERING LITTLE COWARD! GROW A PAIR OF NUTS YOU LITTLE FAGOT! YOU KN..."

Richy sprang forward, smashing his fist into Barbie's face. He shoved Pretty Boy back and pulled a set of hoof nippers off the surgical table.

"Boss!" Tony yelled as he moved toward Richy, "don't!"

Richy jammed the nippers into Barbie Blue's mouth, smashing his teeth, and pinched off Barbie's tongue and pulled it out. Richy backed up a step, still holding the nippers, and bent over at the waist with his hands on his thighs as he tried to regain his composure. Barbie Blue spat blood on Richy's shoes.

"I don't mean to tell you fellas your job," Croc Turd said as he casually leaned on the handle of the crock shit net, "but I'm pretty sure he needed that to tell you, well, anything."

"He can write a fucking note," Richy sounded threatening.

"He might need thumbs for that," Croc Turd drawled, unconcerned about Richy's mood. "Fingers too I suspect. But, hey, that's just me talkin'. *You* guys are the *professionals.*"

Richy jerked his Glock out of the shoulder holster he always wore and shot Barbie Blue in the head. "Clean this shit up," Richy said as he turned and walked out of the room.

Pretty Boy began to wipe down his instruments and put them back in his toolbox.

Luther walked over to Tony, "Man, I don't think I'm cut out for this," he said conspiratorially.

"What the hell are you talking about Luther?" Tony was surprised. "You've been on plenty of these. *Now* you have an issue with it?"

"What? Him?" Luther said indicating what was left of Barbie Blue. "I don't give two good shits about that guy. I'm not talking about that."

"Well thank the Lord above for that at least," Tony said, relieved, "because that's kind of right near the top of your job description.

"No man," Luther said shaking his head. "It's the ear thing."

Tony raised his eyebrows a little. He had no idea where Luther was going with this.

"We're all standing here doing our thing and staying with the program," Luther explained. "Then Richy gives Pretty Boy one of those damnable nods."

Tony dropped his head and slowly shook it as he squeezed the bridge of his nose. This was getting really old, and Tony was tired of holding Luther's hand.

"Now," Luther went on, "I've been around these people quite a lot and I'm trying to keep up with all the sign language. Honestly, it's like standing in the middle of a bunch of Indians while they sign the meaning of the Constitution at me. The nod Richy used looked just like the *slap him in the head* nod. But Pretty Boy rips the guy's ear off, and nobody is the slightest bit surprised. Well, except me, I guess. Is there a gangster handbook or something, because I'm getting really sick of this half-assed communication."

"Look," Tony said taking Luther by the shoulders, "you think too much. Just go with the flow. Besides, you need to save that brain power for when you're thinking with your dick."

"What's that supposed to mean?" Luther asked sounding hurt.

"That cooze Candy dude. She's a manipulator. She'll get you to do stuff you would have never considered doing in your life, then make you think it was your idea in the first place. She's poison, my friend, and she's going to get someone killed." Tony started to walk toward the door. "Poison," he said over his shoulder, holding his index finger aloft for emphasis.

12.

Azi sat like a schoolboy at the far end of the conference room table. The reflection from the screen of his laptop bounced off his glasses, making him look like a psychedelic, deflated Randy Savage. Cutter, Enzo, and Richy sat at the other end, waiting to hear what Azi had to tell them.

"What the hell are you doing all the way down there?" Cutter complained.

"I—ah—I'm sorry boss," Azi stammered. "Where would you like me?"

"Naked bent over a chair," Cutter said blandly. Azi searched for a sign from the three faces in front of him to indicate that Cutter was just kidding. They just sat there like they were posing for an Easter Island sculptor. Azi slowly stood up and began to unbutton his shirt.

"Sit down, shithead," Cutter said as he placed both palms on the table and shot a sidelong glance at Enzo. "Do you believe this guy?" Cutter said to Enzo. Enzo just shook his head. "Get up here so we don't have to shout."

Azi collected his laptop, briefcase, and notepad and walked to the other end of the table. "Is this okay?" he asked as he started to pull out a chair next to Richy.

"Jesus Christ," Cutter exclaimed, "just sit the hell down and tell us what's going on."

Cutter folded his arms, leaned back in his chair, and let out a breath of exasperation.

"Well," Azi started as he finished arranging his things on the table. "Profits are up this quarter, and debits are down. Of course, that's exactly what we expected after Mr. Barbieri graciously gave the entirety of his operation to us."

"I don't think he was that gracious," Richy quipped into his hand. Cutter glared at him.

Azi looked at Richy for a moment, then went back to his briefing. "Some of the clubs are making great money, for example, the Gold Digger. Others, like Piggy's, the Flesh Pot, and the Shiny Monkey are in the hole pretty consistently."

Richy laughed, "In the hole. That's some funny shit right there."

Enzo and Cutter both glared at him.

"What?" Richy said shrugging. "In the hole—a titty bar—in the hole. Get it?"

"Grow up," Cutter chastised.

"Jesus," Richy muttered. "Lighten up a little."

"Go on Azi," Cutter directed his accountant. "I want to know what doesn't add up."

"Well," Azi said nervously, "as I said, the protection cash isn't what it should be. We're down—" Azi scratched at his throat anxiously as he surveyed the numbers on his computer screen. "Let's see here. Yep, we're down just a little over fifteen per cent on those pickups."

"What about everything else?" Cutter asked. "Does everything else add up?"

Azi swallowed hard as he continued to check the numbers. "Yes sir, everything else is up to snuff."

"*Up to snuff?*" Richy mocked. "What are you, Mickey Spillane?"

"When did you learn to read, and just how the hell old are you anyway?" Enzo asked Richy.

"Those books are timeless man," Richy explained. "I read them in high school, and Mike Hammer rocks."

"Shut up," Cutter growled. Then to Azi, "Alright, get lost."

Azi folded his laptop, retrieved his briefcase, and started for the exit.

"Hey," Cutter said, stopping Azi in his tracks, "If I find out there's more to this than what you're telling me, I'm going to personally keep you alive while I feed parts of you to Bianca."

Azi bowed his head slightly in deference and slid out of the door.

"What do you two think?" Cutter asked Enzo and Richy.

"I don't know boss," Enzo said as he rubbed his perpetual five o'clock shadow. "He could be telling the truth, but why hasn't anyone told us the marks are shorting them?"

"Because they're keeping the money," Richy said. "That's kind of the definition of skimming."

Enzo glared at Richy. He secretly hoped this buffoon would screw up royally someday and Cutter would order him taken out. Enzo would be the first one in line to take the job.

"Yeah, it is," Cutter said reflectively. "It's possible the collectors are shitting on us. But that seems too easy."

"Occam's Razor," Enzo said.

"Yeah," Richy quickly chimed in. "The simplest answer is usually the right one."

"Kind of," Enzo corrected Richy's interpretation of the axiom.

"Look," Cutter was irritated, "I'm certain we're all thinking the same thing, and none of us wants to say it. Usually if the books are jacked up, it's the accountant."

"No way," Richy quickly responded. "That turd doesn't have the brass to rip us off."

"If it walks like a duck. . ." Enzo offered.

"I agree," Cutter affirmed. "And I think *that* duck is jamming it in our asses."

"That's crazy talk," Richy said as he stood up. "The guy that was just in here was afraid to pick the wrong chair. Hell Pops, he was going to strip down and let you corn hole him right here. That's how afraid of you he is. *That guy* is never going to even *think* about crossing you."

Enzo looked suspiciously at Richy.

"That could be," Cutter acquiesced. "One thing I know for sure though: someone is ripping us off. Whoever it might be is excellent at what they're doing. After that pompous prick Barbie Blue shot his mouth off, I checked everything for myself, and what Azi's saying is credible."

"He could be able to make it look that way though," Enzo offered. "Before he fucked up with us he was a big time corporate accountant."

"*Was*," Richy said. "That's the operative word here. He *was* a lot of things. Now he's just a coked-out gambler that's afraid to fart unless we give the okay. Besides, Pops here said he checked his work personally and it was fine." Richy stopped for effect then began again. "Look, I agree someone is ripping us off, and Barbie Blue probably wasn't talking about protection money. But Azi has been with us for years. Why would he suddenly decide to concoct a master plan to steal money from us? I say that if we're going to do this right, we keep an eye on Azi, maybe put something goofy in his accounting to see if he mentions it. But the real way we're going to catch this asshole is to have a third party take a look at Azi's material and see if they can find anything, not just in the books but also in our people's spending habits. We find someone, including Azi, that's been buying shit like a coke whore after the fleet pulls in or has amassed more assets than they could possibly afford, then we have our guy. If it's Azi, I'll chop him up myself. I just think this is a smarter approach."

"What about you," Cutter said to Enzo.

"There's merit to what he's saying, Boss," Enzo answered while he eyed Richy. "With his way, we're sure we get the right guy, and I agree, we don't want to cut our nose off to spite our face. Azi does great work and I'd hate to lose him for no reason."

"Okay," Cutter decided. "Who do we get, who we can trust, to look our finances over?"

"Barbie Blue's guy is looking for work," Richy said.

"Are you shitting me?" Enzo erupted, "Your idea is to get the bookkeeper of the guy we just capped to look at our business? That's bullshit!"

"Bullshit?" Richy was incredulous. "We ask the guy that hates us to find one our guys that are currently fucking us. If I were him, I'd jump at the chance to make this family look stupid."

"So, the guy that *you* admit has a hard on for us is going to have access to this family's entire financial history?" Enzo shot back. "Is that about right, or did I miss something there?"

"He has a point, Richy," Cutter interjected. "We can't let an outsider have access to everything regarding our operations. There's no telling how much damage he could do with that kind of knowledge."

"That's why we lock him in a room and tell him he can't come out until he finds something," Richy explained.

"Great plan, Mister *I have all the answers*," Enzo said sarcastically. "What kind of guarantees do we have after he leaves?"

"Jesus," Richy exclaimed, "do I have to hold your hand at every step here? We offer him whores, coke, booze, heroin, whatever his hook is and tell him he'll get a lifetime supply after he's done. That gets him to start working and gives him a goal. Everybody needs a goal bro."

"And when he leaves—bro?" Enzo asked sarcastically.

"Who said he gets to leave?"

That took the wind out of Enzo's sails.

"Good idea," Cutter finally said. "Make it happen."

13.

The inside of the bar next to the Gold Digger was appropriately decorated in shabby postmodern tropical depression. The chipped and bent sign over the door declared this establishment to be "Boat Drinks Pub." The faux grass tiki overhang above the bar held up by plastic bamboo poles fought against the reality of the bare concrete floor and barred windows for descriptive ambiance. In the corner, a man who looked like a bum vacationing in Hawaii, wearing a tropical shirt and shorts, played the guitar badly as he butchered Jimmy Buffets "Son of a Sailor." Azi and Luther sat on shell-backed bar stools, drinking beer out of plastic coconut glasses.

"This place is a real dump," Luther complained. "What the hell do you come in here for?"

"It's within my comfort zone," Azi explained.

"I don't want to be a dick, Azi, but there's nothing in this hole that looks even close to being comfortable."

"Not that kind of comfort, Luther. This is more of a psychological comfort," Azi said, contemplating his coconut. "I have a specific, well-defined area I allow myself to be in, and I never go outside of that."

"Do you mean the boss doesn't let you get too far?" Luther asked. He couldn't imagine Azi would be fenced in like that.

"No," Azi said as he turned his back on the bar, surveying his bleak surroundings. "It's self-imposed."

"You mean you could go wherever you wanted," Luther was skeptical, "but you choose to go to shit holes like this?"

"Yeah," Azi said as he turned back to the bar and took a drink of beer. "I wonder what ingredient they use to make this taste exactly like piss?"

"Why don't you go to decent places?" Luther asked, ignoring the comment.

"These people scare the shit out of me my friend. And I get high as hell then do stupid stuff. Staying around here gives me less of a chance to screw up."

"Damn dude," Luther said leaning back in his chair. "You can screw up anyplace; it doesn't just have to be here. I think that's crazy. You just did four lines of coke in the bathroom. How is that keeping you out of trouble?"

"I can handle my coke," Azi said as he rubbed swollen bloodshot eyes.

"Sure you can," Luther laid on the sarcasm. "What bad things have ever happened when someone snorted coke like it was going to give them life?"

"Get off my ass man," Azi whined. "People are always getting on my ass."

"Speaking of ass," Azi tried to change the subject, "I really appreciate you helping Candy and I out like you do. It really means a lot."

Luther wasn't sure how to handle that statement. He knew Azi was aware of what they did at the valet lot. Luther didn't understand it, but he knew it. As far as Luther knew, Azi just accepted that he and Candy were banging each other on occasion. But why would he bring that up now?

"What exactly are you talking about?" Luther asked suspiciously.

"You know," Azi said casually, "when you guys fuck."

"How much of that do you know about, and why would you thank me?" Candy had told him Azi like to hear about what they did, but he wasn't clear on how far that *talk* went.

"I know *everything* about it," Azi replied casually as he took another sip from the coconut.

"Everything?" Luther didn't want to give up too much in case they weren't talking about the same thing. Luther loved Candy too much to jeopardize her safety.

"Yeah," Azi said raising his coconut to the bartender asking for another. "You guys go at it in those cars and Candy comes home and tells me everything while I fuck her."

Hearing Azi say "I fuck her" felt like an ice-cold slap in the face. It was one of those things that you might already know but sounded hard when someone else said it out loud.

"That makes me crazy," Azi said dreamily. "She tells me what, where, and how you give it to her. I have to tell you, sometimes you guys do things that get me off instantly."

Luther thought about Candy making him ask her to jerk the guy in the club off. He couldn't explain it because he had never thought anything like that before. Candy made him crazy and made him want to do things he didn't even know he wanted to do. But was that really true? She certainly couldn't *make* him say things like that. She couldn't *make* him feel the way she did when he watched her servicing other men. Could she?

"Okay," Luther said staring at the back of the bar, "you know everything. And when she tells you it gets you off."

"Oh yeah, my friend," Azi said smiling. "It gets me off every time. Sometimes so hard my balls hurt for two days afterward. Doesn't she tell you what we do?"

"No," Luther said distantly, "but I also never asked her."

"So," Azi said, tipping his fresh plastic coconut toward Luther for emphasis, "she hooked you with something brother. I can see it in your eyes. What is it?"

"Do you also know what goes on at work?" Luther asked blankly.

"Well, yeah," Azi said slightly surprised. "She does lap dances and some—extracurricular shit. But that's just business."

"And you don't care about that?"

"Why would I?" Azi leaned back in his chair. "She jerks a guy off every once in a while. What of it? It doesn't do shit for her just having some random dick in her hand. But you, sir, you bring her off every single time, and her going out of control on a cock is a beautiful thing. Candy was made for fucking. Hell, she's a fucking machine. And that's why I appreciate what you're doing. You give it to her just like she wants it, and she brings that home to me. But none of that answers the question. What does she make you do? I can see it in your eyes."

Luther thought about that for a second. He didn't want to ruin what he and Candy had. But on the other hand, other than Tony, Azi and Candy were his best friends. If sharing this made the three of them one, he was fine with that.

"She was jerking a guy off in front of me the other day," Luther started. Azi's eyes gleamed in coke-addled bliss. "She wanted me to ask her to take him all the way."

"Oh man!" Azi exclaimed as he leaned back slapping his hands together. "You did it too, didn't you."

"Yeah," Luther whispered. He felt like he was betraying something special he had with Candy, yet at the same time he felt like the three of them were sharing something—magical.

"Did she give you that little "*Why I'd never, unless you want me too*" lip bite of hers? Man, that gets me crazy every time she does it. Usually afterward, I find myself sitting there trying to figure out what the hell just happened." Azi slapped Luther on the back. "You know what I'm talking about, don't you? Of course you do. I bet you took her to the valet and banged the living shit out of her after that, didn't you?"

"Yeah." Luther was getting used to this new relationship.

"Candy," Azi said raising his coconut. Luther picked up his coconut, returning the salute. "You can't kill her, and you can't stay off her. I swear to God she'll be the death of me. Once we get the hell out of here it's all going to be different though."

An ice cold shot of razor-sharp fear tore through Luther's guts. He never considered Candy would leave.

"Are you two leaving?" Luther asked in controlled horror.

"You bet your ass my friend," Azi said confidently. "And we're taking you with us."

"Oh really?" Luther was flailing in a deep ocean of conflicting emotion. "What's going to turn your life around?"

Azi looked around the bar suspiciously, then motioned Luther to get closer to him. "I'm cooking Cutter's books."

"Holy shit!" Luther blurted out.

"Hey," Azi chastised, "keep it down. You never know who's listening."

"The family is working on finding that guy right now," Luther said in a low voice. "They know, Azi. They already know. Oh man this is really bad."

"They know what?" Azi asked confidently. "They know *someone* is stealing from them. I'm currently pushing them toward the bagmen on collections."

"How long is that going to last?" Luther hissed.

"Relax," Azi said. "It doesn't matter. I'm just throwing them a bone. I have to offer something, and that's it."

"What happens after they take that to its obvious dead end?" Luther was frantic. "Candy is going to get hurt, or worse."

"That's the beauty here," Azi said as he took another casual sip of beer. "We have a partner that's going to keep the heat off us."

"That has got to be one hell of a partner," Luther said, still amazed.

"Oh, it is, brother," Azi winked.

"Who?" Luther was ready to tear Azi apart.

Azi smiled, set his coconut on the bar, and pointed at Luther for emphasis. "Richy."

"Oh my God, Azi," Luther stage whispered as he straightened up in his chair. "Are you shitting me? Please say you're just dicking around here. You can't possibly be that stupid."

"I'm not stupid at all," Azi said happily. "Richy gets a far too generous fifty per cent cut to take the heat off us."

"What happens when they figure out what's up?" Luther asked. How many pieces of Richy do think they'll have to feed Bianca before he gives both of you up? Hell, he'll probably do it if they just yell at him. Is Candy on board with all of this?"

"On board?" Azi asked. "She's the one that planned it all. Of course she's on board. I'm laying a paper trail that leads directly away from us. A guy would have to be a genius to figure it out. It's just a matter of time now, brother. You, me, and Candy, living the life on a beach someplace nice and warm."

Luther thought about that. What Azi was saying did sound pretty good. And Azi was one of the smartest people Luther had ever met. If Candy was cool with this, it had to be solid.

14.

If Luther had to list every happy place he had ever known in his life, the list would be painfully short. Foremost, *happy* wasn't actually a place as much as it was a state of mind, because it was anywhere he and Candy spent time together. It didn't matter if it was while she was servicing a customer in the champagne room or when they made love in the back of a Rolls, Luther lived for those moments. Luther's second happy place was actually a place, in the form of his apartment, because it was the only place Good Luther was allowed to exist, although Luther had recently noticed Good Luther seeping into Bad Luther's activities. The third was his current location, the feeding pit, where he spent time with Croc Turd and Bianca.

Luther saw his relationship with Croc Turd as the only one in which he could actually be himself and be honest. His past had left him justifiably suspicious of everyone around him. Candy could have been an exception, but she left Luther perpetually confused, and he didn't like that feeling of helplessness. Tony should have been an exception as well, but Luther could feel that Tony felt obligated to him for something. Croc Turd was a completely broken person who had nothing to hide, nothing to be proud of, nothing to strive for, and no hope of ever getting out of his current situation. In a world filled with head nods and innuendo that could spell the difference between walking through a door or being shot in the face, Croc Turd's childlike honesty was a breath of fresh air.

At first Luther was forced to spend a lot of time with Croc Turd due to his work cleaning crime scenes with Murphy. While Murphy took care of the minutia of a scene, such as blood, small body parts, hair follicles, and fingerprints, Luther did the grunt work. Dissecting large body parts, boiling down evidence on site if it was not possible to transport it to Bianca, removing bloody cloths, etc. were all Luther's bailiwick. While Murphy's time was consumed by the more tedious aspects of evidence removal, Luther was responsible for transporting body parts to Croc Turd. Their friendship flowered from the conversations they had had as they sat by the pit, dropping flesh to a very appreciative crocodile.

Luther took a neatly separated forearm with the hand still attached out of one of the three bulging construction-quality trash bags that sat between them. Before he tossed the appendage in the pit, Luther removed two rings, a solid gold ID bracelet, and a Rolex Cosmography watch and secreted them into a black leather case.

"I hope you're not keeping that shit," Croc Turd cautioned.

"Would you rather I just let Bianca try to digest it?" Luther asked as he dangled the hand by its forefinger over Biancas head. "Who's a good girl?" Luther asked Bianca in a childlike voice. Bianca snapped the arm out of Luther's grasp, "Yes, you're the good girl, aren't you? Yes, you are."

"That's not the point, buddy," Croc Turd replied, "and you know it. We're supposed to take that shit and toss it in the grinder. If Cutter ever caught you with it, he'd rip your dick off on the spot."

"Actually," Luther said as he pulled a foot out of the bag and inspected it, "to be correct, Pretty Boy would pull my dick off after Big Benny or someone like him had beaten the shit out of me. Hell, Cutter probably doesn't even wipe his own ass."

Croc Turd shrugged, tilted his head to one side, and nodded. "True— that is true," he said, contemplating the visual. "Cutter never gets his hands dirty. But that's going to be a small consolation when you're walking around town all beat to shit trying to figure out where your dick got off to."

"It doesn't matter," Luther assured. "I don't pawn that stuff or anything."

"What do you do with shit that could get you killed then?" Croc Turd asked suspiciously. "Do you just let it lay around your place so you can dust it every once in a while? That seems pretty risky for a knick-knack collection. You might want to invest in Hummels or petrified Peeps instead."

"Basically, I destroy it." Luther tried to put Croc Turd at ease. "Yeah, sometimes I give something to Candy, but it's never something that could be identified or anything. I look for things that are engraved, or one-of-a-kind pieces, and put *those* in the grinder. I'm not a complete idiot ya know."

Croc Turd instantly felt bad for bringing it up. Luther was absolutely the only friend he had in the world. Croc Turd was just trying to keep his friend out of trouble, but he certainly didn't want to hurt his feelings. Croc Turd knew everybody in the family shit on Luther and treated him like a moron. He never wanted Luther to think they were anything but the best of friends.

"I'm sorry dude," Croc Turd apologized. "I just don't want anything bad to happen to you."

"I know," Luther sulked. Croc Turd extracted a connected femur, knee, and calf from the bag. He eyed it in disgust and set it aside. "I know you didn't do this shit," Croc Turd said to Luther indicating the family size portion of meat. "You know better that that."

"Yeah," Luther said exasperated. "It's that goddamned Murphy. He does that all the time when I'm not looking. He thinks it's going to get me in trouble. That guy is a real dick hole."

"Yeah, I can't stand him either," Croc Turd confided. "He thinks his shit don't stink, but in reality, he's just a sick lump of shit that mops up blood for a living."

Luther and Croc Turd stared reflectively into the depths of Bianca's pit as they waited for her to finish the unconsumed parts that were still lying around her. A hand protruded from her mouth. She hesitated for a second like she was trying to figure out the physics it would take to get the hand in her mouth. Then suddenly she tossed the hand in the air and clamped down on it before it hit the ground. She smiled a crocodile smile as she chewed on her tidbit.

"Can I talk to you about something that's really bothering me?" Croc Turd finally asked as he continued to watch Bianca.

"Of course," Luther sounded surprised. "You know you can talk to me about anything. I'm sure as hell not going to say anything to the family. Hell, I don't even tell Tony what we talk about."

"This is about you Luther," Croc Turd said cautiously. "I don't want to hurt your feelings or anything."

"You don't have to worry about that brother," Luther said as he reached over a mangled head that was staring blankly across the pit and patted Croc Turd on the back.

"It's Candy, Luther." Croc Turd felt Luther tense up at the mention of her name.

"What about her?" Luther said darkly. He was getting tired of people saying things he didn't like about the woman he loved.

"I just have your best interest at heart here, my friend," Croc Turd said as he tried to smooth ruffled feathers. "I'll stop talking if you don't want to hear it."

"Look," Luther said, consciously ensuring he didn't use the demeaning nickname Croc Turd. "I love her, and she loves me."

"Has she said that?" The words were out of Croc Turd's mouth before he knew it, and he was instantly sorry. "I'm sorry man," Croc Turd said, shaking his head slightly and redirecting his attention to Bianca.

"It's okay," Luther said. "I know you're just looking out for me, and no she hasn't. Sometimes you just know. Do you know what I mean? Neither of you has to say it, you both just feel it, and that's a thing of beauty, brother."

Croc Turd thought back to his time with Evangeline. He thought *that* was real and was a feeling that both of them shared without having to say it. It had been too late by the time he realized Evangeline was just a horny little bitch who was trying to get at her father. She turned on him instantly and helped put him in his current position for the rest of his life.

"I know that, Luther," Croc Turd said sympathetically. "I'm just concerned that you may not be seeing this thing clearly."

"Thanks buddy," Luther said genuinely, "but I'm good."

Both men fell silent for a moment, each wanting to add to the conversation and each not wanting to hurt or implicate the other. Luther could nearly make out a faint, irritating voice that was maddening like a kitten kneading your brain from the inside. *"You know he's right,"* the voice chided. *"That whore is going to get you killed some day."* "She's not a whore," Luther blurted out, and at the same time he realized the voice was Good Luther.

"Hey man," Croc Turd said, raising his hands in surrender, "I never said she was. If that's what you got out of it, I'm truly sorry, buddy."

Luther shook his head in what seemed like deference but was actually an unconscious attempt to force Good Luther out of his head.

"Can I tell you something?" Luther asked hesitantly. "It's kind of a big thing and if you'd rather not, I completely understand."

"You can tell or ask me anything," Croc Turd reassured as he dropped the bruised and beaten head into Biancas open maw. "What is it?"

"Well," Luther began slowly, "it's about something Azi told me." Croc Turd was instantly on guard. He hated Azi and saw him for the sniveling little opportunist he was. Anything that included Azi was dangerous and suspect.

"What about him?" Croc Turd was trying to not be instantly negative at the cost of his friend's feelings.

"Well." Luther didn't want to say it out loud, but he needed outside counsel. "You know Cutter is looking for someone that's skimming, right?"

Croc Turd was pulling half a torso out of the bag and dropped it. "What about it?" Croc Turd said indifferently. He knew what Luther was going to say, but he didn't want to actually believe it.

Luther held Croc Turd in a pleading gaze. "It's Azi." Luther let that drop like a wet sack of old mashed potatoes and waited for the response.

"Oh, my sweet holy shit," Croc Turd said like he was in a trance. "For the love of God, Luther, please tell me you don't have anything to do with this." Croc Turd's fight or flight mode dropped into overdrive. He wanted to distance himself as far away from this information as he possibly could, but he couldn't abandon his friend.

"Not directly," Luther said quietly. Croc Turd threw his hands to his face, leaving bloody smears.

"This is bad," Croc Turd moaned more to himself than to Luther. "This is really, really bad."

"It's not that bad." Luther tried to reason the unreasonable. "Candy and Azi have this all planned out. It's bulletproof."

"It's fucking insane!" Croc Turd yelled. "And it's going to get all three of you killed, at best. Can't you see that?"

"But it's not." Luther tried to get Croc Turd to see the beauty of the plan. "Azi has a partner on the inside, and that guy is going to keep everybody safe."

Croc Turd felt like he was in a dream, floating between the reality of certain death and dismemberment and the fantasy world Luther was trying to convince him of. He hesitated for a moment, unaware he was just staring at Luther with his mouth open. Bianca snapped her jaws together impatiently, but both men ignored her. Luther didn't like where this was going, mostly because he had hoped Croc Turd would reassure him.

"Luther," Croc Turd started slowly, afraid to open Pandora's Box, "who's the partner?"

"Richy," Luther said confidently. "See, nothing bad is going to happen."

"Oh my holy God," Croc Turd moaned as he rocked back and forth on his haunches, "oh my God, oh my God, oh my God." Croc

Turd nearly shouted the last phrase. "These ignorant motherfuckers are going to get you killed!" Croc Turd grabbed Luther by the arm. "Can't you understand? Those two are in bed with *Richy*! Oh my God, *Richy*! They are going to get everyone butchered. This can't be real. Please someone tell me this isn't real. Luther, for the love of God please tell me you're just fucking around here. You can't be serious."

"Calm down man," Luther said smiling as he tried to reassure his friend. "This is all planned out. Right now, they're looking at the protection money. That's going to come back negative. . ."

"What then, Luther?" Croc Turd was frantic. "Where do they start looking?"

"Azi built a paper trail that's going to point at someone else. By then we'll be long gone."

"You're going with them?" Croc Turd was praying this nightmare would just end.

"Yeah," Luther said wistfully, "Azi and Candy invited me. We're all going together."

"Are you out of your fucking mind?!" Croc Turd exploded. "You can't trust either one of those assholes."

"I can trust Candy," Luther said, surprised by Croc Turd's outburst. "She would never do anything to hurt me. She loves me."

"*SHE WILL!*" Good Luther shouted. It gave Luther an astronomical headache. "*She'll gut both of you like a fish and disappear with the money!*" Luther closed his eyes and fought for control.

Croc Turd wanted to punch Luther right in the mouth and toss him in the pit with Bianca, and he was maddeningly conflicted about saying anything bad about that bitch Candy to him.

"I hope you're right, Luther," Croc Turd said involuntarily. "So, who did these criminal masterminds pick to throw to the wolves? Do you know?"

"No," Luther said reflectively, "I never thought to ask. Whoever it is, I'm sure that person has it coming in some way. I mean Candy isn't some kind of a monster, right?"

"*That's exactly what she is,*" spit Good Luther.

Luther stood and walked into the storage closet to retrieve another sterling silver shipping container as he mentally tamped Good Luther back into his box. Good Luther showing up outside the apartment concerned him. When he returned, Croc Turd was absently fishing reptile shit out of the pit with the skimming net.

"Who do you think is traveling to Miami this time?" Luther said, trying to lighten the mood.

"What?" Croc Turd was distracted by visions of horrible vengeance being exacted on Luther.

Luther tipped his head toward the pit. "Who do you think rides to Miami in style?"

"Oh, yeah. That," Croc Turd said bleakly. "Let me see. If I have her digestive cycle down, I think this should be that guy—ah—Caleb Goldberg, I guess."

"Oh man," Luther sounded hurt, "you mean the guy that runs Goldberg's deli?"

"Yeah," Croc Turd sounded sad. "I guess he gave Richy and Big Benny some shit, so they shot him. Now he heads south in a silver box."

"That blows," Luther reflected. "He had the best blintzes in town."

15

Luther and Candy walked along the sidewalk hand in hand, giving the outward appearance of two normal people walking toward a normal restaurant for a normal night out. However, the reality of the scene was much more convoluted and disconnected than even Candy or Luther was willing to accept. This pair shared a twisted *"A Tale of Two Cities"* kinship. To Luther his "dates" with Candy were deep, meaningful, and romantic. To Candy they were an animalistic means to an end, namely, her getting laid by someone that knew all of her buttons. To Luther these trysts were classy, like red roses and candy on Valentine's, or getting your girl's name tattooed on your arm. To Candy they were clinical and detached, a means to a definite end. To Luther he was treating his woman to opulence and luxury. To Candy they were fucking in the back of someone else's car.

"What do you have for us tonight?" Luther asked, slipping a bill into the kid's hand. The valet was a high school senior who looked like he had reached the pinnacle of his entrepreneurial acumen. His pot-selling gig was paying off, valet tips in a place like this could be huge, and the money he was making using the parking lot like a well-appointed hot-pillow joint could have him rolling in money far into his retirement age. Well, in his mind, at least.

"Let me see," the valet pondered while checking random car keys hanging on a pegboard. "Ah, yes. I have a quite lovely Rolls Phantom, black with a white interior, two rows deep on the lot, so plenty of privacy." He gave Luther a conspiratorial wink.

"Isn't that the one with footrests in the back and stars on the ceiling?" Luther asked discerningly.

"You certainly do know your luxury vehicles, Mister LaMotta," the valet shmoozed.

Luther looked at Candy for approval, and she shrugged while she examined a broken nail. "Yes Kenny, we'll take the Rolls," Luther confirmed. "How long would you guess we have?"

Kenny looked at his watch then at the front door of the restaurant. "I would say," Kenny looked skyward, "around two hours." Then he added, "for a small service fee, I can arrange free desserts for the owner. That could add on, say, another forty-five minutes."

Kenny raised his eyebrows to let Luther know this was an excellent deal. Luther didn't understand it, but he slipped another bill into Kenny's hand.

"Very good, sir." Kenny allowed an oily grin to spread across his pimply face. "Down and to your left. Out-of-state plates. You can't miss it."

Luther grabbed the key and placed his hand in the small of Candy's back, allowing her to precede him. After they made the left turn, Luther pressed the "unlock" feature of the fob and located the flashing taillights. Luther opened the back door. "Honey," he said to Candy, motioning for her to get in.

Once in the back seat Luther dropped the fob in the cup holder next to the driver's seat, so there wouldn't be an accidental pressing of the car alarm. As he turned back toward Candy, she was on him like Rick Flare coming off the top rope and started tearing at his belt buckle.

"Jesus!" Luther exclaimed as Candy rolled him into the seat and sat in his lap.

"Give it to me." Candy's voice was low and throaty like a werewolf preparing to tear his prey apart. She jammed her hand down his pants and grabbed him like a junior astronaut trying to land the lunar module for the first time.

"Hey," Luther protested, pulling his mouth away from the suction-like grip of Candy's lips "you're going to tear that thing off like that."

"I've needed this all day," Candy moaned directly into Luther's ear.

Candy dropped herself hard onto Luther's swollen manhood and pressed her face against the top of his shoulder. Her ass went to work like an Oklahoma oil derrick gone berserk. Luther pressed his hands into the luxurious leather on either side, trying to keep his balance while Candy ground on his lap. After the initial shock Luther was all onboard with, well, with whatever this was. He bit Candy on the neck and pulled her hair back, making her quiver with ecstasy.

Luther pulled Candy off him like the banana man peeling off starving monkeys, flipped her onto her hands and knees across the length of the back seat and rammed into her as hard as he could. She dropped her head and growled "Oh. Fuck. Yes." Luther was driving into her with a locomotive rhythm, his eyes clasped shut as he held tightly on to her hips.

"Oooooooooh shit baby," Candy's voice sounded thick and wet now, "pound my ass."

Luther kept the rhythm and violent nature of his love making going, but he opened his eyes and tilted his head like a poodle.

"Pound my ass," Candy begged. "Pound my ass. Pleeeeeeeeeease pound my ass."

Luther took his hand off Candy's side, balled it into a fist and punched her in the ass cheek as hard as he could. They both came at the same time.

They separated into the back seats, both breathing heavily and spent like two fighters going into opposite corners.

"Just what the fuck was that?" Candy complained.

"What, honey?" Luther asked dreamily as he stroked Candy's thigh. She sounded almost pissed off.

"What?" Candy asked incredulously. "Let's see, could it be when you punched the living shit out of me? I think you dislocated my goddamned hip." She squirmed in the chair a little as she winced in pain.

"*I* didn't want to hit you at all," Luther explained.

"Oh, okay," Candy mocked. "I guess I missed the guy holding a gun to your head telling you to beat the hell out of me."

"What?" Luther leaned back aghast. "You said you wanted me to do that. In fact, you begged me too."

"What the actual fuck?" Candy was surprised.

"Yeah," Luther sounded like a child explaining a broken window to his mother. "*Pound my ass, pound my ass,*" Luther said in a high-pitched voice mocking Candy's. "You must have asked me to do that three or four times in fact."

"Jesus Christ, Luther," Candy shook her head, "I wanted you to fuck me harder. That's all, not beat the shit out of me."

"I was already doing that," Luther pouted. "You should have been more specific."

"Yeah," Candy said as she started to get dressed. "I guess I should have. I have no idea how you can be as screwed up as you are and still be a machine in the sack."

Luther was hurt that Candy had said he was screwed up. "I learned about sex in prison," Luther said, sulking.

"Come on baby," Candy attempted to sooth him as she lifted her butt off the seat to zip her pants. "You know I don't think you're stupid. It's just that no one has ever given it to me like you do."

Luther was suddenly exultant. He didn't care what Candy had said before the *screwed-up* part. She had called him baby and complimented him on his sexual prowess. He wanted her all over again, but a thing that was gnawing at his brain put a stop to further coitus.

"I talked to Azi yesterday," Luther said trying to sound as offhanded as he could.

"So did I," Candy said cautiously. "How is that news?"

"He told me something that I'm kind of trying to make sense of. Actually, there's a couple of things."

"*That slimy limp dick little asshole,*" Candy thought. "What might that be?" She smiled coyly at Luther.

"First," Luther was hesitant. He didn't want to say anything that might hurt Candy's feelings, "Azi and I were drinking at Boat Drinks. . ."

"I hate that dump," Candy interrupted. "Azi loves it for some creepy reason.

"It's within his safe zone," Luther explained.

"Yeah, that," Candy said bleakly. "Him and that safe zone bullshit. You guys were drinking in there, right?"

Luther nodded.

"I'm positive Azi did at least two lines of blow in the shithouse."

"Four," Luther corrected.

Candy tossed her palms out by her sides, opened her mouth, and did a short head shake in the universal, "so, what the hell?" pantomime. "He's doing blow and drinking. How does doing that make it a safe zone?"

Luther shrugged, grateful for the reprieve.

"I'm sorry," Candy said. "He and his bullshit just make me nuts sometimes. Anyhow, what did *mister deluded safe zone* say to you?"

"He, ah," Luther stuttered, "well, he thanked me for doing what I just did with you."

"What?" Candy asked laughing sarcastically. "You mean he thanked you for fucking me?"

"Yeah," Luther sounded like a schoolboy. "He said it helps him when—when he does that to you."

Candy was looking out the very expensive window into the really shitty parking lot and shaking her head.

"I don't care," Luther added quickly. "I don't want you to think I have a problem with *anything* you do. I just didn't know he wanted that."

"Look, Luther," Candy said in an instructional tone, "Azi is a weak little man, and he loves to abuse himself. I don't know, maybe it's because he pissed his life away, maybe it's mommy issues, maybe he's just an asshole. He gives me the security I need, and you give me everything else." She didn't mention that *everything else* was simply brutal jailhouse sex in cars. "We make a great trio, don't you think?"

"Candy," Luther said holding her in a deep meaningful gaze, "I don't care how many people are in our relationship. As long as I can have you, on any level, I'm happy. I love you, Candy."

"I know you do honey," Candy deflected as she patted the hand resting on her inner thigh. "So, what else did dic...I mean Azi have to say?"

"Well, Candy," Luther was examining the floor, "that's kind of the most important part. And I'm really worried for you."

"I am going to shove my foot so far up that little turd's ass when I get home," Candy thought. "What's there to worry about?" she asked, kind of sweetly. "Everything is just fine with me. Him I don't know about, but I'm just peachy."

"He said you guys were skimming off the Manchinis."

"THAT FUCKER!" Candy screamed in her head. "He told you *we* were doing that?" Candy asked out loud.

"Yeah," Luther said looking back toward Candy with pleading eyes. "He actually told me it was all your idea, and he's just going along."

Candy was wrestling to control her inner fury like she was trying to kill an Anaconda in the Amazon River. "He said that did he?" Candy lowered her head, looking out of the top of her eyes in that way that made Luther crazy.

"Please, don't start biting your lip," Luther thought. "Yeah, he did," Luther said. "But, like I said before, I don't care or anything, I just don't want you to get wrapped up in something Azi did," he quickly added.

"How much more do you know?" Candy said, trying to pry out information without giving anything important away.

"I think everything," Luther sounded cautious now. Something about the way Candy was reacting put him off. But not far enough off that it distracted him from wanting to ravage her all over again. "I know you have a partner."

"Do you know who?"

"Yeah, Richy." Luther noticed Candy's eyes narrow slightly.

"And?" Candy asked.

"And?" Luther searched for the boundaries of her anger. "I know there's a paper trail going someplace else. But I don't know who."

Candy contemplated her next move. She absently began to rub Luther's crotch to give him something to do while she thought.

"Surprise," Candy said in a voice usually reserved for birthday parties. She threw her hands in the air and Luther opened his eyes. "I guess Azi ruined it for me, but it is what it is. I was going to tell you when we got things a little more straightened out, but we planned on the three of us getting out of here together."

"Seriously?" Luther asked hopefully.

"Sure," Candy said disconnectedly. She was doing the math in her head about how she was going to get rid of two bodies now instead of just Azi's.

"I can't tell you how happy that makes me, honey." Luther kissed her hard. "The three of us free to do whatever we want."

"Yeah, it's going to be great." Candy smiled, but the look in her eyes would have been more appropriate if she had just plunged a bare foot into cold dogshit.

"Hey," Luther asked as he was pulling Candy's pants back off. "Who's the trail go to?"

"I have no idea," Candy lied.

It didn't matter what she said because instead of listening, he was engrossed in violently probing for the leather of the seat through Candy's back.

16.

Luther was sitting, naked except for white boxer shorts and a red headband, in his kitchen/dining room on 1950s-era red padded vinyl stretched across a gently curving chrome frame. The table before him had the same *Father Knows Best* quality, with an off-white Formica top held up by a matching chrome frame. It was hot in that kitchen on the best days in the summer, but the heat from the miniature forge sitting next to him was making it nearly unbearable. In the corner an ancient, caged floor fan hummed asymmetrically as it dutifully hurried hot air around the apartment, until the air eventually found its way back to the starting point.

The last mournful notes of John Fogerty playing the electric piano on "As Long as I Can See the Light" pushed around the inside of Luther's head, leaving him emotionally drained. Rivulets of sweat rolled out from under the headband as he sat in stasis, waiting for the next gut wrencher on his playlist to begin. Long low notes seeped out of the cello like maple sap during a warm Vermont spring day. Luther felt like he could just lay on those notes and drift away to places that didn't even exist in the physical realm. The violins unveiled themselves in the background, unfurling gossamer wings of indigo and violet, then floated up to the musical countdown, beckoning Linda Ronstadt to sweetly advise, *"Love will abide. Take things in stride."*

A tear began to roll down Luther's cheek, mixing with the sweat as it continued down his neck and across his bare chest. The words *"Sonds like good advice. But there's no one at my side,"* ripped up an octave and exploded in his mind. He tilted his head back and shook it slowly, trying to caress and love each and every heartbreaking word. He was in heaven.

He peered at the diamond necklace he was holding through the large glass sphere of a lighted magnifying glass on an adjustable stand clamped to the edge of the table. Using small tools, he gently pried the diamonds out of their settings one at a time, dropping them on a black velvet cloth. Once all of the jewels had been removed, Luther checked the rest of the necklace for other types of metals that might corrupt one of his ingots. Satisfied, he laid the necklace in the forge, then picked a watch out of the large red plastic bucket filled with jewelry next to him on the floor.

"*Buddy,*" Good Luther whispered to him, fading Linda slightly. That annoyed Luther. "*I think we need to have a talk.*"

"We talk all the time," Middle Luther said out loud. "Why do you have to announce this conversation like you're addressing the UN?"

"*This is really important, my friend,*" Good Luther whispered soothingly. "*This is the only place we can talk without that hooligan butting in.*"

"Are you talking about Bad Luther?" Middle Luther asked as he momentarily paused the inspection of the watch.

"*Yeah, him.*" Good Luther sounded genuinely concerned. "*I understand what he does for you—out there. He's your protection and he keeps you steady.*"

"Why do I get the feeling you're about to shit all over that?" Middle Luther asked, placing the watch in a pile, then retrieving a bracelet from the bucket.

"*You need to be putting* a lot *of things together right now, old man.*" Middle Luther could feel Good Luther start to get preachy.

"Oh yeah?" Middle Luther said as he picked up a tiny metal pick. "Like what, exactly?"

"*Let's start at the beginning.*" Good Luther was starting to talk like Candy did when she was trying to explain how Azi wasn't going to get them both killed. "*When was the last time you and I had a conversation like this in your apartment?*"

Luther stopped what he was doing and tilted his head. "Never," he said cautiously.

"*Yeah, buddy,*" Good Luther crooned. "*Never—why do you suppose that is?*"

"How the fuck am I supposed to know?" Middle Luther was getting pissed.

"*Tisk tisk tisk, buddy,*" Good Luther scolded. "*That kind of language has* never *been allowed in here.*"

Luther dropped the bracelet and stopped the music. "No, it hasn't," Middle Luther said to the empty room.

"*Why now?*"

"Ah—it's just, you know, it's just a figure of speech."

"*A filthy figure of speech that's beneath you,*" Good Luther reminded Middle Luther. "*Beneath the real you. And you know it.*"

Luther did know it. The thought that two thirds of him knew it slipped into the periphery of his mind. Bad Luther had no idea what was or what wasn't beneath Middle Luther. This was confusing him.

"*We're all starting to come together buddy,*" Good Luther explained. "*All it's going to take to get good, bad,* and *middle Luther on the same train is a significant emotional experience. I just want you to be prepared. You know I've been with you outside a few times. The three of us could be a much better version of Luther than what's currently sleepwalking around town.*"

Luther leaned back in his chair and rubbed the sweat out of his eyes.

"*That's enough for now buddy,*" Good Luther whispered sweetly. "*I'll let you get back to it.*" Then Good Luther added, "*Oh, one more thing. For the love of God buddy, lose the cooze. She's going to get you killed.*"

Luther punched the continue button on his headset. Linda was gone and Van Morrison was floating through the lyrics of "Into the Mystic." Everything Luther was saying to himself was irritating, interesting, compelling, and annoying all at the same time. It made his head hurt, and he tried to press it out of his consciousness.

He reached into a bowl near the forge and retrieved a pinch of Borax, then sprinkled it over the melting gold. That would lower the temperature it was going to take to burn off impurities. If nothing else, Luther knew what it took to produce good gold out of jewelry, and he had a reputation to protect with the people that bought his product. After the gold was liquid, Luther picked up the crucible with tongs and poured the molten contents into a small ingot mold. After it cooled, he placed the tiny ingots in a stack.

He made himself busy cleaning the kitchen and replacing all of his smelting paraphernalia back on the top shelf in his kitchen. He was correct when he told himself things were changing, but one thing that would never change was the way he lived. Everything had a place, and cleanliness was next to godliness. He wasn't sure about that thing with Candy, though. Just when he was starting to think Good Luther had his best interest at heart, he had to go and say something horrible like that.

He also knew that if the three Luthers ever got together, they would rip each other apart. If what Good Luther was saying turned out to be true, he was going to have to work hard to keep that from happening. That could end him, and he was terrified of that. He was going to start working on a strategy against a joining of the three right now.

"*Good luck with that,*" Good Luther whispered.

17.

Richy and Tony walked along the sidewalk in a neighborhood that was home to the majority of the businesses the Manchini family "protected." Both men were deep into their characters as hardcore mafia muscle just in case people were paying attention and weren't sure who they were. Also, it made it much easier to intimidate when you started right off from a superior level, such as that of a dangerous mob enforcer. A few steps behind them, Luther, deep in his character of "I couldn't care less why I'm even here," walked with his hands in his pockets and B.J. Thomas's sweet melodic voice in his head, telling Luther just how lonesome he was. This was the perfect music for Luther to indulge in his favorite pastime of psychologically beating himself up. "*The midnight train is whining low, I'm so lonesome I could cry,*" B. J. lamented. Luther simply smiled painfully.

A red neon sign proclaiming that "liquor" was available flashed on and off in the front window of the business the trio was approaching. The store front looked sad and depressed, with chipped brick and smudged plate glass windows. Pathetic signs, yellow and warped with age, selling products that no longer existed, leaned lackadaisically against the glass. The shelf they stood on looked like the fly apocalypse had just taken place.

Tony grabbed the handle on the glass door to allow Richy to go first, then followed him in. Luther grabbed the door and entered the drab, cave-like plutonian interior as B.J. moaned "*Like me he's lost the will to live. I'm so lonesome I could cry.*" "*That's perfect timing,*" Luther thought as he scrutinized his surroundings. "*What a pathetic dump.*"

The owner stood behind the counter, giving off body language epitomizing a man who was fed up and wasn't going to take it anymore. "*Your timing, on the other hand, is shit, mister.*" Luther observed. People, starting with this guy, were going to start paying for Richy's indiscretions, and the only ones in the room who realized this were Luther and Richy.

"How's it goin' Mike?" Richy began cordially. Mike DeMaggio had taken ownership of this liquor store from his father, who had received it from *his* father. It was a family institution, and ever since the Manchinis had shown up "offering" protection, DeMaggio was barely able to make ends meet. He had been preaching to the other store owners that if they all told the family to piss off, they could break this ignorant waste of money.

"Fine, Richy," Mike said, not trying to hide his irritation. "How are you gentlemen?"

"Oh," Richy said, looking at Luther and Tony. "We're outstanding actually. Just fucking outstanding."

An uneasy silence fell over the room like a yellow sheet on a dead body, Richy glaring at Mike, Mike glaring at Richy, Tony overdoing his thug persona, and Luther wrapped up in the troubles of B.J. Thomas.

"What can I do for you fellas?" Mike asked evenly.

"For us?" Richy looked around the room again. "What could you possibly do for three guys like us on this fine second Tuesday of the month?" Richy stuffed his hands in his pockets and bounced on his heels a little as Tony theatrically punched his fist into his other hand. Luther rolled his eyes and waited for the next track. Mike placed his hands on the counter as if he was physically trying to either restrain himself or bolster his courage.

A light string intro slid gracefully between Luther's ears and heralded Barry Gibb, explaining to Luther, *"there's a light, a certain kind of light, that never shone on me."* Luther grinned deeply as a tear rolled down his cheek. That grin and Luther's tears terrified Mike. *"What the hell do these three have in mind?"* he thought. The other two were acting normal for people who were probably going to start beating the shit out of him in a few minutes. But the grinning/crying jackass in the corner was a frightening unknown.

Richy realized, dumbfoundedly, that something behind him had Mike's attention. He turned around to see Luther. *"You don't know what it's like, baby you don't know what it's like. . ."* Barry Gibb yelled into Luther's head. Luther had his eyes shut tight, so he didn't see Richy looking at him.

"Is he fucking crying?" Richy asked Tony in disbelief. Mike looked very confused.

Tony shrugged and pointed to his own ear, "It's the music. Luther is very—*emotional*. He'll be fine."

"Son of a bitch," Richy growled. He reached over and slapped Luther lightly across the face to get his attention. Luther's eyes snapped open, revealing Richy's frustration.

He immediately reached up and pulled the Shokz off his head. "Sorry boss," he apologized. "I'm paying attention."

Richy shook his head and turned back to Mike. "Alright," Richy blew himself up as the threatening mafia boss again, "Where were we? Oh yeah, you apparently have zero idea what three fine looking gentlemen like us would be doing in your lovely place of business."

"I know what the other two guys would be doing in here today." Mike was not showing the deference or fear he should have been, and it was pissing Richy off. "*Those* guys would be here to collect. Since you *fine gentlemen* are here instead, I would assume there's an issue."

"You would *assume*?" Richy mimicked Mike. "You know what they say about people that 'assume' don't you Mike?"

Mike shrugged his shoulders and shook his head slightly. "No, what do they say?" he asked.

"They say it makes you look like an asshole," Richy answered, grinning violently.

"Look," Mike started. Tony shot an exasperated look at the ceiling. He knew what was coming next.

"Don't you tell me to 'look,' asshole," Richy pounced. "Do you have any idea what happened to this last asshole that told me to look?" Mike shrugged again.

"Tony," Richy demanded, "tell him."

"It wasn't good," Tony answered obediently.

"Yeah, Mike," Richy glared as he took a step toward the counter, "it wasn't good. Do you know why?"

Mike shrugged again.

"Tell him Tony."

"He beat the hell out of him, I think," Tony searched his memory. "Or did you shoot that one? I get them confused sometimes."

"It don't matter," Richy said, still glaring at Mike. "I think he gets the idea. You *do* get the idea, right Mike?"

"I get it," Mike said still hiding any hint of emotion. "I was just saying you don't usually collect. Two other guys do, so you must want something other than that."

"Some dick hole is shorting us on the collections." Richy sounded as threatening as he could. Luther, who knew exactly where the money was disappearing from, was amazed by how real Richy made his bullshit sound.

"Well," Mike said stoically, "it's not me. But since you're here, Richy, I want to tell you something."

"Oh," Richy said in mock surprise, "stupendous! I'm about to learn some shit." He turned toward Tony and Luther, raising his eyebrows and tilting his head slightly. Luther was instantly confused, but since Tony was just standing there, he figured doing nothing was a good plan for the present time.

"The owners are getting together," Mike said evenly. "We're all tired of this bullshit."

Richy continued smiling as he dropped his arms and folded his fingers together in front of him. "Really?" Richy sounded genuinely interested.

"Look," Mike started to say.

Richy leapt across the counter, grabbing Mike by his shirt front, then tossed him violently into a Fishky Scotch display. Cheap whiskey and broken glass covered the already grubby floor, and Mike slammed hard onto the shards. Tony picked Mike partway off the floor by his shirt and punched him in the face. Mike reached up and belted Tony in the eye. "You miserable mother fucker!" Tony squealed as he rubbed his face. Richy kicked Mike in the side and Luther kicked him in the head. Tony jumped back on Mike and Mike punched him in the face again.

Luther dropped to his knees, sat Mike up against the counter, and started using Mike's head as a punching bag, more out of a sense of job security than to defend his boss. Luther was always mentally stoic about his job as mob muscle. He didn't hate the people he beat up, and he didn't love the people that paid him to do the beating. He would just keep wailing on Mike until someone told him to stop.

Mike's face was a bloody mess by the time Tony pulled Luther off. Luther stood up and kicked Mike in the leg, more for theater than out of irritation. Mike's head lolled on his chest, and he was weeping softly as blood mixed with the whiskey on the floor and pooled around his butt.

Richy walked behind the counter and found the envelope they had come for.

"Is it all there?" Tony asked.

"Yeah, it looks like it," Richy mumbled as he thumbed through the bills. "Stupid prick could have just handed it to me," Richy was exasperated. "But noooo, not him. He has to be some kind of Charlie Bronson and shit."

Richy opened the register and took all of the money that was there as well. He kicked Mike's legs out of the way as he started for the door, making Mike moan. "Shut the fuck up," Richy demanded over his shoulder. Then to Tony and Luther, "Come on, let's get the hell out of here."

18.

Luther had enjoyed the luxury of the last Rolls he and Candy had used, so when Kenny mentioned he had a gold Rolls Ghost with a white interior available, he jumped at it. They had at least an hour and a half to do with it as they wanted, and what they wanted was only going to take thirty minutes or so.

Candy had been acting preoccupied ever since Luther picked her up at the Gold Digger. Not being one for much conversation of any kind, Luther never bothered to ask what she was thinking about. Once in the car the sex was violent and base, just like they both liked it, but Candy had continued to be affectionate even after Luther was through and sitting next to her wrapped in the finest white leather. Affection was new in their sexual history, and it didn't go unnoticed.

"Nobody gets me off like you do, baby," Candy whispered in his ear as she stroked his naked thigh. "You know that don't you?"

"I know that because you tell me," Luther said, absorbed in the feel of Candy's fingertips on his leg. "You and Tony are the only people I trust."

"Then you know how important you are to me also, right?" Candy purred.

"*Get your head out of your crotch*," Good Luther warned.

"*Fuck off*," Bad Luther shot back. "*What the hell are you doing out of the house anyway?*" Only silence echoed in Luther's head.

"Are you okay, baby?" Candy asked as she ran her index finger up to his testicles, then removed it.

"Yeah," Luther said absently, "I just thought of something. That's all."

"Something like this?" Candy asked as she reached up and brushed her hand against growing penis.

"Yeah," Luther croaked. "Just like that."

"I have something I need to ask you baby," Candy said seductively.

"Anything you want," Luther promised.

"It's Azi, baby." Candy had him full in her hand now and was gently working him into blissful ignorance.

"Yeah," Luther whispered, "what about him?"

"*Don't!*" Good Luther shouted into Bad Luther's head. "*There's still time to turn back!*"

"Shut the fuck up, asshole," Luther said out loud.

Candy stopped and leaned back a little.

"No," Luther said excitedly. "Not you. That was for somebody else."

Candy decided to ignore the fact that they were the only two in the car and began stroking him again.

"What were you saying?" Luther asked, trying to be polite while at the same time masking his cerebral "issue."

"It's Azi, baby," Candy said coyly as she bent down and blew a small puff of warm air on the end of his erection.

"Uh huh," Luther said without the least bit of interest in what Candy was saying.

"Well, he's got himself in a little bit of a spot," Luther looked at the back of her head suspiciously. But he decided whatever he was thinking was not important as he felt her tongue search for the inside of his distal urethra, "and he needs our help," she continued as she sat up but kept working on the focus of his attention.

"In what way?" Luther asked. Now his mind was directed at two different things, and Luther did not function well under those circumstances.

"Well," Candy began as offhandedly as she could, "you know all that money Azi has been skimming off the Manchinis' books?"

"Yeah." Both avenues of thought were wrestling for purchase in Luther's head like Frank Gorshin and Lou Antoino in a Star Trek episode.

"He decided he could triple it."

"That's good. Isn't it?" Luther was becoming less interested in what Candy was saying and a lot more interested in what she was doing.

"You would think so," she said as she reached farther under Luther and messaged his rectum with her forefinger. "But you know what they say, the best laid mice have plans."

"Mice—plans—what the?" Luther was floundering.

"It doesn't matter baby," Candy said as she brought her hand back up to continue its original mission. "Let's just say it didn't work out the way it was planned."

"So?" Luther was thinking he should grab her and reenact the previous rutting.

"So," Candy knew it was time to let the other shoe fall, "you know Azi, always thinking about other people. Anyhow, he didn't want to say anything to me about gambling all of our escape money away."

"Gambling?" Somewhere far back in the darkest folds of Luther's mind, Good Luther was screaming through a duct-taped mouth.

"Oh, yeah," Candy said as if the information was irrelevant. "He thought it was a sure thing, whatever it was, and it turned out not to be. At any rate," she was keeping Luther right on the edge of ecstasy now, "he was afraid that I might be disappointed that we had to start all over again from the beginning, but *you* know how I am. I'm a people pleaser. I would never have gotten angry with him. That's just the way life goes sometimes. Well, Azi didn't see it that way, so he wanted to replace all of the money he pissed. . . I mean that he invested poorly, so he borrowed it from Cutter."

"So," Luther was grasping at direct attention. What Candy was saying sounded like something he wanted nothing to do with and most definitely Azi's problem, "now he pays it back."

"Well, that's the thing sweety. When I say he borrowed it, I mean Cutter didn't necessarily know it was a loan." Candy stopped her hand in mid stroke.

"No, don't stop," Luther begged as he squirmed in the seat, trying to force his dick back into Candy's hand without touching it. "How could Cutter not know he loaned Azi money?"

"Ya know that safe in Cutter's office?"

Luther's eyes sprang open, and his erection deflated like the Hindenburg at the mooring mast in New Jersey. Candy clearly had her work cut out for her. She reached back under Luther for a second, then spit in her hand and started all over again. Luther's penis was quickly back in charge of decision-making.

"What the hell did he do?" Luther asked, trying to stay focused.

"He kind of emptied it."

"Kind of?" Luther thought he might not like where this was going.

"Okay, he took it all."

"Then he should put it back," Luther said distractedly as he thrust his hips into Candy's downstroke.

"That money is for *us*, Luther," Candy said like she was a schoolmarm. "How are we going to ever get to spend the rest of our lives together if we don't have any money?" She dropped her head into Luther's lap and ran her lips down the side of the shaft.

"What should we do?" Luther was on the hook now.

"I just don't know baby," Candy whined. "I'm just at my wit's end." She had Luther ready to explode again, and she was expertly delaying it.

"I have some things I could sell," Luther heard himself suggest from under a cloud of sexual expectation. "Maybe sell some jewels or pawn a couple of watches."

"Do you think that's a good idea?" Candy whispered into his ear as she bit down on his ear lobe.

"Yeah, it's a great idea," Luther moaned. He didn't think he could take much more.

"One other thing," Candy added. "Azi can't be seen anywhere around Cutter's office. It would raise alarms. He has no idea how to get the cash back in there."

"I'm in there all the time straightening things up," Luther offered as he ran his hand up to the back of Candy's head. "I can put it back."

"If you think that's a good idea," Candy said as she removed her hand from Luther's crotch.

"Yes!" Luther yelled as he jammed Candy's head into his lap and thrust up.

19.

Luther headed north on 440 toward the Bayonne Bridge and points north loaded down with jewels, mini gold ingots, a box full of very expensive watches, and enough trepidation to stop the Mongol invasion of the west. The dichotomy of what he was about to do was eating him up inside, and he didn't understand where that kind of emotion could have come from. Afterall, this was all his idea, wasn't it? Candy had never actually asked him to do anything specific. She had simply told him what that dipshit Azi had done, and that Azi couldn't see a way out. Luther had simply offered answers to Candy's dilemma.

But he was driving to New Jersey to sell all of the gold he had smelted, fence the jewels, and pawn the watches—all things he had explicitly told himself never to do because of how dangerous it was. He felt as though he was fairly safe, taking his business all the way to another state. He wasn't stupid after all. If he tried to unload this in New York, he'd be on his way south in a silver box in no time at all.

Luther had considered putting Azi down from the first time Candy mentioned he had squandered the money. That was pretty much what Luther did for a living. He thought he might actually enjoy killing, Azi then feeding him to Bianca one piece at a time. Azi would be so much gator shit, Candy would be free, and Luther would be happy for the rest of his natural life. Easy peasy, everybody got what they deserved, God was in his heaven, and all was right with the world. But if Azi went down for this, Candy went down, and Luther could not have lived with that.

Luther had also considered the idea that the three of them living together might become an untenable situation. He also considered that if things got be too much of a problem, he could disappear Azi and act surprised when he inexplicably went missing. He didn't have a crocodile handy that could make the parts vanish, but he was pretty sure he could get his hands on several gallons of acid. He would acquiesce to committing one more act of violence by murdering Azi, but after that, he'd be done with death and dismemberment for the rest of his life, while he and Candy lived in love-filled bliss. Unless, of course, someone were to make Candy's life difficult in any way at all. Then, naturally, they would have to go away also. But that would be it: Azi and whoever might shit on Candy. After that he was done with violence forever. Unless Cutter sent someone after them—THEN he would live the pure and simple life of every Americans.

"Would you like to discuss how everything you just said is a lie?" Good Luther whispered in his head.

"Would you like to go fuck yourself?" Bad Luther shot back.

"Why don't both of you get up off my ass?" Middle Luther said to an empty car.

"Luther, think about what you're doing," Good Luther tried to reason.

"We're taking care of family," Bad Luther chastised.

"That woman. . ."

Luther mentally slapped a giant wad of duct tape over both of their mouths and turned up the music in an attempt to drown out their muffled protests.

Simple guitar notes, three up, then three down, blessedly filled the silence in the car. Luther smiled and rolled the window down. The voice of REM's Michale Snipe wafted through the speakers like a velvet fog from the night: "When your day is long, and the night, the night is yours alone." Michael's words were stabbing Luther in the heart just like he liked it. The breeze swept up from the waters of Kill Van Kull, permeating the interior of the car with bouquets of rotting fish mixed with a tincture of exhaust fumes.

Luther was feeling much lighter of heart and rich in spirit now that his two tormentors were under control. He had been much happier when Good Luther ruled in the apartment and Bad Luther ruled the outside world. Things were simple black and white then, none of those damned shades of grey. Shades of grey confused Luther and made him want to hide in the dark. Before, the Luther that lived between Good and Bad Luther had generally kept quiet and let the other two do the talking. Now things were messy, convoluted, and on the verge of teetering out of control.

He couldn't put a finger on the exact moment his mental stability had begun its smooth metamorphosis, but it seemed to be close to the time he had started to get much more attached to Candy. That idea made Luther far more stalwart in his defense of her. People had started to give him a real hard time about his relationship, the two worst examples of which were the people residing in his head. Why did they all refuse to see that Candy was actually making him better? Hadn't they all treated Luther like a moron because he was different? Now that he was improving thanks to her love and nurturing, people wanted to stomp that goodness out. They were all just jealous that Luther was making such major strides in his life while they were just sitting stagnant.

Luther drove through the seedy part of a seedy part of town and parked in the street next to a bar that made the dust bowl and depression era look like Willy Wonka's dream home. The stench of uncollected garbage fought for control of the senses with the sour scent of vomit and human shit that was creeping out of the alley next door like the first stages of life crawling out of the primordial ooze. Luther hefted the case of gold, Crown Royal bag of jewels, and Tupperware box of watches off the seat, then backed through the broken door of the bar.

The bartender sat on the back self with his feet propped up on the edge of the bar while he read the comics in the newspaper. Greasy black hair whipped up into a pompadour right out of West Side Story perched above glowering eyes; a pockmarked face and thin pale lips were tightly wrapped around an unfiltered Pall Mall. Smoke rose slowly up his face in the stagnant air and hung above his head like a blue/white cloud of carcinogen-laced desperation.

"What the fuck do you want?" he asked Luther, squinting through the self-induced haze.

"Is Tuna back there?" Luther asked flatly.

"Who the fuck wants to know?"

Luther looked around the bar and then behind him making sure he was the only other person in the bar. "I do." Luther never had liked this asshole. After a long Sergio Leone pause that yielded nothing of purpose, Luther said, "Jimmy, quick dicking around and tell Tuna I'd like to see him."

Jimmy used his attitude to push himself off the counter and stalked around the corner. "He says to go on back."

Luther sniffed in indignation and pushed past Jimmy. The door to Big Tuna's office resembled a hobbit hole to hell. Boxes, crates, and barrels that were in the process of biodegrading into a single cell of disgust narrowed and shortened the already inadequate door. Luther knocked and a sloppy wet voice said "Yeah."

Big Tuna had been Big Tuna for so long that no one remembered what his real name had been in the first place. His nick name was foisted on him because of the uncanny resemblance he bore to a more hideous version of Danny DeVito's penguin. Short, fat, and perpetually greasy, Tuna repulsed everyone who had the displeasure of being in the same room with him. A white button on a dingy yellow sport shirt, splattered with food and wine stains, fought against natural physics in a gallant effort to contain his ample girth. Thin, dyed black hair that looked like it had been used to service a Packard laid back tight against his liver-spotted skull and slithered down his back in a poor attempt to mimic a long ponytail. To finish off his air of a festering zombie golfer, a white patent leather belt desperately clung to large plaid patterned pants that stopped two inches short of filthy white patent leather shoes.

"To what do I owe the pleasure?" Tuna asked as Luther bowed through the disappearing door hole. Yellow rotting teeth leered from behind fat grinning lips. Tuna stood and offered Luther his hand. Every time Tuna did that Luther, felt like it would probably be more hygienic to jerk off a roach.

"I bring business," Luther said, squishing his hand into Tuna's, then trying to not wipe it on his pants afterwards.

"Well, well," Tuna said gleefully, "why don't you set it right up here on my desk."

Watching Tuna grin and simultaneously act nearly giddy was like witnessing a psychopathic clown rape a kitten. Luther set the leather satchel on the desktop alongside the Crown Royal bag.

"What about those over there?" Tuna asked, indicating the watches in the Tupperware. "Those look *very* interesting."

"Don't worry about them," Luther shoved as much indifference into that comment as he could. "They're not part of this."

"Then why are they here?" It wouldn't matter if the crown jewels were sitting on his desk and there was a dead wombat in the box. He wanted the thing that he was being told he couldn't have.

"I was going to leave the box sitting on the seat of my car with the keys on top of it, but the valet mentioned this might not be as safe a neighborhood as it looks. Imagine that."

Tuna just shrugged and folded his hands in front of his face. Luther winced at the thought of how horrible those hands had to smell, then opened the satchel, retrieved a handful of ingots, and lined them up on the desktop. Tuna's eyes glittered like a snake getting ready to spring. Luther looked up at Tuna for a moment, then reached in for another handful. When he was finished, gold bars lined the front of Tuna's desk four rows high.

"Ummmm," Tuna licked his lips, mesmerized by what was in front of him. "How many are there, do you know?"

"Yes, I do," Luther said as he continued to glare at Tuna. "Exactly three hundred forty-five."

"How much does each one weigh?"

"Exactly one ounce," Luther said flatly.

"Ah," Tuna said as he reached for his desk drawer.

"Easy," Luther growled as he reached inside his jacket.

Tuna froze. "I was just getting my calculator."

"No need," Luther said still resting his hand on the grip of his pistol. "There's exactly 793,500 dollars' worth of product there."

Tuna relaxed and slowly eased back into his chair. "But I'll bet you're going to tell me how you're going to give me a one-time outstanding deal. Right?"

"I'm not going to tell you shit," Luther said as he poured the jewels out of the Crown bag. "There is 1.5 million dollars' worth of crap piled on your desk right now. You can have it for one mill in cash right now, or I take my toys and go home."

"What makes you think I have that kind of cash here?" Tuna asked trying to look disinterested.

"I *know* what you have here," Luther said taking his hand away from his gun. "Do whatever magical shit you have to do, and put that cash in my hand or I will disappear."

Tuna hesitated as he studied Luther's face. Luther reached down and started to palm everything on the desk back into the satchel. Tuna's clammy hand shot out and grabbed Luther by the wrist.

"Hang on a minute," Tuna said and then hesitated again. Luther jerked his hand free and began to sweep up the loot again.

"Shit or get off the pot Tuna," Luther said sullenly. "I don't have time to dick around here."

"Okay, okay," Tuna said as he eased back into the chair. "Wait here."

Tuna stood up and started to walk out of the door in the back of the office.

"Hey," Luther said stopping him. When Tuna turned around Luther was holding a gun in each hand. "If you walk back in here with anything other than a shit load of cash in your hands, I'm going to shoot you and shithead out front, then I'm going to hurt you."

"Isn't that backwards?" Tuna asked.

"Fuck around and find out," Luther threatened.

Luther could hear noises that sounded like someone was dropping wet sacks of cement on the floor, hammering, a few power tools, then a slow prolonged creeeeeeak like someone was opening a crypt. There was silence for a minute or two, then all the exact same sounds could be heard, except in reverse order. Tuna came back into the office to find Luther pointing a gun in his face.

"You fucking prick!" Tuna spit out.

"It ain't like that Tuna," Luther assured. "This is all straight up. I just like to keep the odds in my favor." Luther put one of his guns back in its holster and pulled a set of handcuffs out of his back pocket. He tossed them on the desk. "Put those on. One on the wrist, one on the arm of the chair."

Tuna glared at him. "Do it," Luther said. "I'll give the key to boy wonder on the way out. I'm just preventing you from getting your face blown off."

Tuna dropped into the chair and snapped the cuffs shut like he was told. Luther smiled, "It's always nice doing business with you Tuna."

"Eat me," Tuna growled. Luther threw up in his mouth a little.

Luther turned his back on the gold and jewels, picked up the case full of money and disappeared through the hobbit hole.

On Luther's way out of the bar, Jimmy was sitting in the exact same manner as he had been when Luther came in.

"He said he doesn't want to be disturbed for the rest of the day," Luther said casually. Once in the street Luther tossed the key to the cuffs into the storm drain. He dropped the suitcase on the passenger side of the front seat, got behind the wheel, and drove off in the direction of his favorite pawn shop. He had watches to sell.

20.

Luther walked into the hallway that led to Cutter's conference room, working very hard to look like he wasn't doing anything hinky. That concerted effort was having exactly the opposite effect on his outward appearance. If anyone had been watching, and there wasn't—Luther had checked, rechecked, then rechecked his rechecking, but, if there had been—they would have noticed he was wound up tighter than a two-dollar watch. He kept telling himself he was putting the money *back* into a safe instead of taking it out, so even if he was caught in the office after he returned the money no one would be the wiser. Unfortunately, the only thing Luther could focus on was what would happen if he was caught walking around with a cleaning cart full of the same amount of money that should have been in the safe.

He was dressed in the same grubby clothes he usually wore on his janitorial days and pushing his usual cleaning cart. Today the cart also contained stacks of hundred-dollar bills in the exact amount of $837,600, matching what Azi had stolen in the first place. Luther was certain the empty safe had yet to be discovered because he hadn't had to cut up anyone into crock bite-sized pieces. All he had to do was get in, get out, job done.

Luther pulled one of the giant double floor-to-ceiling solid walnut doors open, took a breath, and entered the cavernous conference room. The one thing Luther did not know was whether anyone would be present when he got there. He had taken the precaution of finding out exactly where Enzo and Richy were before he started up to the room, but he had no idea where Cutter might have been. Actually, people rarely had any idea where Cutter was. His health seemed to be diminishing slightly, and he had become much more reclusive. The issue wasn't anything you could put their finger on; things were just *different*.

Cutter didn't seem to threaten people with the gusto or delight he usually displayed. And for some inexplicable reason, his eyes were softer, and he didn't say *fuck* nearly as much as he usually had. It was almost as if he were constantly contemplating someplace or someone warm and beautiful. However, a lot of people felt like he was in a constant state of confusion and was trying to figure out what people were saying to him, or like he was trying to understand where the hell he was, and why he was there in the first place.

Richy had mentioned to Big Benny and Tony that Cutter had been forgetting things quite a lot lately. He had forgotten that Barbie Blue and been beaten to death, then fed to Bianca. Richy said Cutter was surprised when he sent for Barbie and Enzo reminded him that Barbie was dead. Cutter was even more surprised when he learned that he himself had given the order. Cutter had tried to cover it up, but it was hard to cover up that look of surprise on your face when you find out someone you had killed was dead.

Tony told Luther things were getting bad in upper management and that they should both be keeping an eye out for a powerplay from another family, or even a management change within the Manchini family. Either of those things could mean the promotion or death of any of the underlings. Tony had also mentioned that Cutter was having a hard time remembering things in his day-to-day life, like tying his shoes, where he put his whiskey glass down, and what the combination to the safe in the conference room was.

Luther understood how Azi had gotten access to the safe in the first place. Candy and Azi had both mentioned that Azi, being Cutter's accountant, had the combination, but Luther had a hard time accepting that excuse. Azi had too many out-of-control vices and was a general shit bag. Luther knew *he* would have never given someone like Azi access to that much money, so he was sure that no matter how far-gone Cutter was, he wouldn't have either. According to Tony, Cutter had written the combo on a sticky note and hidden it under the bonsai tree on the shelf behind his chair. If Tony *and* Luther knew that, then Azi sure as hell knew it too.

Luther pressed the button on his Shokz as soon as he pulled the massive door shut behind him. Low staccato notes bounced in Luther's head as the *Pink Panther* theme began to play. The music would help Luther remember to be constantly vigilant and stealthy. Also, he loved that song.

Luther slowly pushed the cleaning cart around the table and toward the safe. He had been told that haste makes waste and also breeds mistakes. Even though he was only walking to where the un-crime was going to take place, he thought he couldn't be too careful. Halfway across the room he swallowed hard and paused.

"That's right Luther," Good Luther whispered in his ear, *"you shouldn't even be in here. If you get caught you get killed. And for what? For those two manipulating degenerates. Why the hell aren't they doing this themselves."*

"Shut up shit face," Bad Luther growled. *"That's the love of his life you're crapping all over. Give the guy a break. Do it Luther or Cutter is going to dismember your girl while you watch."*

"Will you two assholes *please* get the hell out of my head?" Middle Luther begged out loud. "How the hell am I supposed to get anything done here with you two bitching at me?"

"I'm not bitching at you, buddy." Bad Luther jumped to his own defense. *"It's that other goody-goody dick face making your life difficult."*

"Will you get out of here, you parasite?" Good Luther complained. *"You're confusing him."*

"Both of you shut the fuck up," Luther demanded, "or I'll shove your asses back in the closet." He punched up the volume and the brass portion of Pink Panther lit up his brain.

Luther's hands started to shake as he moved closer to the bonsai. Bad Luther was right: the quicker he went the sooner it would be over. Good Luther was also right: Azi should be doing this bullshit himself.

But the central part of him was also right: Candy was in jeopardy here, and he would do absolutely anything to keep her safe, even if it meant keeping Azi safe as well, at least for the time being. Luther knew he was going to have to kill Azi at some point, but he would cross that bridge when he came to it.

When he reached the bonsai, he gently picked the plant up with one hand and retrieved the code with the other. He was careful not to set the pot down someplace other than where it had been sitting. If he put a mark on the counter or a moisture ring, it might give someone the idea that the plant had been moved by people other than the ones that were authorized to move it. He very carefully put the pot back and carried the sticky note to the safe.

He was trying desperately to control the shaking in his hands as he pushed the first number deliberately; then he rechecked the numbers on the paper and pressed the next number. By the time he got to the fourth number in the six-figure combo, he was beginning to forget what number he had just pressed. He began to panic. What if there were an alarm attached to the safe and it went off if the wrong numbers were pushed? That would certainly bring people into the room, and they would be demanding answers to questions Luther couldn't answer.

Gently he pushed the fifth number and winced when he did. Nothing happened. Luther checked the sixth number and reached for the entry pad. Sweat was dripping freely from his brow, and his finger was shaking as he moved it toward the pad. He rested the tip of his finger on the last number, closed his eyes tight, and jabbed the button.

Click.

He felt the door fall free against the pressure of his still pressing finger and breathed a huge sigh of relief as he swung the safe open. Thankfully it was still empty, so no one knew the crime had been committed. He began to stack the money on the on the safe's floor; then another surge of panic swept through his body, paralyzing him into stasis. What if there had been a certain way the money was stacked? Back to front with a space on one side and another space near the door? Or maybe the other way, front to back with a space in the back? What if it was just tossed in there haphazardly, or stacked across the full bottom of the safe? Luther was terrified; there was no way to know, and all three of them were going down for this.

"Cutter can't remember the last time he had a bowl movement," Good Luther offered helpfully. *"If you're going to go ahead with this, I feel as though I should help when I can."*

"Thanks dude," Middle Luther said. "You saved my ass."

"Quite literally in this case, I'm afraid," Good Luther replied haughtily.

Luther systematically transferred the rest of the bundles of cash from the cleaning cart and stacked them in the safe, closed the door, and hit the "lock" button. He began to reach for the bonsai plant when he heard the door open behind him; he stood up straight but didn't turn around to see who it was.

"Oh, I've got you now," Richy said roughly.

Luther closed his eyes, looked at the ceiling, and waited for the gunshot.

"Come here," Richy ordered.

Luther slowly turned around to see Richy push a woman in a short red dress against the door frame and kiss her deeply. He dropped his face to her neck and began to ravish her. The woman turned her face toward Luther, smiled, and winked. Richy slid his hands down along her sides and began kissing her on the chest.

Luther was horrified. The only thing that Richy's preoccupation offered was a short delay of Luther's life coming to an abrupt and violent end. Luther gulped, blinked his eyes hard, and deftly slid the sticky note back under the bonsai plant.

Richy's hands moved below the seam of the woman's dress, pulling it up then kneading her naked butt. The woman was keeping her eyes on Luther the entire time with that "come hither" smile on her face.

She pulled the clearly drunken Richy closer to her, and he reached between her legs.

"What the fuck?" Richy slurred in wide-eyed amazement. When Richy leaned back Luther could see that he was holding one of the largest erections Luther had ever seen on a woman. Richy did *not* instantly remove his hand or punch the woman in the face. Instead, he just kept holding and looking at the dick protruding from the woman he was trying to bang.

"You never know baby," the woman purred as she reached for Richy's crotch, "you really might like it."

Richy's blurry eyes slowly blinked twice as he started to slowly caress the fema-dick in his hand. He leaned in to kiss her again and caught sight of Luther standing awkwardly near the bonsai plant. Instantly Richy straightened up, realized he was jerking off a man, dropped the penis, and backhanded its owner hard across the face. She fell back out of the door and landed hard on the floor in the hallway. Luther raced to the door as Richy leapt on his date and began to choke her to death. Luther thought about just leaping over the pair to make his escape and hoping Richy would forget he was ever there. However, by the time he reached Richy, his conscience took over, and he pulled Richy off his date, then pushed him back the rest of the way into the conference room.

"Get the fuck out of here," Luther growled at the woman. She got up shakily, coughing and rubbing her throat. She looked at Luther like she was trying to understand what just happened.

"Get the fuck out!" Luther yelled. Then he turned to Richy, who was leaning against the conference table and steadying himself with his hands.

"That piece of shit!" Richy exclaimed. "Did you see that?" He asked Luther as more of an exclamation than the question. "What the fuck was *that*?"

Luther thought it better to not say anything at all until Richy had regained his focus.

"You saw what I did there, didn't you?" Richey said addressing Luther directly. "You saw me smack the shit out of whatever that was as soon as I realized what she was, didn't you?"

"*Cover your butt here son*," Good Luther advised.

"I have no idea what you're talking about Richy," Luther said. "I was in here, then you walked in, for whatever reason, we talked, and then we both left."

"Are you simple or what?" Richy asked as he glared at Luther through alcohol-blurred eyes. "You know exactly what I'm talking about!" Richy was beginning to sound desperate. "And you saw how I handled it too, right?"

Luther decided it was in his best interest not to respond yet. Luther couldn't understand why Richy was having such a hard time understanding. Luther put his hands in his pockets and waited for Richy to catch up.

"You better tell me exactly what your opinion is of the shit that just went down in here asshole." Richy was obviously going for the threat fix instead.

Luther just tilted his head and raised his eyebrows.

"You better say something quick." Richy was nearly apoplectic and becoming far more dangerous. If he didn't catch up pretty soon, Luther might not get out of the conference room alive.

"Okay," Luther said as calmly as he could without sounding condescending, "I'll try this one more time. I was standing over there," Luther pointed to the bonsai plant, "and *you* came in the room from where we're standing right now—alone. You said, 'What the fuck are you doing in here asshole?' and I said, 'Nothing, why?' Then you told me to get the fuck out, I asked why, and you said, 'Get the fuck out retard or I'll kick your ass.' Now does that sound pretty much like what happened according to *your* recollection?"

"Yeah," Richy said slowly. He didn't like being bailed out by someone he saw as inferior to him, and later in the day, he was going to convince himself that what Luther said was exactly what happened. "But what was *I* doing in here?"

"*Jesus Christ*," Good Luther blasphemed, and it didn't go unnoticed by Middle or Bad Luther. "*How far are you going to have to hold this clown's hand?*"

"Well," Luther started carefully, "the honest fact is that the only reason you would have to say what you were doing in here was because you told people about me being in here in the first place, and you caught me. In a perfect world," Luther held Richy's gaze, "I would imagine this would never come up in a conversation. That story is just a, I don't know, a. . ."

"A ruse?" Richy offered.

"Okay," Luther said, "if you're comfortable with that, a—what you said. Because I promise you I sure as hell am not going to say anything about you and I talking in here. Anyway, you came in to try and find Enzo."

"What the hell was Enzo doing in here?" Richy demanded.

"How the fuck am I supposed to know?" Luther was getting tired of this. "I mean, how would you know? You looked for him in here because you couldn't find him anyplace else."

Richy thought about that for a moment. "So, you aren't going to say anything to anyone. Is that right?" Richy said through narrowing eyes.

"About what?"

"About—" Richy started to get excited again. "Oh yeah, that's good. Yeah, that's real good."

"I think we're all on the same page now," Luther said smiling.

Richy thought about that for a minute, now that he could relax a little more. "Aside from this bullshit, you know I slapped the shit out of her, him, whatever, as soon as I knew it had a dick."

"That's exactly what I saw," Luther said. "That's why I had to pull you off her, so you didn't kill her when you found out what she was."

"Yeah," Richy said as he rubbed his face, mulling over the circumstances, "yeah, this is all good. It's lucky I straightened you out. I might have had to make you go away."

"I really appreciate you looking out for me like that," Luther was trying to be as contrite as he could.

"Okay," Richy was getting back to his old self. "Let's get the hell out of here."

"Sounds good," Luther said as he went to retrieve his cleaning cart.

"Hey," Richy called to Luther, stopping him in his tracks, "just what the hell *were* you doing in here anyway?"

"Cleaning," Luther smiled as he pointed at the cart.

"Oh, yeah," Richy said. "I always wondered who did that shit."

21.

Luther could feel the coolness of the bathroom tile through the black plastic sheet he was kneeling on. The buds of his Shokz resting against his temples fabricated the sweet soul-mending voice of K.D. lang as she taught Luther about tragic love through the lyrics to Leonard Cohen's "Hallelujah." The words sliced into his brain like beautiful shards of milk glass. "Now I've heard there was a secret chord that David played, and it pleased the Lord." He gripped the ankle of the leg laying in his lap harder against the beautiful pain he was filled with. The saw in his other hand rested on the dead hooker's shin bone just below the knee. K.D's voice produced a smooth and warm sound in a way that no human vocal cords should ever be able to. The chorus sailed away, and the verse began again. "Your faith was strong, but you needed proof, you saw her bathing on the roof. . ." Luther began to saw back and forth across the tibia in wide fluid motions, keeping time with the string section. His head bobbed and nodded with the rhythm, and he clenched his eyes even tighter at the most emotional moments of the music. Luther was surprised when the leg came free, and a needless downstroke of the saw ripped through his coveralls.

"Son of a bitch," Luther complained as he rubbed his bleeding thigh.

"What happened?" Murphy yelled from another room.

Luther dropped the leg into a large heavy-duty garbage bag and examined the woman's torso to see just how much work he still had to do. He stood up and walked to the bathroom door, leaning on the frame. Murphy was busy moving the bodies of a coke dealer and another naked hooker closer to the bathroom so he could begin cleaning. Tony, who had been part of the hit, had stayed in the room to catch up with Luther.

"Do you ever get tired of this?" Luther asked Tony as he wiped his hands with a red shop towel.

Tony smiled and looked around the room. "I'm not sure which part of *this* you're talking about. Is it the Tony Montana-sized pile of coke on the coffee table over there, or the amazing view we get to see every time we have to tweak one of these rich clowns?" Tony made a wide sweeping gesture with his arms, indicating the amazing view of the New York skyline through floor-to-ceiling windows in a penthouse apartment. "Or is it the top shelf booze we take with us, or the money we get paid to do this kind of shit? If it's any of that, then I would have to say no, I don't get tired of it."

"I think your boyfriend is having an attack of conscience," Murphy offered as he laid his own plastic sheet on the dining room tile.

"What I mean is the killing, butchering, beating, and feeding people's parts to a crocodile." Luther sounded sad and reflective.

"What's bothering you buddy?" Tony asked, genuinely concerned.

"While you contemplate that," Murphy said sarcastically, "give me a hand here."

Luther moved next to a naked fat man wearing enough gold jewelry to sink a Chinese junk and got down on his knees.

"I don't know," Luther began as he propped the back of the dead man's neck on a blood-stained piece of four-by-four and began to saw across the throat. "The money's good and all, but I used to think we were the good guys, and the people we turned into gator shit were bad."

Murphy stopped clipping fingers off a hand and gave Tony a look. Luther would have never understood the nuance, but the *look* was definitely one of "*Are we going to be cutting up this shithead next?*"

"It's really starting to seem like we're all bad," Luther continued. "Like, we kill them, they kill us, we kill each other. It just doesn't seem normal. I see people walking down the street every day, and you can tell just by the looks on their faces that they're not worried about being tied to a chair while someone razor slices their eyeballs and rubs salt into the cuts."

"It's the life we've chosen, brother," Tony said apologetically as Luther dropped the dealer's head into a bag with as much interest as he would have shown in wiping his ass.

"What if we un-choose it?" Luther clearly had a lot on his mind, and Tony didn't like the sound of any of it.

"You had better unplug your head from your asshole, buddy," Murphy advised Luther.

"I'm just sayin'," Luther defended himself.

"Well," Murphy said as he stacked fingers in piles like little pieces of cord wood. "Just *sayin'* shit like that will get you killed."

"See," Luther said, dropping the arm he was cutting off at the elbow and pointing at Tony with the bloody saw, "see, that's the kind of shit I'm talking about right there. I can't even *think* about things, or I might be headed south in a silver shit box. People should be able to be what they are," Luther complained, "We *work* for these people. They don't own us."

"Oh fuck me hard," Murphy exclaimed as he removed a second fingerless hand and placed it next to his finger stack.

"They kind of do own us Luther," Tony said concerned. "Are you thinking about leaving or something?"

"No," Luther lied, "nothing like that. I just don't know why, if we're doing everything they want us to do, why we can't just live the way we want. Everything just seems so, I don't know, restrictive."

Murphy stood up, retrieved the dealer's head from the bag, and set it next to the original owner's hips. He took a karambit out of his tool bag, grabbed the body's dick and balls, sliced them off at the pubic bone, and stuffed them in the head's mouth."

"What the fuck?" Tony asked, surprised.

"The head goes to Red Fred in a box," Murphy explained, "then the hookers and the rest of his fat ass goes to Bianca."

"That's the kind of shit I'm talking about too," Luther said, pointing at the end of a penis peeking out from between dead goatee-lined lips, giving it a look of a dick coming *out* of a vagina.

"What," Tony was confused, "you have an issue with stuffing a dick in a guy's mouth all of a sudden? We do that kind of shit all the time."

"Not that," Luther was acting like he thought he never should have brought any of this up in the first place. "Murphy just had a dick and a set of nuts in his hand."

"What the hell are you trying to say?" Murphy was pissed off.

"Come on Luther," Tony pleaded. "Talking like that isn't a good idea."

"Why not?" Luther said defiantly. "Am I going to be killed because life shit confuses me? If that same guy was laying there on the floor alive and Murphy grabbed his dick..."

"Look shithead," Murphy stood up, holding the karambit in a threatening manner.

"Take it easy," Tony said, motioning Murphy back.

"See what I mean?" Luther spread his hands out and shrugged his shoulders. "If that dick was warm, Murphy would be gay."

"I suggest you move this conversation someplace else," Murphy growled, "and keep my name the fuck out of it."

Tony motioned Luther toward the bedroom. "We'll just be a second," he said to Murphy.

Once they were in the other room, Tony grabbed Luther by the shoulders. "What the hell is wrong with you?" Tony hissed an angry whisper.

"Nothing," Luther said defensively. "I mean none of us really knows how we're going to handle something given the right set of circumstances."

"What did you do, Luther?" Tony didn't like where this was going at all.

"I didn't do anything," Luther assured him. "I'm just sayin', I'm not gay or anything, but given a certain set of circumstances, I might find myself with a dick in my hand. That's all."

"Were you jerking guys off someplace?" Tony asked in a low voice. "Because that would be a problem."

"What the hell for?" Luther asked a little louder than he should have. "It's *my* hand. I'm not asking Cutter to jerk him off. Why would he care?"

"Keep your voice down," Tony cautioned. "Where the hell is this coming from then?"

"All I'm saying is these people treat us, and each other, like shit," Luther said angrily. "Who cares if one of us sucks a cock or jerks off a dog? How is that any business of Cutter's?"

"It just is, my friend," Tony was becoming borderline frantic. "Look, I don't know what's gotten into you right now. Hell for that matter, I never know what's going on with you, but you better get yourself straightened out."

"I'm not sure I want to," Luther sounded like a pouting child. "I don't care about cutting people up or torturing someone. Hell, I'm just fine with murder. Most of these people need to be removed from the face of the earth anyway. It just doesn't make sense to me that if we're doing great work for Cutter, why would he give a shit if you and I were married?"

Tony took a step back and examined Luther for a moment. "Is there something you want to tell me?" he asked cautiously.

"What?" Luther sounded confused, then he caught on. "Jesus Christ, no! I'm just asking a question. I don't want to get out of this bullshit, but I don't know why we can't just live our own lives."

"We just can't, goddamn it." Tony was getting irritated. "Let's just go back in there and finish this up."

They both walked back into the room just in time to see Murphy pulling guts out of an open torso. "Are you two assholes about finished?" Murphy asked.

Luther began to pick up smaller body parts, dropping them in the bag. "Can I get these," he asked Murphy sarcastically, "or are you going to sell them on eBay or some shit?"

Murphy just glared at him.

"I gotta go," Tony said uneasily. "Do we have an understanding?" he asked Luther. Luther just nodded his head.

After Tony left, Murphy and Luther finished the rest of the cleaning in silence. As they hoisted the garbage bags onto the cart, Luther asked Murphy, "Why do you suppose Richy drinks so much?"

"Boy," Murphy said disconnectedly, "you're just full of shit you need to get off your chest today, aren't you?"

"It just seems like he's really lonely, even with all the different women he hangs out with."

"Richy had a real tough time after his mother got eaten," Murphy began with an air of indifference. "His father bringing that fucking monster back from Colombia didn't help. Then those bullshit rituals with shipping off box after box of croc shit to the family mausoleum didn't do anything to straighten that kid out either. It just looks to me like that he's trying overly hard to be a tough guy to make his father proud him."

"You think Cutter wouldn't love him if he didn't act tough?" Luther couldn't begin to grasp that idea.

"Are you shitting me?" Murphy laughed as he dropped the last bag of body parts onto the cart. "If Richy didn't act exactly like he does, Cutter would disown him at best or knock him off at worst."

"Man," Luther said as he grappled with the concept, "can't you see how totally fucked up that is?"

"Of course I can," Murphy said as he took his surgical gloves off and dropped them in an empty bag. "It's just the way it is, and I don't know what you and your boyfriend were shooting the shit about back there, but for both your sakes, you better get your head on straight. Things are what they are, and you know the rules, but for some reason you want to get all touchy feely about it. You're in this forever because you know too much. You're not getting out, and the mob is never going to be flying the LGBTQ flag over any of their houses. So buck up, quit thinking about dicks, and do your fucking job."

22.

Luther and Tony followed Big Benny as they navigated the top floor of a plush Manhattan hotel on the way to someplace and to do something about which neither one of them had a clue. When Luther walked into the monumental lobby of the hotel, he was struck with a mild case of agoraphobia. The ceilings were held up by gigantic pink marble pillars that rose two stories in the air, and each pillar was easily twice as big around as he could reach. The real mindblower to Luther was the highly polished black granite floor. It didn't seem to bother Tony or Big Benny, but the reflection combined with tiny gold flecks made Luther feel like he was floating in an endless field of golden stars. He instantly wished he was by himself with his music. He could float around this place for days, leaving a trail of tears everywhere he went.

"How amazing would that be?" Good Luther crooned wistfully.

Big Benny hadn't said a word when they met in the lobby; he just tilted his head toward the elevators and began to walk in that direction. The aurora around Benny was dark, heavy, and threatening, so both the other men knew to keep their mouths shut and do what they were told. Benny stopped in front of a door, hesitated, then turned to the two men with him.

"Once we get in here," Benny said darkly as he jerked his finger over his shoulder, indicating the door to the room, "whatever you see will never leave that room. Do you two completely understand that?"

"Sure Benny," Tony said, shrugging his shoulders to indicate that that had always been a given in his line of work. Luther simply nodded.

Benny shifted his feet, took a breath, and pointed an index finger directly in Luther's face. "See, it don't seem like you do—completely. So, let me lay it down for you like this. When Cutter told me what was in this room, we both figured the best thing to do was put you two and Pretty Boy on it, then shoot all three of you in the head just to make sure there wasn't an issue. Then Cutter figured that plan would leave him light three guys, and he can't afford that right now. I told him we could get three cracked out monkeys to do the shit you clowns do." Benny stopped to take his cigarettes out of his jacket pocket. He jammed one in his mouth and glared at both men as he lit it. Benny took a deep drag, pulled the cigarette out of his mouth, and made a broad gesture. "Cutter didn't see it that way. So for now, you two assholes are safe. Have I made my point?"

"Yeah," Tony said. "Take care of it and forget it. No problem."

Benny looked at the flush white Luther. "And you?" Luther simply nodded again. "I want to hear those words come out of your dick-catcher right now or you'll never see the outside of this place again."

"I understand," Luther stuttered. "After I walk back out of that door, I won't remember anything that went on in there."

Benny studied them for a second, letting a cloud of smoke swim out of his mouth and up his face. "Okay," he finally said. "There are no grey areas here. If *Cutter* ever asks you what happened in here, you tell him you have no idea what he's talking about. If he threatens to kill you, you still don't know. Got it?"

They both nodded. Tony turned around and pushed the door open.

When Luther stepped inside, he was dumbstruck. First the opulence of the room was the definition of breathtaking, but the thing that made it even more amazing was the destruction that had been wrought in there. It wasn't what he was used to. There were no dead hookers or drug dealers, there was no blood splattered floor to ceiling, and there were no bullet holes in the walls to patch. This was an all-out party that had gotten out of control. Cushions from furniture were scattered around the room like someone had used them for a round of disc golf. Red lace panties hung from a lamp, and a matching bra lay on the floor about ten feet away, sopping up the contents of an open bottle of Anal Ease that had been overturned next to it. Lamps were overturned and shades crushed. Empty wine, liquor, and champagne bottles lay haphazardly around the room, some broken and others laying on their side. All were empty.

"Goddamn it," Benny murmured. "Richy! Where the fuck are you?"

Right then Tony and Luther were both wishing themselves anyplace other than this. They heard sobbing coming from the bedroom that sounded like Richy. As they stepped inside, they all three froze. The bedroom was even more trashed than the rest of the place. Richy sat on the floor, covered in blood as he leaned against the foot of the bed with his face in his hands and wept uncontrollably. Luther recognized the woman on the bed with a knife sticking out of her chest as the same one Richy had been jerking off in the conference room a few days before.

"Out," Benny ordered. Once they all three got into the other room, Benny said, "You two don't move, don't touch anything, and DON'T go in that bedroom. I have to make a call."

Benny walked into the bathroom and closed the door, but Tony and Luther could still make out what he was saying.

"Yeah, boss," Benny's muted voice bled through the door, "we have a real problem here. . . Well, this bitch has a dick." There was a long pause, then Benny said, "Boss?" Short pause, "Yeah, I'm sure." Pause. "Well, if I had a dick that looked like that, I would have gone into the porn business. So, yeah, I'm sure." There was another long pause, then, "They're both here with me right now. No, he hasn't gotten here yet." Luther and Tony were petrified. The number two for the Manchini family was on one side of them crying over a transsexual he had murdered after at least three days of alcohol-laden sex, and their lives were being decided by a mob lieutenant in a bathroom.

"Boss," Benny continued in a low threatening voice not directed at Cutter. "Boss, I'm telling you, we need to wait until he gets here, takes care of the place, and then we need to take all three of them back to the office and drop a bullet in their brain pans." Another long pause. "Yes,

I do, Cutter. Pure and simple." A long pause. "Are you certain? Because there's no coming back from this." Pause. "Come on, boss, you can't ask me something like that. It's not my place." Pause. "Yes, I know he did, and yes, I know he has. But I'm not the one. . ."

There was a very long moment of silence, and Luther could hear Benny pacing back and forth. "Okay boss. Here it is: if that's what the other three get, then all four do. If not, no one does. But remember you forced me to give my blunt, emotionless opinion."

There was a moment that seemed to stretch into an eternity. What the person on the other end of that phone said next would determine whether the rest of their lives lasted 30 minutes or until their demise from natural causes.

"Okay boss," Benny finally said. "If that's what you want, that's what you'll get." Then. "Yeah, I'll let you know when it's done." When the door opened Luther jumped like he had been goosed by a welding torch.

Benny stepped into the room and didn't even acknowledge Luther or Tony. He started into the bedroom and said over his shoulder. "Let's get this shit done." Luther and Tony still didn't know what the final answer was, but they were sure they would find out as soon as the mess was cleaned up.

Benny stood over Richy with one foot on either side of him. "Hey!" Benny bellowed. Richy didn't respond and just kept crying into his hands. "GODDAMN IT RICHY!" Benny yelled more forcefully this time but only received the same result as before. Benny pulled back one meaty hand so far that he twisted at the waist. When he let it fly, his open hand rolled Richy across the floor in a ball, landing him in a lump against the wall. Luther had never seen anyone slapped that hard in his life.

Benny strode purposefully across the floor, kicked Richy in the ass, then jerked him off the floor by his shirt. Once Richy was standing Benny smacked him twice and kept him from sliding back down the wall. Luther and Tony were both thinking that if this was what the boss's kid was getting, they were as good as dead.

Benny screamed into Richy's face, "Get your shit together, fuck head!" Richy quit crying and stared dumbly into Benny's face. Snot ran freely down the sides of Richy's lips, and he was shaking. "What happened here?" Benny demanded.

"What?" Richy croaked.

Benny grabbed him by the hair and shoved him toward the body on the bed. "Once you had your fill of cum wads shot down your throat and up your ass. . . what the fuck happened?"

"I don't know?" Richy managed to get out, trying to defend himself.

Benny picked a used condom off the mattress and swung it back and forth in front of Richy's face. "Okay, we have that bullshit remark out of the way now. You're saying you didn't notice that when you had your dick three feet up this bitch's ass *your* balls were slapping up against another set that didn't belong to you?"

Richy gazed into Benny's glare, pleading for a way out.

"Great," Benny said, releasing Richy's hair. "We can dispense with the horseshit now." Richy stumbled forward and sat on the bed. "How did that knife end up in your butt buddy's chest," Benny paused as he silently counted, "five, no, six times?"

"She," Richy started to say but Benny cut him off.

"He,"

"What?" Richy asked blankly, then began again. "She. . ."

"*He*," Benny cut him off again. "Say *she* one more fucking time and you'll be laying right next to him."

Luther and Tony were standing at the end of the bed, visibly shaking. There was a knock at the door. Benny froze and reached for his gun. "Get that," he said to Tony.

Tony began to sleepwalk toward the door, and there was another knock, a little more frantic this time. "If you don't recognize them,"

Benny ordered, "put a hole in their head and drag them in here. No, drag them in here, *then* put a bullet in their head."

Tony rested his hand on the grip of his gun and looked out through the peephole, then opened the door.

"What the hell took so long?" Murphy complained. "Did I interrupt a circle jerk?"

"This is really bad," Tony whispered. "I'd keep the smart-ass remarks to a minimum."

"You can say that shit again," Murphy said loudly. "Cutter briefed me personally over the phone on the way here."

"Did he say what happens to us?" Tony whispered again.

"Funny," Murphy said sarcastically. "When I was talking to Cutter about his son sucking cock in the family's own hotel suite, your name never came up. Go figure."

Murphy pushed passed Tony dragging two huge roller suitcases in either hand. "You want me to set up in here or out there?" Murphy asked Benny.

"Right here on the bed," Benny instantly said. "I don't want to get any more blood than there already is on this white carpet."

Benny turned his attention back to Richy. "Spill it."

"Sh. . ." Richy started but thought better of it when Benny raised his hand. "He, well, he was going to blackmail me," Richy whined.

"Did he say that?" Benny asked strongly.

"Yeah," Richy said, trying to sound convincing.

"Were there any pictures or proof?"

"Well, no," Richy stuttered.

"How do you know for sure?"

"We both locked our phones in the hotel safe, and I was the only one with the combination," Richy explained hopefully.

"How long were you two lovebirds up here?" Benny asked as he was trying to put things together.

"Two," Richy started, "no, three days."

"Did anyone see you with him?" Benny was doing his best to stay calm. His fists were balled so tightly there were only deep red or dead fish-white splotches on them.

"No," Richy assured. "I came up here alone. Every time room service came up, Tulip stayed in the bedroom."

"Fucking Tulip?" Murphy exclaimed, trying to suppress a laugh.

Benny ignored Murphy. "Exactly what did he say when he threatened to blackmail you?" Benny was trying to find out if one of the other mob families had set Richy up. "Exactly," Benny repeated.

"He said. . ." Richy began searching for memories. "We were laying on the bed and he said, 'Wouldn't your father just shit if he saw us here?'"

"That's it?" Benny looked like a cartoon pressure gauge that had been riding above the redline for a long time.

"Yeah, Benny," Richy said hopefully. "That's all, I swear."

"And then," Benny murmured, his voice shaking on the edge of an explosion, "You went out there, you got a knife, and you used this shithead as a pincushion. Is that about right?" The last four words came out like Benny had been constipated for six months.

"Yeah," Richy answered very slowly.

"JESUS MOTHERFUCKING CHRIST!" Benny screamed at the ceiling. Everyone else stood frozen in place. "This fucking homo gave you a little fucking offhand pillow talk, AND YOU STAB HIM SIX FUCKING TIMES?!" Benny sprang at Richy, jerking him off the bed by the front of his shirt.

"It was the coke," Richy said weakly.

Benny flung Richy into the corner like a sack of wet laundry.

"You—" Richy whined trying to protect himself, "you can't do that. When my father finds out. . ."

Benny jerked his gun out of its holster, squatted in front of Richy, and jammed the barrel into Richy's nose hole so hard his head hit the wall. Blood oozed down the gun barrel and Richy yelped pathetically.

"What?" Benny screamed into Richy's face, "He'll *what,* you sniveling little lump of dog shit? He gave me some leverage here, so if I pull this trigger and blast that empty space in your head all over this nice white wall, what do you think is going to happen?" Benny pushed harder and yelled, "What motherfucker?!" Benny pulled the hammer back. "WHAT?" he yelled again.

Luther and Tony winced and closed their eyes tight. Murphy kept laying out plastic sheeting like it was a day at the park.

Benny stood up, lowered the hammer on his gun, and returned it to its holster. "You three," he said without taking his eyes off Richy, "clean this shit up. Take your time and do it right." Then he turned to face them. "Cut him up small. The parts go to Bianca, and there should be two baggage trolleys in the hall. Take it all out the service entrance."

Benny reached down and pulled Richy up by his shirt again. "I'm going to take little Chief Fuck-My-Ass here back to his old man."

Benny and Richy pushed past the still shaking Tony and Luther. "Is that it?" Tony asked quietly. "Oh yeah," Benny said. He jerked his pistol out and shoved it in Tony's face so fast Tony didn't have time to react. "I almost forgot the fun part."

Benny held the gun there for what seemed like an eternity, steely eyed and stoic. Then he started to laugh. "Oh man, look at your face! You two assholes are too easy." Then, seriously again, "Clean this shit up, and keep your mouth shut."

"About what?" Luther asked.

Benny turned around ready to beat the shit out of everyone in front of him. When he saw Luther's benign smiling face, he understood. "Yeah," Benny said, "*about what?* For a moron, you fucking kill me sometimes."

23.

Cutter leaned easily back in his overstuffed office chair, holding a glass of bourbon in one hand while strumming the fingers of the other on the desktop. Across from him Richy relaxed in one of two identical traditional brown sheepskin library chairs. Richy had his legs crossed at the knee, so his shin pointed almost directly at the floor. His foot impatiently bounced up and down in time with his heart, which was pounding. He also held a bourbon glass in his hand and was trying very hard to allow it to hang indifferently off his knee.

"Are you comfortable, son?" Cutter asked with a slight edge in his voice. He had never referred to Richy in that way.

"Yes," Richy tried to sound nonchalant and was failing miserably. He took a sip of bourbon to accentuate his cavalier demeaner.

"Tell me," Cutter began as he leaned forward, setting his glass on the desk, "have you always sat like that? I never noticed it before."

Richy tilted his head and narrowed his eyes. "Like what?"

"Like *that*," Cutter waved a finger toward Richy's leg. "You know, like a bitch."

"Dad," Richy began.

"You," Cutter said forcefully cutting Richy off, "keep your fucking mouth shut until I tell you to open it." Cutter was still pointing a finger at Richy, which shook with rage.

"I," Cutter stood up, calming himself as he walked around his desk and sat on a corner of it, facing Richy, "I was kind of wondering," Cutter said smoothly. Then, spreading his arms out at his side, "Have you always been a fag, or is this just some new lifestyle you're—" Cutter paused, placing his hands on the desk edge, "I don't know. *Exploring,* I guess?"

Richy put both feet on the floor and leaned forward like he was going to respond. Cutter cut him off with a raised index finger. Cutter dropped his head and shook it slowly twice, and then he pushed himself off the desk and walked back to his chair.

"Three days," Cutter peaked his fingers against his chin. "That, my friend, is quite a lot of dick-sucking and ass-fucking. Hell, I'm amazed you can even sit in that chair." Richy remained quiet.

"It was the coke," Richy defended himself. "That's all."

"Ya know," Cutter said after a short pause, "I've done quite a lot of coke in my time." He put his hands back on the desktop, lowered his head, and shot Richy a glance out of the top of his eyes. Almost like he was just telling a story to the guys at a bar. "By that I don't mean *a lot*, I mean a queen's metric shitload of coke. Know what I'm sayin'? But it's funny, you know, in that way that's not funny at all, but not one time was I *ever* so blasted out of my mind I said, 'Man, ya know what really would hit the spot right now? A nice stiff dick and a hot load of cum.' Maybe it's just me, but coke just never turned me into a cocksucker."

Richy and Cutter sat in uneasy silence for a protracted amount of time. Richy could hear the grandfather clock behind Cutter ticking.

"Feel free to respond," Cutter finally acquiesced.

Richy started to talk about the beginning of his relationship with Tulip, at the party, then in the conference room, and instantly thought better of it. "This woman was beautiful. . ."

"Man," Cutter stopped him.

"That's just it," Richy placed his hands on the chair and leaned forward, "I met *her* at a party I was throwing at the house, and this bitch was drop dead gorgeous. Before *she* left, she gave me her number," Richy lied. "I called her and told her to meet me at the hotel. I got there before she did so I could set things up. . ."

"What *things*?" Cutter interrupted.

"Shit like blow and weed," Richy explained. "I just didn't want to look like an asshole digging coke out of a bag in front of her."

"Interesting choice of words there," Cutter muttered.

"By the time she got there, I was already blasted," Richy lied again. "We started fooling around, I was playing with her tits. Then the next thing I know she has my dick in her mouth. It was crazy. That was the best head I've ever had in my life. I shot my load down her throat, and we took a break," he lied. "I don't like to kiss a bitch for a little while after she does that."

Cutter raised his eyebrows in acknowledgement.

"We did a lot more blow and drank quite a bit." Richy didn't want to reach the end of this story, but he knew it was inevitable. "That's when I found *her* dick."

"Okay," Cutter said, pursing his lips, "that explains the first, what, three hours. Then there you are with a guy that has really great tits and an elephant dick, and the first thought that comes into your head is, 'Wow, that thing really looks like it needs to be in my ass.' Am I keeping up so far?"

Richy dropped his head and slumped back in his chair. There was no more for him to say. He couldn't think of a single way to explain what happened and make it sound like he didn't just have a homosexual relationship in the company hotel for three straight days. He remained silent.

Cutter let the silence hang like an atheist at an Evangelical potluck. "I know that Big Benny was pissed off that you stabbed this bitch, guy, bitch guy, whatever. I'm not mad at you about that part." Richy looked up hopefully. "Hell," Cutter went on, "you just did what I would have had to do eventually. At least you did it before this degenerate could get out of the hotel. Benny finally came around after he tried to talk me into putting a bullet in your head."

"That motherfucker!" Richy said wide eyed.

"Shut up," Cutter demanded. "Do you think that wasn't *my* first thought?"

"But," Richy was dumbfounded.

"Do you have even the slightest idea of what potential harm you could have done to this family?"

"I," Richy started.

"Shut the fuck up," Cutter was standing again. "You aren't really stupid enough to think that was a question, are you?" Cutter didn't wait for an answer. "This family business has been handed down through five generations! Five! There is nothing, I repeat, nothing that I wouldn't do to preserve that legacy." Cutter slammed his fist down on the table. Richy jumped. "Then here your dumb ass comes. Richard Manchini carries the tradition on to the sixth generation." Cutter hesitated for effect. "Well, that's after he takes a little side trip to get fucked up, suck a few cocks, and get ass-reamed! And none of this bullshit even *begins* to deal with what these other families, families that *all* answer to me by the way, are going to do when they find out how weak we are. How weak *you* are"

"I don't think," Richy started to defend himself again.

"That is the first fucking intelligent thing you've said since you came in here!" There were veins standing out on Cutter's forehead Richy had never seen before. "You don't fucking think! EVER!"

Cutter sat back down in his chair, adjusted his jacket, and composed himself.

"You're right," Richy placated. "About every single thing you just said. I fucked up huge and put everyone in jeopardy. Including me."

"Especially you," Cutter corrected calmly.

"Yes," Richy continued, "I realize that as well. And I realize that I need to quit fucking around and grow up." Cutter looked at his son hopefully. "So I'm not going to blow smoke up your ass. I'm probably still going to snort a line from time to time, and I'm certainly not going to stop drinking. But I know my limits, just like you do, and I'm going to take responsibility for myself AND this family."

Cutter was at least happy Richy didn't try to sell him some bullshit about staying sober for the rest of his life. If he was going to say something like he just had at a time like this, there might be some hope.

"Just one thing," Richy added. Cutter tilted his head slightly. "Do you really think it's a good idea to let the people who were there continue to walk around?"

Cutter thought about that for a moment. "So," he began slowly, "you're suggesting that I murder three, no, four of my own people to the cover your fuckup."

"Yes," Richy pled his case. "I know it's super fucked up, and it's my fault. But especially those two shitheads, Luther and Tony."

Cutter considered what Richy had just said. "It's not something I hadn't already thought of, and what you're saying is true. But if I just start killing my own guys, for no reason. . ."

"But there is a reason," Richy said, cutting him off.

"Not one I can advertise," Cutter explained. "Those people that have done good work for us in the past wind up dead and the word gets out we did it ourselves, people will start jumping ship like crazy. Then what do I do, kill the guys that killed the guys? Eventually I run out of guys to kill. No, I'm going to let all of this go the way it is for now. If it becomes an issue, I'll deal with it."

Cutter leaned over the desk and pressed a button. "Send him in," he said. "We have other shit to deal with right now."

Enzo walked through the door and greeted them both, "Boss, Richy. What's up?"

"Sit down Enzo," Cutter said, indicating the other library chair. "I've been dealing with this thing for too long now and I'm getting nowhere."

"What thing?" Enzo asked.

"Yeah," Richy added. "What's going on?"

"You see," Cutter was clearly unhappy, "that's the shit I'm talking about right there," Enzo and Richy looked at each other confused. "This skimming shit has gone on so long with no answer that most of the people here have forgotten about it."

"We pressured the marks for protection money," Enzo said. "If you want us to do more we will. Azi's books are fine, so I don't even know if someone *is* skimming, or maybe that bitch Barbie Blue was just trying to get to you."

"Yeah," Richy quickly added, "Azi's books are fine. So how do we know someone is skimming off us in the first place?"

"After that shit with Barbie, I did some checking on my own," Cutter said conspiratorially. Richy swallowed hard.

"What kind of checking?" Richy asked, trying to sound nonchalant.

"Yeah, Boss," Enzo added. "I didn't know anything about this."

"No one does," Cutter explained. "I asked to have all business income reported directly to me before it goes to Azi. It's not a lot, but it doesn't balance. And Azi didn't mention it."

"Maybe your math was wrong," Richy said hopefully. "Or maybe Azi did catch it and was tracking it down before he said anything to you."

Enzo shot Richy a glance.

"I've thought about all of that," Cutter answered. "And at this point I don't have enough to go on, so I don't want to alert Azi. The only people that know about this are you two. If the skim suddenly stops, then I know it's one of you guys."

"Hey," Enzo protested.

"I'm just fucking with you," Cutter smiled. "But rest assured there is a skim, and I am going to personally filet the shit bag that's doing it when I catch him."

"Do you have a plan then?" Enzo asked.

"I have a couple," Cutter divulged. "I think the first thing I'm going to do is throw a little bait out for Azi. If he fucks up and takes it, problem solved."

Richy was unmoved by that. If Cutter laid a trap, Richy would know about it and warn Azi off. But it would be better if he could direct Cutter in another direction.

"Do you want me to put something together to trap Azi?" Richy asked.

"Yeah," Cutter said. "Work something up and let me know what it is. Just don't tell anyone else."

"Not a word," Richy falsely promised.

"Do you want to do something else also in case it's not him?" Enzo asked.

Richy was ready for that too. "I really think that's a good idea. If someone is taking money from us, I doubt they're just putting it in a 401k."

Cutter smiled. He could see where Richy was going, and it made him feel a little proud he was stepping up like this. "Go on," Cutter prodded.

"Well," Richy sat up in his chair a little more, "We know what we pay these guys, right? So we get into all of their financial records and see who it is that's pissing money away faster than it's coming in."

"Do we even have that capability?" Enzo asked.

Cutter waved his hand in the air dismissively. "That's not going to be a problem."

Nothing in the fabric of the universe happens in a vacuum; one thing affects another, which affects another, and so on until one innocuous event becomes a global catastrophe. Communication has this same odd property, like a childhood game of telephone. Richy knew no limits to his hypocrisy when it came to matters of self-preservation or amassing wealth. He was in bed with Azi and Candy in a criminal sense, just as Luther was in bed with Candy and, by extension, Azi in a coital sense. Also, Luther's best friend was Tony Ferrari. Information passed through this web of relationships seemingly disconnected and uncollected.

After the incident in the hotel room, Richy had thought about little other than getting rid of four problem children that could ruin him. Luther would be the simplest of the issues to correct. Usually, people in the family only realized Luther existed when he was in view. If Richy popped him, no one would notice until the body washed up someplace, and even then, the most engaged reaction would amount to little more than "*OH yeah, I remember that guy.*" Richy also held an ace he could use against Luther anytime he wanted.

Not only did Richy know about Azi taking the money out of the safe, but he had also been the architect of that plan. There had been no gambling debt Azi was trying to repay, and a more astute person than Luther might have called bullshit on the very idea right from the beginning. Richy just had no idea when Luther was going to "put it back," hence the surprise in the conference room. Richy took his cut of the original safe money, and Azi and Candy received theirs. Now Richy had the knowledge of that, *and* the knowledge of Luther pawning the watches in his arsenal, to use whenever he needed it. And he needed it now. All he had to do was find the pawn shop in New Jersey that had the extremely expensive engraved watch that was connected to a murder scene, and Luther was nothing more than a memory.

Tony was an easy mark also. Through Luther, Candy had learned that Tony had invested in several of the businesses the family used as fronts for their less-than-legal activities. That money was really paying off for Tony, and, according to Candy, Tony was working pretty hard at hiding that income from Cutter. Richy was, at the present time, setting Tony up for the fall in connection with the skimming *and* taking care of a second of the hotel witnesses all in one move.

Big Benny was going to be a lot harder. He wasn't stupid, and as far as the family was concerned, he was squeaky clean. Richy figured when the hit went out for either Tony or Luther, he would drive his father toward giving the job to him and Benny. The hit goes bad, Benny catches a bullet, and all is wrapped up. Well, except for Murphy, but Richy could basically walk into Murphy's apartment and blow his brains out for all anyone cared about him. Strike four and the smell of life is sweet.

"I, ah," Richy started to put his plan into motion, "I think I might have a handle on someone that fits into the filthy-rich-for-no-reason category."

"Oh," Cutter raised his eyebrows hopefully. "Who might that be?"

"Yeah," Enzo added, "and why is this the first we're hearing about it?"

"It didn't seem like a big deal to me at first," Richy explained. "The guy buys nice shit, and you forget that he bought nice shit a few times before. I just think this is worth looking into."

"Who?" Cutter asked.

"Tony Ferrari." Richy had just signed one of his problems' death warrants.

"You guys get Azi and figure this shit out," Cutter said angrily. "I don't want any fuckups. Make absolutely sure you have the right guy, then find out who's been working with him. This shit is going to stop right fucking now. Don't say anything to anyone about this."

Richy couldn't believe his luck. His partner in crime was going to help him produce the evidence that would start his roll down easy street.

24.

For Luther the inside of the champagne room had become as comfortable and secure as if he were sitting on his own toilet in his apartment with the door shut. It was warm, dim, slightly humid, familiar, and possessed the wafting mixed bouquet of body odor, sweat, semen, mildew, and deep depression. Disappointment that bordered uneasily on the brink of a necessary hospitalization rounded off the motif, settling Luther into a coma of uneasy comfort. However, the two most important things the champagne room had to offer that his personal latrine lacked was Candy's smell and the intoxicating, throaty way she talked when she was servicing a penis.

Candy, clad only in her gold lamé G-string, had her back to Luther as she straddled a quasi-unconscious patron sprawled on the bench as structureless as an overused crash test dummy. She had all of her weight on her knees and stabilized herself with her hands on the back of the bench as she worked her client's face using her breasts like a lai gua sha facial lifting tool. The client let out a low luxurious moan that sounded like a euphoric Darth Vader wearing a gas mask. Next to them a small square mirror, dusted by the remnants of seven or eight lines of blow, reflected the bleak blackness of the ceiling that was only free from grime due to elevation and gravity. Next to that were three hundred-dollar bills fanned out like a poker hand.

"Are you about done there?" Luther asked, showing uncharacteristic impatience.

"My craft knows no time limits, baby," Candy said dreamily. Luther watched as Candy's hands disappeared in front of her. Her elbows jerked back a little and the client thrust his hips up and against her. "*Jesus Christ,*" he blasphemed. Candy slowly did her rhythmically erotic hand dance, then looked over her shoulder at Luther. She smiled seductively as her eyes wandered down to her ass, begging Luther to follow. Luther could see the thin booby-trap-esque wire of gold G-string move out of Candy's ass crack as she pulled it aside from the front. The client hissed out a long low exclamation like a beachball with a pinhole leak. As Candy rode the object of her financial affection, she continued to watch Luther wistfully. Unconsciously Luther grabbed for his own swelling crotch and held it in anticipation of a promised climax.

The client jammed his ass off the bench so hard it lifted Candy in the air. She closed her eyes gently and mouthed *"Oh Luther,"*

"Okay," Candy said nonchalantly to Luther as she lifted herself off the well-lubricated member, "now I'm done. Ooops, one more thing."

The client was lolling in post-coital and current drug-addled bliss, pants still unzipped and open, as his rapidly flagging phallus slid down his thigh and left a post-passionate snail trail on his very expensive, dark blue slacks. Candy stood up straight, grabbed him by the front of the shirt, pulled him off the bench, then marched him to the door. His pants had fallen around his ankles, forcing him into a ridiculous penguin walk. As Candy hustled him out the door, he noticed Luther through blurry slits.

"How long has he been sitting there?" the client slurred.

"Who?" Candy said indifferently as she steadied him with one hand and opened the door with the other.

"Him," he said, pointing toward Luther with his chin.

"No idea what you're talking about," Candy said flatly as she pulled the door open and shoved the client forward. The last thing she saw as she closed the door was his feet getting tangled in his pants, forcing him to fall on his face.

"Huh," Candy observed nonchalantly, then she closed and locked the door. She allowed her hand to lightly run along Luther's shoulder as she passed and took a seat on the bench. Seductively she rubbed her hands down her thighs, pulled her knees apart, bit her lip and whispered, "Want some, daddy?"

"No," Luther instinctively answered. Then after some afterthought and a short staring contest with Candy's recently abused vagina, he qualified that remark with, "Not right now."

Candy crossed her legs tightly, retrieved a cigarette from a pack on the side stand, lit it, drew a deep drag, folded her other arm across her naked chest, and asked impassively, "What's on your mind, honey?"

"Do you have any idea what's going on around here?" Luther sounded very concerned, and Candy was pretty sure she didn't want to talk about whatever he was going to say next. She scooted her butt to the edge of the bench, leaned far forward, and drug one liquid red fingernail up the length of Luther's tethered erection. Luther grabbed her finger pressing, it tighter around the object of his confusion. He wanted her with every fiber of his physical and metaphysical self, but what he had to say couldn't wait. He pried her finger away like pulling a leech off his shin. Candy sat back and smoked while she pouted.

"I can't wait to hear what's more important than *that*," she said, pointing to Luther's crotch with her cigarette fingers.

"I asked you if you had any idea what's going on around here," Luther said again.

"I know what's *not*," Candy said as she nipped at the edge of one overdone fingernail.

"I'm serious Goddamn it," Luther said sharply. Candy snapped out of her *catch me fuck me* persona and sat up a little straighter.

"All right," Candy said defensively, "Jesus, take a pill. What's going on?"

"A LOT!" Luther said, knowing he was being a little overly dramatic as the words leapt out of his mouth. "Look," he went on with a more level air, "people are being killed, tortured, and hunted as we speak."

"*Look at this whore*," Good Luther chided. Luther didn't like the sound of his voice. Good Luther seemed more assertive, and a little more like Bad Luther. It confused him. "*She doesn't give two good donkey shits about what happens to other people. She. Is. Going. To. Get you killed, Buster Brown."*

Luther shook the inner him off without the customary *"Shut the fuck up."*

"Who?" Candy asked as though she honestly had no idea what he was talking about. If this dick manipulation gig were to not pan out, she could have a great career in the world of stage and screen.

"Who?" Luther mocked with that "what the hell is wrong with you" voice. "Are you going to tell me you have no idea what kind of shit storm is going on in the family right now?"

"I know that apparently Richy is a cocksucker now," Candy said with a shrug. "You know, I've always suspected that he might be a little light in his loafers. He loves to stick it my ass too much."

Luther sat there for a second, examining Candy with his mouth hanging open. That comment opened a Pandora's box of questions that Luther was pretty sure he wasn't ready to hear the answers to.

"What?" Candy eased back with her head tilted to one side. "You had to have known Richy was fucking me too. I mean, I do pretty much belong to the mob, and I am pretty good at what I do."

Luther shook his head a little to clear it. He didn't have a problem with Richy banging his girl; after all, he had just moments before watched her ride a complete stranger. He wasn't really good at changing thought streams in the middle of an idea though.

"You mean you really thought he might be?" Luther searched for the word, "You know."

"Gay?" Candy asked chuckling. "Luther, you have to understand that people are basically all bi-sexual beings. Men just can't wrap their heads around being submissive to another man, that's all. The fact that we have to put a label on it doesn't really say much for how far we've grown as a species, does it?"

"None of that matters, Candy," Luther was swimming in the deep end of lost concentration and going under for the third, possibly fourth time. "People are dying and having parts cut off them for things that you're directly in the middle of."

"I know about everything that's going down around this shithole," Candy said blankly. "But none of it revolves around me. I'm just an innocent bystander."

"Nobody is innocent in this!" Luther exploded.

"*About fucking time you got your nuts back*," Good Luther said supportively. "*Don't let this bitch manipulate you.*" Luther was surprised into a near-auditory response. Good Luther was getting quite a mouth on him.

"What the hell are you talking about?" Candy was irritated by being held to anyone's scrutiny. "Some money is changing hands, and that's it. *I'm* not cooking the books; *I'm* not stealing money from right under Cutter's nose. In fact, I'm about the only clean person in this whole mess."

"*Oh, for the love of God, dude*," Good Luther complained, "*would you please just strangle this whore to death and put us all out of our misery?*"

"It's funny," Luther began. Candy had never heard this tone in Luther's voice. It was not a good thing. "I tried to have this same conversation with Azi. Of course, that was before the bodies started piling up, and the manhunt was on. Do you know what he told me?"

"I can't wait." Candy's voice dripped with sarcasm.

"He told me that *you* were actually the mastermind behind all of this," Luther was stern. "He said that *you* planned the entire thing, and he is just following *your* orders."

"That little treasonous fuck," Candy shot out under her breath.

"Cutter is onto the fact that the skim isn't coming from the protection rackets," Luther advised. "They've beaten the shit out of almost all of the people that are paying them and have found nothing."

"How do you know that?" Candy asked with a look like she was struggling to put a plan together.

"I was there for most of them," Luther answered, "but how the hell does that matter, Candy? They are done looking at the protection side. That's all that matters now. They're looking for who's responsible."

"What exactly do they have to go on?" The look on Candy's face was last seen at the planning table for D-day. She gazed directly at Luther, "I mean, exactly what even makes them think there *is* a skim in the first place? They may be wrong."

"What the fuck?" Luther said. His face pinched together as it gave in to massive incredulity. "Are you out of your mind? Maybe they're wrong? They're not wrong, and do you want to know how I know that? I know that because I was told that by the two people that are currently stealing from the mob!"

"Keep your voice down Goddamn it," Candy hissed. "I know how *you* know it, but maybe there's some way to convince them it isn't actually happening."

"Candy," Luther was pleading now, "you're going to get hurt, and I couldn't live with that. You have to do something. You have to stop this and hope they quit looking."

"Baby," Candy cajoled, "Nothing is going to happen to you, or me, or Azi for that matter."

"The only one I care about is you," Luther moaned. Then, "I love you, Candy."

"*Sweet holy mother of fucking Christ!*" Good Luther screamed into his head. "*That's your dick talking, you dumb shit, not love!*"

"Shut the fuck up!" Luther demanded. Candy had seen him do this before, so the outburst didn't seem odd. But right now she couldn't have crazy Luther fucking things up.

"I love you too baby," Candy said ignoring the outburst. "When this is over it's going to be just me and you. I promise," she lied.

"When is that going to be?" Luther sounded desperate.

"Soon," she said as she patted his leg in a motherly fashion.

"How can you be so sure you're not going to be caught?" Luther floundered in a tempest of insecurity as he begged for a life preserver from a barbell salesman.

"Azi has it all set up." Candy was able to say that with mountains of assuredness.

"How?" Luther sounded cautious. "Azi is the first one Pretty Boy is going to start cutting pieces off. I don't mean to be a dick, but I think Azi doesn't have what it takes to protect you."

"He doesn't have to baby," Candy soothed. "From the beginning he's been pointing the paper trail away from us. Richy is on board too."

"Pointing at who?" Luther asked cautiously.

"I honestly have no idea," Candy's words festered in dishonesty. "Why, does it matter?"

"Not if it keeps you safe, it doesn't." Luther believed that with his entire being. He had never loved anyone else at all, let alone as deeply as he loved Candy. He wanted her to have his children when this was all over, and they both could live a normal life.

"*Oh my God, oh my great God in heaven!*" Good Luther lamented in Luther's head. "*This is so wrong! She is going to get us chopped into little tiny pieces, Luther. Hell, she'll probably hand the nippers to Pretty Boy herself.*"

"But Richy though," Luther pushed back a little as he ignored the wailing in his head. "That guy is not right."

"Don't worry about Richy," Candy smiled. "This is business, and I have everybo. . . I mean I have *Richy* right where I want him."

25.

The reality of the human animal is that of a much more delicate and instinct-driven entity than the members of its kingdom, or even phylum, want to admit. In the animalistic world of earth, there are certain aspects of species, or subspecies, that run true across the board with very few exceptions. Predators, for example, tend to have their eyes mounted on the front of their head. Lions, tigers, polecats, humans, etc. all share forward-operating vision. Creationists will say, "That's so they can see their prey better," but who knows, at one time there may have been predators with eyes on the sides of their heads; consequently, they were really shitty hunters and eventually died out.

Prey, on the other hand, tend to have their eyes on either side of their head, for example, deer, horses, sheep, goats, whatever. The fascinating arena in which humans thrive forces them to live in various other substrata that are usually reserved for simpler, less complicated, less deadly animals. For example, you would never expect an elk walking down the street minding its own business to be jumped by another elk that wants his cell phone and cash. Nor would you expect a prairie dog to whip out a Glock and bust caps into some bitch ass other prairie dog when he caught him banging Mrs. Prairie Dog. The animal world, aside from humans, is not that complex. When a human is threatened, the only action you can expect from it is to do the unexpected, and that is just one of the many things that make the human the most dangerous animal on the planet.

In the bowels of a dank, musty, and rotting alley that lay off a street of the same qualities, just not in the same quantities, stood a door marking time in quiet desperation. This particular door was ageless and painfully unassuming. It might have been the same portal Jesus passed through on his way to Jerusalem or, more likely, based on its beaten and battered façade, it may have been the door the Goths and Vandals beat on in an attempt to sack Rome. If one were to judge the interior of this building according to the door, they would be neither surprised nor disappointed.

The alley door opened into the grill/storage room/employee changing room/janitor's closet of the "Thirteenth Step" bar. A pedestrian path of dull grey depressing concrete crawled along between the layers of built-up grease that, if cut through, could mark the age of the bar like growth rings in a redwood. This path of hopelessness wound through the accoutrements of the bar business and passed under an unfinished metal door with a small porthole at face level, meant to preempt it from swinging open into someone on the other side.

On the other side of that door was the idea of a drinking establishment that had at one time been a front for the Manchini family. The neighborhood in the area had also at one time been vibrant and filled with possibilities. However, the crime, drug sales, gang hits, and unexplained explosions and fires found the majority of the local population seeking more stable climes. The clientele disappeared, income vanished, and in the end, after the bar had been entirely used up by the mob, they also left for more financially stable venues, abandoning the Thirteenth Step to the current manager.

Another equally desolate hallway on the other side of the bar led back to the restrooms. The door to the men's room had a crude drawing of a cock and balls, and the ladies' facilities were adorned with a drawing of a cat that looked like it might have been drawn by a first grader with a heroin addiction. The men's room made the backroom area look like the lobby of the Mirage in Las Vegas. Two ends of a broken neon tube clung to their respective outlets in a fixture that was held to the ceiling by magic and willpower. The walls had been painted hundreds of times by people who could not have cared less about aesthetics and had never been introduced to the wonderful world of masking tape.

The sink bore an astounding resemblance to a Cy Twombly painting, if Cy had only worked in earthtones. The corner had been broken off either by a head during a fight or an ass during deep romance. Across from the mirrorless sink stood a stall that had character but no structural integrity. The sign on the cockeyed door mislabeled that stall as "out of service." The factual title should have been, "Current residence of one Anthony Ferrari."

The faint glow of a flashlight app on a cell phone came alive, seeping through the cracks around the door as the rusted hasp creaked like the lid on a vampire's coffin. Slowly the stall door slid open just far enough so the dark eyes of the dweller within could examine the area for anyone that may have stayed behind after closing, such as hobos, vagrants, or hitmen.

Tony came out of the stall like a bashful ten-year-old taking the stage in a school play. When he was fully out of his new home, he let the door gently slide back into its natural spot, balanced between the fulcrum of a broken hinge and the force of gravity. He stepped quietly to the restroom door and pushed it open in the same fashion as the stall. Tony had chosen the mole approach to defense when he learned he was being set up to take the fall for the skimming operation and gone to ground. The current owner of the Thirteenth Step was a friend of Tony's from back in the day who also still had some loose connection to the family. Consequently Tony could get a little news on how close the boogeyman was to finding him.

His plan didn't extend past his hiding in a seedy shitter stall. The owner made it perfectly clear that if anyone from the organization came in searching for Tony, he would do nothing to stop them. He also made it clear that when they found him, he would act surprised and expose Tony for the deceptive little fucker he was.

Tony's life had become a punchline that he lived out like the man that had fallen off a twenty-story office building. As he passed each floor he could be heard saying, "So far, so good."

26.

The basement of the Manchini building was the definition of dichotomy for Luther. The atmosphere would make a dark, humid alley in Poe City, Philippines, seem like an airy walk along the main thoroughfare at Disneyland. The stench of crocodile shit was perpetual and overpowering, but Luther had become used to it, even welcoming it at times. That was the scent permeating the air when he and Croc Turd would have their philosophical discussions about life as they fed bits of flesh and sundry parts of anatomy to Bianca. He and Tony had spent quite a lot of time in that dump as well after a hit or a cleanup, separating what Bianca could and couldn't eat.

Unlike the deeply personal talks he and Croc Turd had, Luther and Tony talked about the old days when they were kids. Back before there had been three Luthers to deal with in the dark confines of his head. Way back when the one Luther, the first Luther, had been smarter, more well-bred, and actually had some options in life. Tony also spent hours with Luther standing around the croc pit while they waited for Bianca to finish the last helping of human as he carefully explained or tried to explain the nuances of mob life.

It was at that croc pit that Luther learned he should wait for Tony to use some type of signal before he reacted to one of those dumbass subtle gestures mobsters used that could mean the difference between life or death, not just for the person the Manchinis were directing their wrath toward, but for Luther as well. The day Cutter had nodded toward Luther, apparently signaling him to let Barbie Blue out of the conference room, Luther could have started a blood bath in there. If he had put a bullet in Barbie's head like he had planned, everybody in that room would have started shooting.

As an antithesis, the room adjacent to the croc pit had an entirely different sensory effect on Luther. That room was generally referred to as the "operating room" by everyone in the organization due to the number of amputations that had been exacted on "patients" suspected of wronging the Manchinis in some way. Luther had never been bothered by gore, torture, agonizing animalistic screams of pain, or the sound of extremities being snipped, clipped, sawed, or torn off a body. Instead, it was the reek and the overwhelming permeance of the hundreds of gallons of blood that had flowed across the concrete and snaked into the drain. The stench was so thick and overbearing that you could taste the thick coppery tang of blood as soon as you walked through the door.

As Luther and Murphy walked past the croc pit, they could hear the unholy screams of someone being tortured in the operating room. That certainly wasn't surprising because they had both been summoned to clean up a mess after the tormentors were finished extracting information.

"Man," Muphy said as the ripping sounds of someone being abused grew louder, "someone sure is getting their soul torn out in there. Any idea who fucked up?"

"None," Luther answered honestly. He knew it was whoever had been unlucky enough to be the scapegoat for Azi, but neither he nor Candy had ever divulged that information. Actually though, when Luther thought about it, that wasn't true. Every time he had asked who was going down for their crimes, she had been evasive. By the time they reached the operating room door, Luther had already convinced himself that Candy hadn't said who it was because she was just trying to protect him.

When they first entered the room, Luther had to let his eyes adjust to the poor quality of the lighting. It wasn't like Cutter couldn't have afforded to add a few fixtures in there in order to help Pretty Boy see what he was doing. The first person Luther could make out was the back of a bloody, whimpering man who had been duct taped to a chair. Pretty Boy stood off to one side next to a red Craftsman rolling tool chest. Apparently, he had chosen the Village People's Dave Hodo "construction guy" persona for this job. A red plaid flannel shirt draped over his shoulders, untucked and unbuttoned, revealed a ribbed white wifebeater t-shirt underneath. A clear plastic half-bubble eye protector that covered his good eye like a safety monocle rode under the visor of a white construction helmet. Jeans over engineer boots finished out the ensemble, with a red railroad hanky flowing artfully from his right back pocket.

Enzo and Richy stood facing the victim in practiced poses of righteous indignation.

"You into fisting, there, Pretty Boy?" Richy asked, smiling.

"What did you just say to me?" Pretty Boy asked in disbelief.

"I asked, in essence," Richy repeated slowly, "do you like to have a fist shoved up your ass on occasion?"

Pretty Boy had a claw hammer in his hand and took his attention entirely off the victim as he took a step toward Richy.

"What the fuck is wrong with you?" Enzo asked Richy, irritated.

"I'm not sayin'," Richy began, "I'm just sayin'. He has a big ass red handkerchief hanging out of his back right pocket, and he's obviously dressed up like one of the Village People."

Everyone in the room just looked at Richy disinterested, waiting for whatever this current stream of bullshit was to run its course.

"Red—right," Richy said with his hands spread out and his shoulders hunched in the international "do I really have to explain myself?" expression.

"Jesus," Richy exclaimed. "What a bunch of fucking Philistines. Right receives, left gives. Red for fisting, brown for ass-fucking, yellow for being pissed on, whatever. You know, clandestine gay code."

"Are you shitting me?" Enzo asked as he looked at Richy like he had two heads.

"What?" Richy asked innocently.

"What?!" Enzo exclaimed. "We have this fuck head in the chair, Pretty Boy is working, and you ask bullshit like that? What the fuck is wrong with you?"

"Jesus, calm down," Richy said, sounding hurt. He looked at Pretty Boy and nodded toward the man in the chair.

"Eat my shit," Pretty Boy said sullenly.

"See," Enzo said as he threw his hands up in the air. "Now *this* bullshit."

"Come on dude," Richy tried to placate Pretty Boy, "I was just fucking with you a little."

Pretty Boy stood looking like a pissed off statue of himself.

"Okay, okay," Richy said impatiently, "I'm sorry already. Is that what you want to hear?"

"You sure do know quite a lot about men's assholes." Pretty Boy sounded guttural and threatening. His eye flared with anger through the safety monocle.

"Knock this shit off!" Enzo bellowed. "And just where the hell have you two assholes been?" he asked Luther and Murphy. "We started without you."

"I had to wait for Murphy," Luther said distracted. There was something about the guy in the chair that he couldn't quite put his finger on.

"Hey, fuck you, retard," Murphy shot back at Luther.

"Shut the fuck up!" Enzo ordered. "I've had enough of this bullshit already. Jesus, I hate you jerkoffs." Then he pointed at Pretty Boy, "You have shit to do. Get busy."

"Honestly, Enzo," Chair guy croaked out.

"*That voice,*" Good Luther whispered. "*It can't be.*"

Pretty Boy snapped a backhand across chair guy's face hard enough to snap his head to one side. Luther instantly went steel rod rigid and his lip began to quiver. Chair guy was Tony.

"*Oh my God!*" Good Luther roared in horror. "*Oh my God Luther. It's Tony! They are going to beat Tony to death. You can't just stand here with your dick in your hand. Do something for Christ's sake!*"

Luther was vibrating all over now—not shaking uncontrollably but vibrating as if he was attached to a 220-volt outlet. Every nerve ending was firing, making his skin crawl. What could Tony possibly have done to deserve this? Pretty Boy reached into his toolbox and pulled out a pair of nippers.

"THEY ARE GOING TO START CUTTING PIECES OFF! STOP THEM!" Good Luther's voice ricocheted off the recesses of Luther brain. His head was pounding, and he was terrified.

Enzo said a single word to Tony, "Why?"

"I'm not the guy," Tony begged as tears rolled down his face. "I swear to God I'm not the guYYYYYYYYYYYY." Pretty Boy snipped Tony's pinky off with as much emotion as you would use while cutting carrots for a charcuterie board.

The human mind is an amazing machine, and the power of justification is one of its best magical tricks. The reality of a hopeless situation comes slow to the human consciousness. That one thing that is going to rescue someone from of a life-or-death situation is always just a millisecond away in the mind of the threatened. A human mind can convince its person that a car barreling toward it is going to swerve at the last minute, or that a fall from a cliff is going to be broken by an unseen tree limb, or any minute the rescue ship is going to come over the horizon and pluck my ass out of these shark infested waters. Never in the history of powered flight has a pilot become a smoking hole in the ground while giving in to the inevitable. Control inputs and plans will keep coming fast and furious until the earth shall rise and smite thee.

Currently the earth was rising at an incredible rate with the singular plan of smiting the shit out of Tony. In the vague haze of what was left of his consciousness, Tony completely understood how this situation was going to end. But the animal instinct for survival was still running hot and heavy through his slowly emptying veins. Deep inside his lizard brain, down in that place where he was pretty sure he was still going to be able to get out of this, he was strategizing like a man possessed. Which is exactly what he currently was.

He knew what, and who, they wanted, and he was still sane enough to understand the person that they really wanted was the one who had just started a conversation about fist-fucking with the monster who had clipped his finger off. If he tried to give Richy up, Richy would beat him to death before he ever finished the sentence. He knew that if he gave them what they wanted, which was Azi and Candy, Luther would be implicated before they ever finished duct-taping Azi's arm to the chair. Tony had ruined Luther's life and put him here, and if Tony had to go out like this to protect him, then so be it.

With each finger Pretty Boy clipped off, Tony thought through the fog of blazing pain and the distracting sound of his own screaming that he was going to be okay. He didn't really need that finger; he had others. As each finger fell to the filthy concrete, one at a time, and he realized that they were going to take them all, he justified his interminable refusal to accept his imminent death by rationalizing that he never really used those fingers that much anyway. Everything was going to be fine.

With each part of Tony that fell into an ever-widening pool of blood, urine, and excrement surrounding, Good Luther screamed, begged, and wept into Luther's brain. "*Please*," Good Luther pled through choking sobs, "*please don't just let this happen. It's TONY you sniveling lump of shit. You know what it takes to fix this, you pathetic excuse for a human being. GIVE THAT CUNT UP YOU FUCKING COWARD! Oh my God Luther, please give them up—these animals are killing him one piece at a time.*"

"Looks like your boy done fucked up," Murphy said to Luther blandly.

Luther stood as though he were paralyzed. The rhythmic hum of the universe vibrated through him, connecting him to the vast reaches of the whole of creation at once. There was nowhere to hide in all of that blackness, no place to escape the howls of the essence of his best friend's soul being wrenched free of its physical self.

The subhuman screeching wail started low and unshaped in the depths of what used to be Tony as Pretty Boy sat in his lap and sliced both eyelids off Tony's right eye with a box cutter. The gripping barbed howl rose in volume and pitch as Pretty Boy stood, shoved Tony's head back savagely, and sliced his eyeball open. The articulation of Tony's torment and pain exploded up through his throat like a million needles ripping him apart from the inside, then erupted past his lips and smashed itself pitifully against the dank hateful ceiling.

Good Luther lay prostrate as he wept uncontrollably inside the prison of Luther's mind. "*I fucking hate you!*" Good Luther wailed, "*I fucking hate you and I hope you die a painful miserable death in some shithole, alone and unloved!*"

"SHUT UP!" Luther yelled outwardly. "JUST SHUT THE FUCK UP ONCE AND FOR ALL!"

"See," Enzo said conversationally to Tony, "even your buddy is tired of this horseshit."

Pretty Boy took an eye dropper out of the toolbox, shoved Tony's head back again, and squirted gasoline into the open eyeball. Tony raged and cursed the heavens in a way now that wasn't nearly human. Good Luther rocked in a fetal ball and cursed Luther. "*I'm gone, you heartless, soulless motherfucker!!*" Good Luther collected enough control out of his gut-wrenching sorrow to say his last words to his jailer. "*You're on your own now. You and that motherless whore you stick your festering cock into.*" The last words drifted back into infinity, floated on the whisper of the cosmos, and vanished. Good Luther was no more, and Bad Luther was nowhere to be seen. The only thing left was Luther and the weight of his inaction that would buckle his knees every single day for the rest of his life.

As if it were punctuation on the end of Luther's life as he knew it, Enzo drew his gun, motioned Pretty Boy out of the way, and shot Tony in the head.

"Clean this shit up," Enzo directed Luther and Murphy.

27.

Luther and Murphy were left alone in the poorly lit hell that had changed Luther for the rest of his life. For better or worse, and time would only tell which, there was only one Luther now. Good Luther had been absorbing Bad Luther for several days and was picking up too many of his bad habits, like swearing a lot. Luther hated watching the transformation and missed the times he had living only one existence, allowing Good Luther to completely take over, filling him with peace and bliss. Now he was certain that Good Luther was gone forever, and he sensed that Good Luther had taken Bad Luther with him.

Now, for the first time in his life, he was truly on his own. He had had his parents as a child, then he had had Tony, and while he was in prison, he had had Bad Luther. Bad Luther was the only Luther that was allowed to exist for the time he was incarcerated. Luther was beaten, swindled, raped, belittled, and torn down when he first went inside. Once Bad Luther showed up, he became the person who exacted pain and discomfort on others. Everyone knew to give Bad Luther a wide berth, and that's just the way Bad Luther wanted it.

Luther had had Tony in his life again as soon as he had been released from prison, and the only person Luther allowed Tony or anyone else to see was Bad Luther. The fact that he didn't trust Tony enough to let him see regular Luther didn't stem from anything Tony had done; it was because Luther had been painfully taught that it didn't matter what people did or even what they said to you. Eventually everyone he knew let him down at best or completely betrayed him at worst.

The birth of Good Luther had been slow and cautious. In the confines of his apartment, Luther eventually gave in to the insatiable craving he had to get back the part of himself that had been crushed into oblivion so long ago. Good Luther blossomed with each and every heinous act Bad Luther was forced to carry out for the mob. Although he had reason to do so, Luther never held his situation with the mob against Tony. Instead he felt it was one more thing that he would never be able to repay his best friend for. The money had made him independent, and Tony had been there at every turn to guide Luther through the ever-changing and deadly life of a mobster.

Now pieces of that friend were being tossed into a black, construction-quality trash bag while Luther squeegeed pools of the fluid that had articulated Tony's body into the disgusting, bacteria-ridden drain in the center of the operating room floor. Luther couldn't stand the sound of Murphy sawing and chopping Tony's body apart, so he hooked his Shokz over his ears and started the play list on his cell phone. Van Morrison began to tell of a voyage into the mystic.

"We were born before the wind, also younger than the sun..."

Those words personified the relationship Tony and Luther had in the early days. They were young, and life and the entire universe were available for their taking. They certainly had been before the wind. Tears stung Luther's, eyes making it hard to see what he was doing. But that was possibly for the better. If he could clearly see the mess he was cleaning up—a mess that he had possessed the information to stop—he might have gone completely mad.

"Let your soul and spirit fly, into the mystic."

"Hey," Luther could hear Murphy calling to him, but he wasn't ready to let the outside world invade his sorrow. "Hey, shitbird," Murphy called again. He was being his usual vulgar self, but there was no edge or malice to it. Even the perpetually caustic Murphy felt the weight of what had just happened in this room. He hadn't even given Luther a hard time about helping him separate the body for Bianca.

"I know you can hear me, Luther," Murphy said again. This time it was more even and less demanding. Luther drug the Shokz off his ears and looked up at Murphy through eyes that had given up.

"Hey man," Murphy said, looking away. The pain in Luther's eyes cut too deep. "Take this in to Croc Turd," he said, indicating the cart carrying the trash bags containing the sliced and diced Tony. "He's waiting for them."

Luther allowed the squeegee to fall to the floor and zombie-walked the cart into Bianca's pit room. Croc Turd stood next to the pit, shoulders slumped as though he was supporting the weight of the world on them. Red swollen eyes indicated he had been crying.

"I don't even know what to say, brother," Croc Turd said sadly with a hint of pleading in his voice. "I'm just so sorry, Luther."

"About what?" Luther asked blankly.

Croc Turd examined him closely for a moment. It was clear that what Luther had just been a part of had bent him psychologically. So much so that he wasn't even sure Luther was registering what he was doing. It was like he had just turned off and was running on automatic.

"Nothing, my friend," Murphy finally said. "Let's get this taken care of." Croc Turd took control of the cart and moved it to the area he always fed Bianca from. Luther dropped himself into his usual chair and leaned forward with his forearms on his thighs.

"Hey man," Croc Turd said, "you don't have to do this you know."

"Don't you want me here?" Luther sounded hurt.

Croc Turd looked at the bulging trash bags then back at Luther. There was certainly something different that Croc Turd couldn't define, but this wasn't the same Luther he had always known. It was clear Luther had checked out, but whether it was temporary or permanent was yet to be seen.

"No man," Croc Turd said, "it ain't like that. Of course I want you down here. This place would be unbearable if I didn't have someone I trusted to talk to. I just thought, you know," Croc Turd glanced at the bags and back to Luther again, "in light of the job we have to do and all."

"Yeah," Luther said as though he was disconnected from the planet, "let's get to it."

"Are you sure you're okay?"

"Jesus Christ, are we going to do this or what?" Luther didn't seem irritated because he was about to do something no one should ever have to endure. Instead it was more like he was anxious to accomplish a task, like mopping the floor or making his bed.

Both men sat in their timeless lawn chairs and focused on the task at hand. Croc Turd rolled the edges of the first bag down, and Luther whistled for Bianca. The reptile, off color from the lack of sunshine and bloated from too much flesh and lack of exercise, slid through the fetid water of her Olympic-sized pound, tail gracefully moving back and forth through the murk propelling her giant flat head and piercing dark eyes forward. All of the grace of movement in the water fell away as Bianca drug her full weight up the slight ramp and waddled into the feeding pit. Just like a well-trained Great Dane, she settled at her handlers' feet, tilted her head up, and opened her gaping maw in expectation of her first feeding in almost a week. This was going to be quick.

Luther reached into the bag, retrieved a finger, and tossed it into Bianca's mouth like he was feeding pigeons at the park. Croc Turd's heart was breaking, and it took every shred of intestinal fortitude he possessed to hold back his tears.

"If this gets to be too much, buddy," Croc Turd said softly, "I can finish by myself."

"Thanks," Luther said as he dropped a fingerless palm into the pit. Both men sat, leaning forward with forearms on thighs like they were sitting at a campfire after a long day hunting. Then Luther began to open up a little, speaking without facing Croc Turd.

"I know what you're trying to do," Luther finally muttered.

"You do?" In Luther's current state, Croc Turd wasn't sure he understood anything.

"Yeah man," Luther said as he continued to toss small portions of Tony into the pit. "I'm not catatonic or anything."

"*Catatonic?*" Croc Turd was shocked. He wasn't sure he had ever heard Luther using anything larger than a two-syllable word since he first met him.

"This," Luther continued indicating the bag of parts, "isn't Tony."

Croc Turd considered explaining to Luther that in fact it was, and he needed to accept the reality of that. But there was something odd about the tone of Luther's voice that made Croc Turd feel as though he may be about to learn something deep and beautiful.

"This is just the organic package that allowed us to interact with Tony." Croc Turd had stopped everything he was doing and was just staring at Luther in puzzled amazement. "Have you ever watched the moment someone stopped living?"

"Yeah," Croc Turd answered slowly, "once or twice."

"That person is *there*, talking to you, screaming at you, begging for their life, or whatever, then you shoot them or cut their throat or something like that and they just—fade out. You know? I've never seen anyone just snap out of existence. I guess maybe if someone was blown up or something they might drop out pretty quick, but with that it happens in a blinding flash of light and they're gone, but nobody sees how they go out. I've seen a lot of people fade out in my time here, and it has really taught me something about life."

Croc Turd realized that he was hanging on every word and prayed that this new version of Luther would not stop baring his soul.

"People may look like each other," Luther went on like there was no one else in the room. "They may share physical attributes, but their mannerisms are their own. You might see someone on the street or something like that and think '*Hey, that's Bob over there.*' Then you see them move or something, scratch their nose, or raise an eyebrow, or the way they tilt their head, and you realize that person is not who you thought it was. That's because the essence, or whatever you want to call it, that articulates Bob is only his. If Bob and the other guy were standing next to each other and they both died on the spot, you wouldn't be able to tell the difference between them because the vessels are the same, but the contents are gone.

"That's why people fade out when they '*die*,' for lack of a better term. That essence is being released back into the ethereal space that surrounds us. So, this isn't Tony, Tony is diffusing into the area around us right now. It's like water in a clay pot. If you have a pot that is full of water, then you break that pot, the water doesn't just disappear. It's still water, it just spreads out and evaporates into the atmosphere or combines with puddles or whatever. So it's not like that 'Tony's in heaven looking down on us right now' horse shit. That's just the product of a lazy mind making shit up that's easy for them to accept. Tony is around us, moving through us, and diffusing into the rest of the energy that makes up the universe."

Croc Turd was speechless, and Luther lapsed back into reflective silence.

"The problem I have is something else," Luther finally confided. Croc Turd couldn't wait to hear the thing that was more of a problem than watching your childhood friend beaten, mutilated, and shot in front of you, then feeding that friend to a fat, depressed, endangered, and domesticated crocodile. "It's about the money-skimming."

Croc Turd felt like he had just been punched in the forehead then tazed. "What about it?"

"I know about it," Luther said off handedly like what he just said wasn't the *real* issue.

"Oh, Luther," Croc Turd forced out. "What are you saying? How much do you know?"

"Everything, I guess," Luther shrugged.

"Oh shit," Croc Turd was staring at Luther in amazement laced with large amounts of horror. "You didn't—you know—take that money, did you?"

"What?" Luther seemed to snap out of his reverie. "Of course not. First of all I wouldn't have any idea how to even *start* something like that, let alone keep it secret for as long as it was."

"Do you mean," Croc Turd was dumbfounded, "it really *was* Tony?"

"Fuck no." Luther was instantly irritated by the simple fact that *anyone* would think Tony was capable of something that stupid and dishonest. "Tony would have never done anything like that. And if he ever caught me pulling that shit, he would have beat the hell out of me for it."

"Then who did it?" Croc Turd didn't want to ask the other question, like why he didn't use that information to save his friend. His head was reeling like he had just found out that field mice were actually in charge of the planet.

"Azi," Luther said blankly.

"That little shithead?!" Croc Turd was amazed. "Why in the name of God would you not give that little rat fuck up to save Tony?"

"It's complicated, man," Luther explained. "I'm not sure how much you want to know just in case they come for you."

"Half of these assholes don't even remember I'm down here." Croc Turd rationalized.

"You can't say anything," Luther realized he sounded like a kid telling a friend not to tell he was the one that threw a rock through the neighbor's window. Croc Turd didn't respond.

"Azi is ripping off Cutter and he's implicated Candy," Luther really needed to get this off his chest, but at the same time he felt like he was betraying Candy. "If I say anything at all, Candy is going to get hurt, and I can't let that happen."

"That fucking cu…!" Croc Turd began then cut himself off. He deeply wanted tell Luther exactly who he was really protecting, but he knew better than that. He had tried to get Luther to see the light about that toxic bitch ever since he became entangled in her web of shit and lies. Luther wasn't hearing any of it because Candy was the only lifeline that was keeping Luther from opening a vein. "If she's implicated in this thing, I can promise you she's in deeper than she's telling you."

"She's telling me everything," Luther said. "So is Azi, that's how I know all of the things I know about this."

"Wait a minute," Croc Turd interrupted, "if Azi and Candy really are the ones running this scam, how can they possibly have kept it a secret so long? Azi would have been the very first person they looked at for this and that shit bird could never stand up to that kind of scrutiny."

"You're right about that," Luter agreed. "They have someone on the inside that's protecting them."

"If anyone was keeping those morons' asses in one piece and out of a silver box, they would have to have some serious clout in this family."

Luther stayed quiet for an uncomfortably long time. "It's Richy," he said softly like he was revealing Jesus was a bookie.

"What the fuck did you just say to me?" Croc Turd felt as though he should run like he was trying to stay in front of the magma at Pompeii. "Did you really just tell me that the bookkeeper is stealing money from the most dangerous man on the planet, and his *son* isn't just part of it, but he's keeping the heat off the people responsible?"

"Yeah," Luther answered with no emotion or conviction. "That about says it, I guess."

"Oh shit, oh shit, oh shit," Croc Turd said. He had tucked his head between his knees and laced his fingers over it. "This is bad, man. This is so, so bad." He suddenly snapped his head up. "Wait, if those three are wrapped up in this, how did Tony get involved?"

"That had to be some kind of serious screwup," Luther said as if he were trying to solve a complex math problem in his head. "Candy told me they were making it look like someone else was responsible just in case Richy wasn't able to keep the heat off of them. But it was someone that was spending more money than they were making."

"Luther," Croc Turd was trying extremely hard to get Luther to understand what had happened, "why on earth don't you think Tony was the one those clowns set up? That's the only thing that makes sense. You see that, right?"

"Candy couldn't have done something like that." Luther's tone was matter of fact. "I asked her several times who they were pinning this on, and she said she didn't know. Even if she did know who it was and didn't want to tell me, she and Azi know how much Tony means to me, and she would never consciously do anything to hurt me like that. We're too much in love." Luther would have never fathomed the idea that Candy had no idea who was a big deal in his life, or any personal information about Luther at all. She certainly had been told many times what was in Luther's heart and who the people were that he held close, but if what he was saying wasn't directly connected to her, and her alone, his words were nothing more than white noise she had to endure until she was able to say something relating to herself.

"A mistake?" Croc Turd was trying with everything he had to not talk down to Luther. "You think the three of them set someone up, and through some astounding tear in the fabric of the universe, they grabbed Tony out of a crowd of people and killed him for a crime that the guy asking him the questions had actually committed?"

"I know how it sounds," Luther was doing the breaststroke through a vast pool of denial, "but Candy would have *never* done anything like that to me. And there is no way I could have thrown her under the bus. Believe me, the entire time I was in that room, I wanted to just blurt it out. But I never would have finished that sentence before Richy put a bullet in my head, and Candy would have been next. It was the same reason Tony didn't say anything."

"What would Tony have to say?" Croc Turd couldn't believe where this was going.

"I told him everything I knew," Luther explained. "Tony could have said who it was, but Richy wouldn't have let him finish. Barbie

Blue tried that, and Richy cut his tongue out in mid-sentence. Besides, if he let on that he knew anything, I would be the next one in the chair because we were so close. Richy couldn't let me live. Tony was protecting me."

"Luther, you have to get out of here. Azi," he meant Candy, but he knew Luther wouldn't hear anything after that, "is going to turn on you. You are not safe here."

"Where the hell am I going to go?" Luther asked. "Besides, if it were that easy why didn't you take off years ago?"

Croc Turd didn't have an answer for that.

"I'm going to see Candy tonight," Luther said thoughtfully. "I'm going to ask her what happened. I'm sure she'll be able to clear everything up."

28.

A 1956 black Bentley S1 Standard Steel Saloon rested exactly where the owner had paid extra for it to be kept safe. Not too close to other cars to avoid scratches or dings. Marks like that on a car of this caliber would have been sheer heresy and an afront to fine antique car owners everywhere. The parking space had been personally selected by the owner after a walk through the lot with the valet before he was willing to hand the keys over. Not too close to the street or alley, so there would be a lot of other very expensive cars that hooligans bent on destruction for kicks would get to first. No billboards, antennas, windowsills, or power lines, so nothing would inadvertently fall on it, and no birds would point their uncontrolled cloaca in the Bentley's direction and drop vile pools of birdshit on the five-coat lacquer finish.

The interesting thing about this particular parking space is that the perfect spot for an anal-retentive car owner is the exact same place two people looking for some undisturbed personal time would choose. The valet had been kind of a prick about giving Luther and Candy their usual spot because he was pretty sure the owner of the car they wanted was a "sue your ass off" type of guy. Luther was undaunted; he needed time with Candy, and he didn't need to get it in some shitty parking spot they both weren't used to. Luther doubled his usual bribe, then threatened to beat the living shit out of the valet, and eventually just ripped the keys out of the kid's hand. This just wasn't the valet's night.

Once in the back seat Luther and Candy kind of connected. They didn't make love because that would assume something bordering on romance, and they didn't fuck, because that would assume fulfilling some sort of animalistic need. Luther simply entered Candy and moved around some until he was finished.

"Where the hell were you?" Candy asked as she rearranged her clothing and lit a cigarette in a car that had only ever felt a wisp of cigarette smoke when it was passing laborers on the assembly line.

"What do you mean?" Luther asked in a disconnected manner as he pushed all of his weight onto his shoulder blades, hiked his ass off the seat and shimmied his pants back on.

"You weren't here with me when we were fucking, and you're not here now," Candy said as she pulled a deep drag on the Marlboro, then coated the roof fabric with the exhale. "So what's going on?" The tone that Candy was using would have fit perfectly when used by a bored listener trying to be polite as someone explained the sex life of the south Floridian Iguana.

"A lot happened today," Luther said from a thousand miles away, "I just haven't figured how to best cope with it."

"*What the hell was that?*" Candy was confused. Luther, the basic animal power-fucker had just had sex with her like she was his sister, and the way he was talking was odd. It almost had an educated quality to it—almost.

"Like what?" Candy asked, more interested in understanding the twilight episode she was currently in. "I haven't heard about anything big happening, and I haven't seen Azi."

"I'm not surprised," Luther said. "So you have no idea what all went down since this morning?"

"Nope. I've been hanging off the pole all day for the breakfast pervert club. What's up?"

"Honestly, baby, I'm pretty conflicted about saying anything to you," Luther noticed an odd look spread across Candy's face when he said that. He took it to mean that she might be in a vulnerable place right now for some other reason, so he was even more hesitant to bare his soul.

"*What the fuck did he just say?*" Candy thought as she struggled to gain purchase in this conversation. "*Did this dumbass just use 'conflicted' in a sentence? And correctly, no less?*"

"I'm worried that you are going to get really upset about part of this," Luther was facing Candy now, with his hand on her thigh like he was going to tell her an AIDS test came back positive. "And I'm even more worried you're going to feel responsible for some of it. But I know you had no way of knowing anything, and it's all just a big mistake."

Candy currently had more evil shit balanced in the air than a plate spinner on Ed Sullivan. Consequently, Luther could be talking about *anything* she might actually be responsible for. But, for the life of her, she couldn't think of a single thing she was doing, aside from the skimming, that would affect him. Well, there was the replacing money in Cutter's office thing. And now that she thought about it, she had talked him into pawning jewelry to bail Azi out. But that was it; how could any of that be what he was talking about?

"You don't have to worry about me being upset about anything," Candy said, in what served as a sweet voice in Candy world, as she covered Luther's hand with hers.

"I don't know," Luther said staring at the floor. "This is pretty big. It has to do with the skimming thing."

Candy jerked her hand off Luther's like it was on fire. A boulder rolled down her throat and slammed into the pit of her stomach, nearly causing her to throw up in Luther's face. How much do they know? Did Richy roll over on them? Were they cutting up Azi right this minute? Were they coming for her next? Was that why Luther had been so weird? Was there a hit out for her, and was Luther the guy that was going to do it? Was her life really going to end seeing her freshly fucked in the back seat of some old-ass car?

Luther felt her stiffen up and saw the look of wild animal fear in her eyes. "See," he said soothingly, "that's exactly why I didn't want to say anything to you. I knew you would get upset."

"Luther," Candy said slowly, "we did an excellent job of covering our asses with this thing. Jesus, we even have Richy. . ." Candy stopped in mid-sentence. What she was thinking was too heinous to ever consider. "Luther, did something happen to Richy, or did that little piece of shit roll over on us? What the hell is going on? You are scaring the shit out of me."

"Honestly, baby," Luther said quickly, trying to smooth things out, "you're fine. I know you are, and as far as I know, Azi is in the clear also. I haven't seen him today, and with the day I've had that's a really, really good thing. I just think a mistake was made this morning, and I think you are going to be extremely upset when I tell you. But you have to understand I don't hold anything against you. There was no way you could know. I mean with all of the Goddamned head-tilting and chin-pointing these assholes are in love with, something like this was bound to happen.

"They make life and death decisions every day and let some dumbass eye twitch or nose pick decide who dies and who gets the door opened for them. Eventually the wrong person is going to be beaten to death, cut into small pieces, and fed to that fucking lizard in the basement. I guess it's not really Bianca's fault, but holy shit. . ."

"Jesus, Luther!" Candy cut in. "You're making me crazy here! I couldn't give a shit less about that shit-eating gator. . ."

"Crocodile" Luther corrected. "Endangered."

"I DON'T GIVE A FUCK!" Candy yelled. Luther knew this was going to go badly and he was going to hurt her feelings. "Luther, tell me what happened or I'm going to rip your dick off and feed it to you."

"Please don't be mad at me, baby," Luther whined.

"Luther," Candy was vibrating, trying to control her temper, "I'm not mad. Scared to death, yeah, but not mad. I could never be mad at you, baby." Candy knew that grabbing Luther's dick wasn't going to fix anything immediately, so she was forced to go the much more complex route of mental manipulation. "Please, just tell me what the hell is going on. No matter what it is we can work it out. Okay?"

Luther had to consider that for a bit. He was pretty sure that when he told her Tony had been killed instead of the real person they were setting up, she was going to be crushed. He wasn't certain she could come back from that.

"Look," Candy said, trying to spark some information, "Why don't you start by telling me what happened with Richy? Is he still in one piece, and has Cutter figured out what Richy's doing behind his back?"

"That lump of shit Richy will always be okay," Luther said miserably. "That asshole stood there asking questions of a guy that Richy knew damn good and well had no idea what he was talking about. You know, I realize that this was always Richy's position in this operation; keep Cutter off balance and looking in the wrong direction. But holy shit, the way he was asking questions and telling Pretty Boy to torture this guy had *me* believing Richy was clean as a whistle. That prick sure can lie."

"Okay," Candy was grasping at straws now, "Richy is still good, and you didn't see Azi anyplace and never heard his, or my name, mentioned in connection with this operation. Right so far?"

"No," Luther said, "I mean yes. Shit, I mean neither of you ever came up."

"Oh thank God," Candy breathed a sigh of relief and collapsed into the upholstery. "Hey, wait. What was the part that was going to upset me? Because all of this is actually pretty good news."

"It was the part about the guy they beat, shot, and cut into pieces, and who I fed to Bianca." Luther really wanted to stop now that Candy was relieved. He knew she was going to lose her mind when she found out they did all that to the wrong guy.

"What about it?" Candy said with an inquisitive look.

"Well," Luther stumbled through his words, "it was Tony. I know you couldn't have known that," he added quickly. "That's why I was afraid you would be devastated when you found out they had the wrong guy. I don't blame you at all; honestly, you have to believe me. I don't hold any of this against you. I never could."

"Who the fuck is Tony?" Candy asked, genuinely stumped as to who Tony was and why Luther gave a shit.

"You see," Luther said joyously as he grabbed Candy's hand. "I was absolutely positive you had nothing to do with it."

"Oh shit," Candy said absently. "Are you talking about Anthony Ferrari? They call him Tony the tongue sometimes."

"Yeah, baby," Luther said apologetically. "Please don't be upset."

"Damn, Luther," Candy said with a chuckle, "I'm not upset at all, and you shouldn't be either. Everything is just fine. That's the guy Azi set up. Oh man, you scared the shit out of me. Everything is perfect."

Every warning that people had given Luther about this bitch came crashing into his head all at once. It hit him hard enough to make him feel dizzy. His face burned as he remembered all of the things he had told this whore about his friend Tony, about how Tony was the only friend he had until he found her. Everyone had been right about her, and he had been too stupid to pick up on what they were saying. The only things that crossed his mind was how she made him feel when they made love and the plans they were making for the future. Just like every other slimeball in his life, she had used him, and he could see clearly now that as soon as she got what she wanted, she and Azi were going to knock him off.

"Hey, baby," Candy said tilting her head slightly, "is everyth. . ."

Luther snapped both hands out, grabbed her by the throat, and slammed her head into the roof, denting it outward.

Candy grabbed both of his wrists and fought to speak, "Tighter," she croaked. Luther's eyes blazed into her face, but something in his head that was inexplicable was having a life-or-death wrestling match for his emotions. "Tighter," Candy croaked again, "then fuck me as hard as you can."

Luther glared at her as spittle hung to his quivering lip.

"Do it," Candy managed to get out. "Fuck me like an animal."

Luther held her neck with one hand and tore his pants open with the other. He reached up to continue throttling her. When he slammed himself into her, it crammed her head violently against the roof and bent her neck over slightly. Luther continued to abuse her with unbridled sexual violence. Every time he bashed her up against the roof again, he grunted, and she moaned. He jerked himself out of her harder than he had been pounding into her, forced her onto her knees, and jammed her head against the side window as he stabbed into her again with all the hatred and viciousness he could garner.

Luther accosted her vagina over and over again. At one point Candy passed out, so Luther slapped her across the back of the head as hard as he could and began to sodomize her. When he finally reached his climax and his venom exploded into her, he was crying uncontrollably. He jerked his rapidly deflating member out of Candy, put his hand on her hip, and pushed her into the back of the driver's seat so hard it broke forward, laying on the steering wheel. The horn began to scream indignantly.

Luther opened the door, backed out, and dressed himself. Candy lay on the broken seat-back, moaning roughly and breathing heavily but otherwise unresponsive. "Stay the fuck away from me you worthless cunt," Luther cursed her, then spit on her and slammed the door shut. He was done.

29.

Richy sat behind his desk in a poorly acted out version of his father in deep thought. Big Benny filled the entirety of an overstuffed leather chair in front of Richy's as he slowly spun the ice cubes around in a bourbon glass he had draped over one knee. Richy was thinking, and Benny was waiting. Finally Richy unfolded his hands, placed them on the edge of the desk, and leaned forward.

"We have an issue here, Benny," Richy said.

"We always have an issue in this fucking place now," Benny groused. Richy did have a point though. At the rate they were cutting people up, they were going to have to get one, maybe two more crocodiles in that basement to take up Bianca's slack. Eventually the mausoleum in Miami was going to be so full of gangster shit in silver boxes they were going to have to either build an annex or convince Cutter of how ignorant the croc shit thing was. And good luck finding anyone that was brave or ignorant enough to bring that shit up to Cutter.

"Yeah," Richy agreed with a disconnected air, "I'm afraid that's true. But *this* issue hits a little closer to home for me."

"*If you're talking about sucking cock in a hotel room for three days,*" Benny thought, "*then fucking a ditty bag, we have an issue.*"

Benny relaxed in the chair, set his glass on the side table, and folded his arms, "Whatever could you be talking about, Mr. Manchini?" Benny said blandly. In his mind he was calculating the physics problem of getting his gun out of its shoulder holster before this little shit-stain could clear the desk with his.

"You have done nothing but good for this family for decades, Benny," Richy started to say.

"I'm glad you remember that," Benny glowered. "I hope your father realizes that also."

"What the hell are you talking about him for?" Richy said, annoyed by Benny bringing Cutter into this conversation. "He has nothing to do with this, dude," Richy set Benny straight. "I know I can trust you, Benny. You've proven that over and over again."

"Why do I get the feeling I'm about to have to prove it again?"

"Goddamn it, Benny!" Richy growled. "Knock it the fuck off. I'm trying to talk to you here. I need to run something by you that you and I are going to have to take care of and I don't know how to go about it. I don't need your fat ass getting all paranoid and shit while I try to work it out."

"Okay," Benny said hesitantly. He decided listening to whatever bullshit was about to come out of Richy's mouth would give him time to work the kinks out of his gun draw problem.

"You and I haven't talked about the, ah, unfortunate happenings in the company suite the other day," Richy began to lay out. Benny was unmoved. "I know I don't have to explain myself any further to you about what really happened in there. I also know that I don't ever have to worry about you bringing it up again. Ever."

Benny didn't twitch as much as an eyebrow, which made Richy extremely uncomfortable.

"That all being said," Richy went on, "I—*we*—have three other assholes that were in that room who I'm not one hundred per cent sure are going to be straight up about this shit. I—*this family*—can't afford to take a chance with that."

Benny remained as stoic as Michelangelo's David.

"We need to finalize things," Richy finished.

"And *exactly* how do you want to accomplish this?" Benny asked, then added for clarity. "Exactly."

"Jesus, what the fuck is up your ass?" Richy wanted cooperation and all he was getting was hesitation.

"Well," Benny began, "since you asked and all, I'm feeling just a little bit vulnerable here. I assume we're talking about the ultimate type of assurance, right?"

"Yeah," Richy said with a small impatient shake of his head as he shrugged his shoulders. "What the hell else would I be talking about?"

"See, Richy," Benny began slowly, using WAY less enthusiasm than Richy would have liked to see, "when you start talking about whacking witnesses, there were four people in that room other than you and the guy you were fucking. You stabbed the living shit out of him, and Tony fucked up on his own, taking him out of the picture. Once we knock off Murphy and the idiot, what's to keep you from doing the exact same shit to me at some point?"

"What in the fuck do you think all the shit I said at the beginning of this meeting was about?" Richy was getting tired of all this "soothing feelings" bullshit.

"Alright," Benny finally acquiesced. "But you *do* see a few issues with this plan other than getting me to believe you're not coming after me next, don't you?"

"Like what?" Richy asked exasperatedly.

"Well," Benny started. He hated dealing with Richy. Everything Richy did was a knee-jerk reaction to something that needed at least a little consideration first. "For starters, in order of 'who gives a shit?' and ascending, the idiot is going to need to be replaced. Yes, I know you could replace him with a sign spinner supporting a crack addiction, but you're never going to find anyone with that clean of a background. Another thing, Luther and Croc Turd work together great; they always have Bianca's best interest at heart. Hell, I'm not sure that fucking monster would still be alive if it wasn't for them."

Richy had his head resting on the back of his office chair, staring at the ceiling like a first grader during a lecture about the letter "B." "What else?" he asked without raising his head.

"You might want to pay attention here," Benny chided, and Richy raised his head to look at Benny. "Murphy is a real issue. He's the best cleaner we ever had and replacing him is going to be right next to impossible."

"Fuck him," Richy said. He really hated having his plans shit on with logic like this. "We can replace him with the Monster. That living horror story would be perfect in that position."

"Okay," Benny said irritably, "we can't simply *'fuck him'* as you so thoughtfully put it. Cutter is never going to let his body man out of his sight. That is not negotiable."

"Oh, for the love of Christ here," Richy whined, "can we just kill a motherfucker or what? I'm not asking for the world or anything. In fact I'm not *asking* for shit. I want two shit-birds that are so far down on the totem pole they're underground to die. How is that so fucking complicated?"

"Have you brought this up to Cutter?" Benny wanted to say "*Have you asked Cutter?*" but he knew that would push this child over the edge.

"Why?"

"Because if you're going to start dropping members of Cutter's crew, I think he might want to know about it. Call me crazy, but he could get a little pissed about it if he were to find out after the fact."

Richy thought about that for a moment. What he wanted to do right now was shoot Benny in the forehead, call Murphy and Luther up to his office to clean it, then shoot both of them. There, problem solved. Some place WAY, way back in the recesses of his infantile mind, the question of who would clean up the cleaners nagged at his conscience. But piss on that. He could figure that out when the time came.

"Richy," Benny was going to give it one last shot, "you simply can't go around knocking off soldiers because they have something on you." Richy started to protest but Benny cut him off with a wave of his hand. "I'm afraid that's just not up for debate, brother. You get Cutter's okay on this, and I'll shoot those assholes myself. I'm afraid that until then, I can't help you."

"And," Richy fumed as he attempted to give Benny the most threatening look he could muster, "what if I told you I already *had* my father's approval for this?"

Benny contemplated that statement for a moment. He was tired of playing games with this spoiled brat, and Richy was starting to write checks with his mouth that his ass couldn't cash.

"*If* you were to tell me something like that," Benny sounded like a timber wolf that was cornered, "of course we're just talking here, but *if* you did, I would have to say you were a lying son-of-a-bitch." Benny moved his hand sightly closer to the butt of his Glock.

Richy tried to pierce Benny with a riveting glare but only managed to make that squashed-up face a baby gets when it shits its diaper. Benny's look conveyed his all-consuming need to blow Richy's head off.

"Okay," Richy finally assented, "you're right. I'll talk to the old man and get back to you."

"Sure," Benny said as he rose to his full height, "you do that. Let me know what he says."

Richy watched Benny walk out of his office with a smile on his face. As soon as the door closed, he slammed his fist on the desktop in a short tantrum. So, Benny was going to be a dick about this; that was okay. He would just have to set that prick up later, after he cleaned up the other two. Plan A hadn't worked, and he had no intention of going to his father about shit. He guessed it was time for plan B. Now all he had to do was get the name of that pawn shop in New Jersey from Candy.

30.

Luther punched the button on his Shokz and dropped his head. Dean Ford began the soft and mournful words as The Marmalade backed him. "*The changing of sunlight to moonlight, reflections of my life, oh how they fill my eyes.*" Luther dropped his face into his hands and wept with a soul-cleansing ferocity he hadn't known for decades. The last time he cried like this had been the first night he spent in prison, feeling deserted by his family and alone in the dark of his cell. His roommate sat on the bunk next to him and wrapped a huge arm across Luther's back to console him. He said he understood and would take care of Luther. Then, to prove his commitment to Luther's well-being, he stood, slapped Luther across the face, and jabbed his dick against Luther's lips.

Luther protested, so his cell mate punched him in the face again as hard as he could. When Luther came to, his face was pushed tightly against the bars of his cell and he was being raped. A guard walked past, and Luther begged for help. The guard kept walking along the corridor as if nothing was happening. That was the first of very many betrayals, beatings, and rapes that would fill Luther's life. From that time on all Luther had to comfort him was Good Luther and Tony. Then he opened himself up to Candy. Now, in the ultimate betrayal, Tony was dead at the hands of Candy, Good Luther had turned his back on him, and Bad Luther had slipped away in an unannounced departure. Luther was truly and completely on his own and drowning in desperation.

"*Oh my sorrows, sad tomorrows, take me back to my own home.*"

Tears burned his face and soaked into his palms. He heaved in huge pathetic and painful sighs, trying to grasp onto anything that would give him reason to continue living. He had been so careful since his incarceration when it came to relationships. He had been sleepwalking through the duties the Manchini family had thrust upon him. In the commission of whatever crimes he committed for his superiors, he was completely emotionally disconnected. He could murder, maim, beat, rob, dissect, and feed body parts to a crocodile in his day-to-day life, and it never affected him. But when he was with Candy or Tony, he could be himself—to a point. When he was working with Tony, he knew he would be taken care of, and his friend would keep him from doing something stupid that could get him killed. Now, all of that had been ripped away from him.

"I'm changing, arranging, I'm changing, I'm changing everything. Everything around me."

Luther looked to the ceiling for answers and found nothing. He wanted out, completely out. He wanted out the only way people have been able to get completely out since the beginning of time. And that sounded *so* good. That sounded like the warmth of a quilt on a cold winter day. He could wrap himself in death and revel in sweet descent as his essence was finally released into the jetsam of life that swam around humanity every day. That sounded like the beautiful song of the sirens calling him to the rocks of finality.

But he couldn't leave yet. He couldn't move into the only plane of reality that he could now accept. He had things to finish and dues that needed to be paid.

"The world is a bad place, a bad place, a terrible place to live. . ."

"Yeah, Dean," Luther thought, "you hit that shit right on the head. This world is a festering shithole, and everyone in it deserves to fucking die. Everyone!"

Every time Luther had been fucked, both literally and figuratively, came boiling up from deep within his bowels. Every single slight, every degrading name, every beating, every time he was used for others' benefit: all of it pressed into Luther and dug at his ability to control it. Tony needed to be avenged. The death of his love for Candy needed to be championed. The sick and twisted world that Azi had pulled him into had to be torn down and crushed.

There was going to be some motherfucking biblical vengeance unleashed in this city, and Luther was going to be the one swinging the flaming sword of righteous redemption. And that shit was going to start right fucking now.

31.

Richy walked into the receiving room for his father's office and found Enzo already waiting.

"What's going on?" Richy asked as he passed the secretary's desk and approached Enzo.

"I was pretty much hoping you could shed some light on that," Enzo answered. "All I know is the old man told me to 'get my ass' up to his office, don't talk to anybody on the way, and make it quick."

"Yeah," Richy agreed, "that was pretty much the exact same thing I got. He sounded pissed off, but then he aways sounds pissed off now." In reality Richy knew exactly what his father wanted. He had worked hard to put all the cards in place so they would fall precisely the way Richy wanted them to. He was beginning to get very good at this subterfuge and setup thing. He was already putting together plans for his next operation that would put him directly into Cutter's chair, and he wouldn't even have to get his hands dirty. Of course his father would be dead when the smoke settled, but you know what they say about making an omelet: sometimes you need to blow someone's brains out.

"Do you blame him?" Enzo said, taking Cutter's side in an argument that hadn't even started yet. Richy felt the most minuscule sting of remorse in the new realization that Enzo was going to have to go as well. Oh well, as they say in Spain, "que sera, sera."

"I'm just sayin'," Richy said glumly, "I'm getting tired of him being up my ass."

"You're tired of *him* being up your ass, huh?" Enzo always thought the right thing to do in the Richy-and-the-homo situation would have been to roll two bodies up in a rug. Richy was nothing but a problem anyway, and that's all he was ever going to be.

"What the fuck is that supposed to mean?" Richy shot back.

"Take it anyway you like," Enzo smiled. "Oh, wait, you've already done *that*, haven't you?"

On the inside Richy was apoplectic with rage. He envisioned the rapturous joy he would experience pulling his gun out and shooting Enzo right in his smug-ass face. At least now he no longer felt bad about Enzo checking out along with his father. Actually he was already formulating a plan that would have Enzo taking the long ride south in a sterling silver box with gold handles. On the outside he just smiled at Enzo and hoped he wouldn't notice Richy's chin quiver in furious smoldering delirium.

The two men floated around in an uneasy mutual loathing as they waited for Cutter to call them in, Richy planning Enzo's demise and Enzo perfecting the story he was going to have to tell Cutter when he accidently shoved his gun up Richy's ass and pulled the trigger till it went click.

"You can both go in now," Cutter's secretary advised.

"What's up, Pops?" Richy said lightly as he strolled into the office first. Enzo, understanding the gravity of the moment, simply walked in and took a seat across from Cutter's desk.

"Sit the fuck down," Cutter growled. With his second in command and his son seated across from him, Cutter held each one in his gaze for a moment before speaking. The gloom was so heavy in the room there should have been a foghorn in the distance proclaiming danger.

Cutter took in a breath to speak and stopped. After a few seconds ticked off the clock. he began again. "I started to say that things are fucked up, but that doesn't come close to describing the state of our daily operations. This business," he jabbed his index finger into the desk for emphasis, "is on the rocks. Shit that should only happen once a decade in a business like ours is happening every other goddamned day, and it is going to *cease* right now. I don't care how many sad sons-a-bitches have to go into the pit. I don't give a shit if we have to get fifteen more crocodiles and open a fucking pig farm in the basement. I want this shit in line *yesterday*!"

"What's the issue?" Richy asked cavalierly as he lounged in the leather chair, knowing exactly what was 'up.'

Enzo looked at Richy then back to Cutter, switched the silver toothpick to the other side of his mouth, and tilted his head to one side as if to telegraph to Cutter the understanding that Richy had to go.

Cutter stood, walked around his desk, and sat on the corner of it directly in front of Richy. "For anyone in this room that is a big enough dipshit to have no idea what the *issue* might be," he started, looking directly at Richy. Richy pressed back farther into the padded leather chair back, unconsciously trying to put more distance between him and his father. "Let me break it down for you. One of our lieutenants had to tell me we had a money theft issue. Then, in an act of desperation, and for some inexplicable reason, he had his tongue cut out by some asshole that doesn't understand the concept of torturing for information." Cutter was still addressing only Richy. "Then another asshole decides getting fucked in the ass by a tranny FOR THREE GODDAMNED DAYS in the family penthouse is a pretty good idea, *but* stabbing the shit out of the tranny would put a fucking cherry on top of the first idea. And, we still have a skimming issue, even after we murdered one of our own soldiers to stop it."

"We do?" Richy asked, genuinely surprised. He was going to have to stuff his foot into Azi's ass after this meeting. Richy had specifically told him to lay low for a while. At least he thought he had told him that. At any rate, he would certainly make sure he told him after this bullshit meeting was over.

"Yeah," Cutter said sarcastically, "we do."

"What happened, boss?" Enzo asked, trying to put the "Richy is a dumbass comedy hour" to bed.

Cutter stood, straightened his jacket, and returned to his chair. "Some ignorant-ass, low-life, not-following-the-rules, opportunist piece of dog shit has been taking jewelry off the stiffs we make go away and pawning it."

"*Finally,*" Richy thought.

"Did we catch it in time?" Enzo asked. Richy looked at him like he had no idea what Enzo was asking.

"No," Cutter answered with a low irritated voice. "We didn't."

"*Oh, thank God,*" Richy thought. "*This is all going so well!*"

"What's the damage, and what do you want us to do to fix it?" Enzo asked. Before Cutter answered, Enzo slowly looked toward Richy and wondered whether Cutter found it odd that Richy didn't seem surprised and wasn't asking any questions at all.

"The only ray of sunshine in this monkey fuck is that there is no way it could get worse," Cutter sounded almost defeated. "The pawn shop owner has a guy come in dumping some really expensive watches for however much the pawn guy offered. Of course, he thinks that's suspicious right off the bat but, he also thinks the guy acted a little 'slow.'"

"*Perfect,*" Richy blissfully thought. Enzo remained quiet.

"The pawn guy, being the suspicious sort, examines the more expensive of the group of watches and finds one of them engraved. The he calls the cops."

"Did he say what the engraving was?" Enzo asked.

"Yeah," Cutter said as he looked at Richy suspiciously. "It said '*to Jason from Amber, together forever*.'"

"Do we know them?" Richy figured he had better start getting involved.

"Everybody knows them," Cutter growled. "Jason and Amber Jackson are the owners of the largest investment firm in the country. Amber also has a maiden name that is the same as the most powerful Senator in the US Senate's."

"Daughter?" Enzo asked.

"Yeah," Cutter responded as he hung his head for a second.

"How did we get involved in this bullshit?" Richy asked, already knowing the answer.

"Cops show up, check the surveillance video, and guess who is handing over the watches?"

Richy shrugged and Enzo remained stoic.

"That fucking retard Luther LaMotta." Cutter's words dripped with diseased requital. "There's an APB out on that asshole, if they still do that, right now. If they pick him up, there's a connection to us. If there's a connection to us, it won't be long before they figure out that the Jacksons were deeply in debt to us for a number of dumbass things Jason had pulled over the years."

"What does Luther know?" Enzo asked as he crossed his other leg.

"He *knows*," Cutter began, "that Benny cut both of their throats because he was standing there when Benny did it. He *knows* Murphy cleaned the scene because he helped. And he *knows* they were cut into small pieces then fed to Bianca because *he* was the one who did *that*."

"What do you want us to do, Pops?" Richy asked. No matter what Cutter said Richy already knew Luther wasn't coming out of the back end of this mess still breathing.

"I don't want this fucked up," Cutter said. "I want the two of you to take care of this personally. Go get that shithead. Pick him up at his place, and don't fuck up his face. I don't want people to remember two mobsters dragging some bloody asshole down the street."

"Do we bring him back here?" Enzo asked.

"Oh, you bet your ass," Cutter commanded. "You drag his dumb ass right back here. Don't let anybody see you bring him into the building, then tape his ass in a chair right next to the pit."

32.

It was a rare occasion when Luther had to go more than one or two blocks away from his apartment, but today he had to pick a few things up from the hardware store, so he could fix a few things before he put this misery behind him. As he walked, he slouched like a man constantly carrying a load of bricks on his back. The weight of the decisions he was struggling with was nearly unbearable. He was fighting the intellectual idea to just run. With everything that had transpired in the last few days, he knew his life could very easily be measured in hours or even minutes. He could possibly take whatever money he had left, take one of the cars from the valet, and hit the road. But he would have felt bad about leaving the valet to answer for a stolen car, especially after recently leaving an unconscious hooker in a car he had damaged with her head.

With that thought, it was the first time he realized he may not even be able to get a car from the valet anymore. Hell, even if he wasn't in jail, the kid probably didn't have a job there anymore. So his transportation needs were up in the air, but that didn't change the fact that people needed to pay for the wrongs exacted against Luther and the people he cared for. If he died in the process, then so be it. But he couldn't just go in guns blazing. He couldn't take the chance of being killed before everyone got their just due.

Every time he thought about Tony in that chair, he found himself seething out of control, and being out of control in any way right now could get him killed. He had to formulate well thought out plans, and now that he had quite a few of his old faculties back, planning was going to be so much easier. Azi and Candy had their payback coming; he just hadn't figured out how yet. Richy needed to pay, as well as Big Benny. That was a lot of well-protected people Luther was going to need to take out, but he would find a way. He no longer cared whether he lived or died in the process. He just wanted to make sure that everybody got their specific brand of dismemberment or murder before he was killed himself. He couldn't do that and run away at the same time.

Luther set his packages on the filthy carpet, fished in his pocket for his keys, shoved one into the lock, and pushed the door open. When he retrieved his bags from the floor, they made soft sucking sounds as their plastic stuck to the grime of the floor. Luther set his bags next to the counter just inside the door, then closed and locked it.

"Hey shithead," Richy said menacingly.

Luther's head snapped up and he instantly cursed himself for being in such a fog, planning everyone else's demise, he hadn't even noticed the men in his kitchen until the door was shut. Enzo leaned on the counter close to the opposite wall, and Richy rested his shoulder on the refrigerator.

"Richy," Luther said, slowly acknowledging his guests, "Enzo. What's up?"

Luther felt his waistband with his elbow and remembered he had left his gun in the nightstand next to the bed. That wasn't good because current Luther knew exactly what was going on.

"What's up?" Richy said with a mocking tone. "Why, you are asshole."

Luther looked at Enzo for clarification. "We need you to come with us Luther," Enzo said sympathetically.

"Do I have a job?" Luther said, trying to sound like stupid Luther. "Tony usually comes to get me for that, but now I'm not sure how that works."

"No, dipshit," Richy said impatiently, "you don't have a job."

"Am I in trouble for something?" Luther asked meekly.

Richy pushed himself off the refrigerator and started to say something, but Enzo stopped him. There was no reason to make this difficult. "No Luther," Enzo answered easily, "you don't have a job and you're not in trouble. Cutter wants to talk to you is all. No big deal."

Luther stood still as he looked back and forth between Enzo and Richy like he was trying to make a decision or form a thought. "How long do you think I'll be gone?"

"Goddamn it!" Richy cursed.

"I'm not sure," Enzo answered, still trying to control Richy's impatience.

"Do you think it will be okay if I water my plants real quick then?" Luther asked passively.

"Sure," Enzo quickly defused. He'd let Luther water his plants, then they'd walk out to the car. No big deal.

"Thanks," Luther said brightly. "I need to get the watering can first."

"I am going to beat his fucking ass, Enzo," Richy growled. Luther tried to look afraid of Richy.

"Where is it?" Enzo asked.

"In there," Luther said pointing through the serving window into the living room.

"Yeah," Enzo said. "Go ahead."

"Jesus Christ!" Richy complained. "How long are we going to put up with this bullshit?"

"Shut up," Enzo ordered. "Just let him do it and we can leave. If you can't handle that, go wait in the car."

Richy leaned back against the refrigerated and pouted. Enzo filled his time by imagining how great it might feel to break Richy's nose.

Luther moved into the living room slowly, hoping that no one would ask why the watering can would be on a shelf in the living room instead of in the kitchen under the sink. Once he got to the shelf, he slowly slid the watering can toward him with his one hand as he slid a Glock out of a hard case holster he had screwed into the bottom of the shelf with the other, shielding it from view with the watering can.

"I would like to express my appreciation to you fine gentlemen for allowing me the opportunity to water my ficus," Luther said, facing the kitchen through the serving window.

"What the fuck?" Richy said confused. He couldn't figure out when shit-for-brains learned to talk right.

Luther let the watering can fall away. Before it hit the floor he put a bullet in Enzo's chest. As Enzo deflated off the counter and down the front of the cupboards like a flattened cat in a cartoon, he managed to get his gun out and drilled two holes in the ceiling above Luther's head. As ancient, dried plaster rained down on and around Luther, he aimed the Glock at his next target.

Richy already had his gun out and was in the middle of a screaming spray-and-pray magazine-emptying fit. Bullets zipped past Luther, taking out potted plants, breaking windows, and splintering plaster on the wall. Debris was still flying around the living room as Richy's hammer dropped on an empty chamber. Luther pulled the trigger and the nine-millimeter hollow point, personification of great vengeance and furious anger, leapt through the open space of the serving window and slammed into Richy's shoulder at the same time as he knocked over the kitchen table and ducked behind it.

"YOU MISERABLE MOTHER FUCKER!" Richy screamed in pain. "You shot me! You are so fucking dead!"

Luther was still standing in the middle of the living room, pointing his gun at the kitchen table. "Is that a different kind of dead than the one I would have been after you two pricks took me back to Cutter, or would it be the same? I get confused sometimes, you vile little dick sucker."

"Oooooh," Richy howled. "That hurts like a bastard!"

"I bet it does," Luther said plainly as he pulled the trigger and sent another bullet through the table in a place he knew Richy wasn't hiding.

"Son-of-a-bitch!" Richy yelped.

"That was just to let you know I could end this anytime I wanted. But I really need to see the hole open up in your face just before you die. It will be—you know—cathartic and shit. By the way, as long as we have some time here before you finally give up and accept what's coming, what happened? How did you talk Cutter into taking me out, and how are you going to punch Murphy's ticket?"

"It was the watch, you ignorant lump of shit," Richy spat.

"What watch?" Luther wasn't sure what he was talking about.

"The watch you pawned you dumb fuck," Richy laughed a little. "You know, for your girlfriend."

Luther thought about that for a second. "How did the cops find it? That sleazeball I pawned it to would have *never* called the cops"

"You ignorant piece of shit," Richy laughed. "The three of us set that up so we'd have someone to deflect heat onto if we needed it. After that thing in the hotel room, you had to go, fuckhead. Candy gave me the name of the pawn shop you used in Jersey, and I paid him a visit."

"I'll be damned," Luther said matter-of-factly and with only slight surprise. "You just went to Candy, asked her where the watch was, and she gave it up just like that?"

"No, dickhead," Richy sounded weak, "I went to Candy, fucked her in the ass because she asked me to, then she told me where it was just like we were planning to do all along."

"Of course you did," Luther said with all the emotion you would use taking the garbage out to the can at night. Luther stood there for a second. Richy took that to mean that he was getting into Luther's head, when in fact Luther was just waiting for him to stand up.

"You're not ever going to stand up, are you?" Luther asked.

"Fuck you, retard!" Richy screamed.

"Okay then," Luther said as he released a breath of frustration. He raised the Glock and took aim at the shelf above Richy's head where he kept his smelting equipment. The bullet snapped out of the barrel and raced into the kitchen, slamming into the box of Borax directly above Richy. Richy looked up to see where the shot went just in time to receive a torrent of the corrosive base powder in his wide-open eyeballs.

Richy shrieked a high-pitched inhuman scream and stood up, clawing at his eyes. The first shot went through Richy's hand before it destroyed his eyeball and that side of his brain. The rest of the shots followed Richy to the floor, each finding their mark, until the gun went click.

33.

Candy had a lot on her mind as she entered her apartment. She still couldn't walk right after that fiasco in the Bentley with Luther, and she wasn't sure if her neck would ever stop hurting. Everything in her life that she had been working so hard on was unraveling because she hadn't remembered some trivial bullshit a mark had said to her. Who gave a shit what friends Luther had? And with all the shitty luck in the world, she had to pick the one prick on the planet to have knocked off that would send the key to her operation around the bend.

If she didn't have Luther to freely accept the fall for everything she and Azi had been responsible for, she was going to be as busy as a cat covering up shit, trying to either bring him around again or finding someone else that stupid. She needed Luther to take out Richy just before they hit the road, then she would give Luther up to Cutter, and Azi would eventually die in some horrible accident, and of course she would be grief stricken until she got far enough away from the scene of the crime: then the world would be her oyster.

She opened the door and stepped into the living room. Sitting in a chair directly in front of her in the middle of the room, Azi looked insane and had a swath of silver duct tape covering his mouth. His eyes bulged in terror, and he was frantically mumbling something into the tape as he furiously pointed behind her with his chin.

"What the fuck?" Candy whispered in deep confusion. She heard the door close and turned to see Luther towering over her.

One of the things that had protected Candy through her career as a lying, thieving sack of shit was her ability to assess, formulate, and deflect at lightning-fast speed. When the only thing you had to worry about was protecting yourself above everything else, things like that were much easier.

"Holy shit, baby," Candy said breathlessly as she placed her hand over her heart. "You scared the living shit out of me." Luther was amazed at how good she really was at this. Her instant reaction to seeing her partner in crime tied to a chair and gagged by the guy that she had betrayed, by the guy that had tried to kill her then brutally raped her, was the same as it would have been if a friend of hers had jumped out of a closet and said "boo."

"I'm sure I did," Luther said, smiling in a way that chilled her.

"How long have you been waiting for me?" she asked, trying, but failing, desperately to sound nonchalant. "If you had told me you were coming over, I would have made sure to be here for you."

"You really are an amazing woman," Luther complimented, and Candy smiled. "You *really* are going to stand here and shoot the shit as if everything were lollypops and roses and your boyfriend weren't taped to a chair behind you with a gag in his mouth." Candy just blinked in amazement. It was the first time in her life she was at a loss for words. "You are actually going to act like the guy you just shit on, the guy that just tried to fuck you to death because you killed his lifelong friend, just stopped by for a visit. And like *I* didn't tie that shit stain in that chair, then wait for you to get home."

"Baby. . ." Candy struggled.

"Shut the fuck up, bitch," Luther said evenly.

"Baby," Candy pushed through, "whatever this is, you and I can work it out. I am so sorry about Tony, and I'll do anything you want to make up for it."

"Anything?" Luther said, raising both eyebrows.

"Yeah baby," Candy begged, "anything you want. You know how I feel about you. How I have felt about you from the very first time I ever met you."

"Oh yeah," Luther said moving closer to her, "I know exactly how you felt." Luther stopped and looked over her shoulder toward the struggling Azi. "What about him? Somebody has to pay for Tony, and I want you to myself anyway."

Candy didn't turn around and continued to work feverishly, trying to seduce Luther. "We don't need him, baby," Candy said, trying to overcome terror with sexual electricity. "He was just the guy that had to get the money off Cutter's books." Behind her a muffled voice tried to shout restrained words that sounded a lot like *"you fucking bitch."*

"Okay," Luther sounded agreeable, "but we can't just leave him here. As soon as we're gone he'll roll over on us in a heartbeat. How do you propose we make sure he doesn't?"

Azi was screaming uncontrollably through his tape and shaking his head as he violently struggled against the bindings. Luther dropped his hands into his pockets comfortably.

"You know a lot about cleaning, baby," Candy whispered seductively as she twisted her hips slightly. "I'm sure you can come up with *something*."

"Hear that old buddy," Luther said to the hysterical Azi over Candy's shoulder. "Looks like you're out and I'm in. That kind of blows for you, dude. And not in the good way."

"I am going to fuck the living shit out of you right in front of him before I tear his guts out," Luther said as he moved closer to Candy.

"Do it," Candy moaned.

"Oh," Luther said in a low voice with a humorless smile, "you are one evil bitch, aren't you?"

Candy reached out and touched Luther's crotch lightly as she closed her eyes. Luther's hand shot out of his pocket so fast Candy wouldn't have had time to react even if she was looking right at it. The needlepoint of the double-edged stiletto shot out of the handle in Luther's hand like a silver viper's tongue, and Luther jammed it deep into Candy's arm. He savagely ripped it back out and with one fluid motion jerked Candy off her feet by her throat and slammed her painfully into a chair right next to Azi. Candy howled in pain.

Luther continued to hold her in place by her neck as he brought his face close to Candy's as if he were going to kiss her. "If you fucking move, I'll cut your tits off." For emphasis he pushed the tip of the stiletto into the bottom of her left breast. Luther had transformed into the incarnation of death and vengeance. "Blink once if you understand me, whore," Candy blinked. Luther loosened his grip and retrieved a roll of duct tape from a table next to Candy. He roughly taped her arms down, then forced her legs apart and taped one to each leg of the chair. "*Please Luther,*" Candy begged and wept uncontrollably. "We can work this out. *Please,* listen to me, we can fix this." Luther backhanded her mercilessly across the face.

"Funny you should use those words," he said flatly as he finished taping her last leg to the chair and stood up. "That is exactly what I'm going to do." He smacked a strip of tape brutally across her mouth, snapping her head back. "I'm going to fix you two worthless assholes.

"I have to say, though," Luther said, moving behind Azi, "this guy is really just one of your pawns. You know, just like I was. And Richy for that matter." Candy had her neck twisted as far around as she could, trying to see Luther. She was manically shaking her head and protesting through the tape. "I don't see any reason he should have to suffer the same fate as you," Luther placed his hand on Azi's shoulder. "How do you feel about that buddy?" Azi had his head tilted back at a wild angle as his eyes bulged, and his head nodded spastically up and down, affirming that he should not have to go through whatever Candy was about to suffer.

"You two fucking people," Luther chuckled as he shook his head slightly. "Okay then, so be it. You get the easy way buddy." Luther grabbed Azi by the hair, jerked his head back as far as it would go, and jammed the stiletto into Azi's carotid artery, then violently jerked the blade forward. Blood spit spasmodically from the gash in Azi's neck as his heart pumped his life essence into the atmosphere around him. Candy stared wide eyed as the tape on her mouth flexed back and forth with her hyperventilation. The fountains of blood slowed as Azi's heart lost pressure and interest, until it stopped altogether. Luther let go of Azi's hair and shoved his lifeless head into his chest.

"Wow," Luther said off handedly, "what a mess," then to Candy, "I guess it needs to be washed down a little."

Luther went to the back of the apartment as Candy struggled wildly, trying to see what he was doing. Suddenly torrents of water poured over her head, but she vaguely noticed that it didn't actually smell like water. Luther stepped around her, upended the rest of the contents of the gas can on Azi, and dropped it on the floor between them.

Luther walked to the door as Candy strained against the tape and pleaded with unintelligible words. "What's that?" Luther asked as he pulled a lighter out of his pocket and flipped the top off with his thumb. "I couldn't understand you." Candy became even more agitated in wide-eyed horror. "I guess it doesn't really matter though," Luther said as he spun the knurled wheel over the small stick of flint, in turn igniting a small yellow flame on the wick, "it would all be just more lying bullshit. Right?" He tilted his head and held the lighter in front of his face for a moment; then he smiled and tossed it directly into Candy's lap.

34.

Croc Turd was surprised when he walked around the corner to the pit. Luther was sitting there alone in his usual chair, feeding marshmallows to Bianca. He didn't look up when Croc Turd sat next to him.

"What's up, buddy?" Croc Turd asked uneasily.

"Nothing, Marty," Luther said indifferently. Croc Turd was shocked.

"Okay," Croc Turd replied cautiously. "Exactly what the hell is going on?"

"What do you mean, buddy?" Luther asked as he dropped the rest of the bag into the pit.

"Neither you nor anyone else has used my real name since Cutter put the word out. So, I say again, what the hell is going on, Luther?"

"It's funny, Marty," Luther said smiling genuinely, "I have also never called you Croc Turd. It's time for a change. No matter what happens right here and now, today marks the end of you working for that fucking reptile." Nothing Luther was saying was doing anything to put Croc Turd at ease. "It's been a very long day, Marty," Luther went on as he stretched back in his chair. "A very long day indeed. Quite a number of people that desperately needed sorting out are no longer converting oxygen to bullshit."

"What have you done, Luther?" Croc Turd asked, "And what's up with the way you're talking?"

"I used to have—issues, Marty. There was a version of me that I allowed the public to see. I called that shithead Bad Luther, and then there was a version of me who was a good person, intelligent, thoughtful, and moved by the beauty in life. Do you know what I called that version of me?"

"Good Luther," Croc Turd guessed, shrugging his shoulders.

"Give that man a ceegar!" Luther exclaimed. "That's absolutely correct, Marty. And there was a Middle Luther in there who was horrified by Bad Luther and jealous of Good Luther. I don't mind telling you, Marty," Luther folded his arms across his chest, "the inside of my head was one complicated shit show." He leaned toward Croc Turd conspiratorially. "Just between you and me, I think I might have been a little, you know," Luther whistled and spun his index finger in small circles next to his temple.

"Tell me what happened today, Luther," Croc Turd said again.

"I guess I should go in order." Luther gazed at the ceiling for a moment in thought. "Yeah, that would be best." Then turning to face Croc Turd, he said, "First, the love of my life, Candy Barr, late of the Lancaster Pennsylvania Barrs, or whatever, gave me up to Richy when I pawned an engraved watch for her. Richy, in turn, scamp that he is, *was*, I guess, called the cops. Well, as you can only imagine, Cutter pretty much lost his shit and sent Enzo and Richy to kill me. I have to say, it was touch-and-go for a second. Anyway, I shot Enzo in the chest, then I played a short game of "whack-a-mole" with Richy, dumbass game by the way, and then I emptied a clip in him. Do you know Enzo died with that fucking toothpick still in his mouth?" Luther produced the bloodstained silver toothpick from his pocket and examined it in the dim light of the pit.

"Oh sweet baby Jesus, Luther," Croc Turd breathed.

"I know," Luther said as he smiled and tilted his head a little, "Pretty cool. Right? Any old how, I grabbed some shit I had picked up that morning and set off for my original destination, Candy and Azi's place. Azi was the only one there, and I had to beat on him a little to get him to sit in the chair so I could tape him to it and gag him. But as you can imagine," Luther chuckled a little, "I didn't have to beat him that hard. If you look in the dictionary under the word 'chickenshit,' there's a picture of Azi right next to it."

Croc Turd was staring blankly with his mouth hanging open. Luther reached over and gently closed Croc Turd's mouth by pressing his chin up. "You might want to keep that closed in here, Marty. Flies might lay eggs in it.

"But I digress. Where was I? Oh yeah. Azi taped in the chair. So, I waited until Candy arrived." Luther leaned forward and looked at Croc Turd. "Can you believe she thought she could fuck her way out of it?" Luther laughed out loud. "Man, she was something else. To shorten things up here, cut to the chase as they say, I taped her into a chair, and then I set both of those slimeballs on fire." Luther's eyes gleamed, "Pretty cool, huh?"

"Jesus Christ," Croc Turd quietly blurted in amazement.

"Hey, I'm not some kind of soulless Philistine," Luther said defensively. "I slit Azi's throat first. He just needed to die, not burn to death like the epitome of evil Candy was. Damn, what kind of animal do you think I am anyway?"

"What happens now, Luther?" Croc Turd asked with a shaky voice.

"Well, sir," Luther said as he stood up and reached behind him. Croc Turd leapt off the chair and pulled his gun out of the back of his belt, pointing it at Luther.

"Marty," Luther said in mock surprise as he spread his arms out at his sides. Luther's Glock was resting lightly in his right hand. "You have a gun; I have a gun. We all have guns. So what now?"

"What are you going to do, Luther?" Croc Turd asked, still pointing his gun at Luther's chest. "Are you going to kill me and feed me to Bianca?"

"I'm not going to kill you, Marty. Hell, you're probably the only friend I have in the world right now." Luther said as he steadied the gun in his hand. "I'm going to shoot that fucking monster in the pit. I think I'll be doing that evil pile of shit a favor anyway."

"I can't let you do that, Luther," Croc Turd said shakily, still pointing his gun at Luther's chest.

"Sure you can, Marty," Luther said, smiling with half of his mouth. He pointed his gun into the pit.

Tears streamed down Croc Turd's face. "Luther, please don't make me shoot you!!"

"Everything is going to be fine, Marty," Luther whispered.

The report of a single gunshot bounced across the concrete room in deafening remorse. Then everything was silent.

36.

The sun burned hot and bright out of the New York sky, reflecting off the midnight black paint of a brand-new Lincoln Town Car. Every turn of the spotless tires propelled it farther along the Verrazano Bridge, out of the stink of the city and toward the promise of a new life someplace far away and remote. The valet tag still hung off the key chain, and all of the windows were down.

Luther stretched his arm out the window and did the up-and-down airplane action with his hand for a little while, then he propped it on the windowsill and placed his palm on the roof. On the bench seat next to him a beautiful sterling silver box with gold handles rode easily. Across the top, written with black marker on a stretch of white medical tape, were the letters T-O-N-Y. Luther reached down to the phone laying in front of Tony's box and pressed a button. Cajun fiddling filled the car.

Luther looked across Tony's box at Marty and smiled. "What did that asshole Greeley say?" Luther asked.

"Go west, young man!" Marty shouted and pointed his index finger forward. Mary Chapin Carpenter's voice ricocheted off the expensive upholstery. "Saturday night and the moon is out, I wanna head on over to the twist and shout!" Luther pounded the roof of the car to the beat, and Marty backed him up, playing drums on the dash.

Both men sang at the top of their lungs, "When I hear that fiddle wanna beg for more, wanna dance to a band from a-Lou'sian tonight!"

Even the air smelled sweeter.